THE AMIS
ANTHOLOGY

BY THE SAME AUTHOR

THE
AMIS
ANTHOLOGY

CHOSEN AND EDITED BY KINGSLEY AMIS

Hutchinson

London Sydney Auckland Johannesburg

First published in Great Britain in 1988 by Hutchinson Ltd,
an imprint of Century Hutchinson Ltd, Brookmount House,
62–65 Chandos Place, London WC2N 4NW

Century Hutchinson Australia Pty Ltd,
89–91 Albion Street, Surry Hills,
NSW 2010, Australia

Century Hutchinson New Zealand Limited
PO Box 40-086, Glenfield, Auckland 10, New Zealand

Century Hutchinson South Africa (Pty) Ltd
PO Box 337, Bergvlei, 2012 South Africa

Photoset in Linotron Palatino by Rowland Phototypesetting Ltd,
Bury St Edmunds, Suffolk
Printed and bound in Great Britain by
Butler and Tanner Ltd, Frome, Somerset

British Library Cataloguing in Publication Data
The Amis anthology: a personal choice of
English verse.
1. Poetry in English. Anthologies
I. Amis, Kingsley, *1922–*
821'.008

ISBN 0-09-173525-4

CONTENTS

INTRODUCTION

This is a collection of my favourite poems, which is not the same thing as a collection of the couple of hundred English poems I may happen to think are the best. A favourite poem, like a favourite human being, is attractive partly for reasons that are the stronger for being unfathomable. There has to be a personal element about such a poem, something producing the illusion that it was written specially for me, however well I may know that it was in fact written for the whole nation, or for an individual member of the poet's circle, or for nobody in particular. I believe that what appeals to me in this way is likely to appeal to others in the same way, hence this anthology.

Many of the poems here will be unfamiliar to many readers, but that is, so to speak, accidental. Poems of great repute, even as well known as no. **38** (Gray's 'Elegy Written in a Country Churchyard'), can equally exert a personal appeal after countless rereadings, and there are many of those here too. Other regulars, just as admirable in all ways except that indefinable one, are firmly dropped. Yet others I ignore because I dislike them or consider them overrated; nothing is here because I think it ought to be here. The reader is free to speculate which of these considerations kept out the entire works of Shelley, say, or Ezra Pound.

Shakespeare is out for a couple of reasons (not including the last-mentioned). His non-dramatic poems are not favourite of mine. Even his sonnets, especially his sonnets, lack my personal factor, a deficiency I feel is connected with something else that is missing from them or wrong with them – but this is not the place to start on that. And while I do indeed feel, have always felt, that *Hamlet* was written specially for me, I cannot include it all here, and nothing less than all of it would be enough.

On similar grounds, or those of justice to the author, I have resisted the temptation to put in pieces of long poems, though I bend this rule in a few cases like no. **61**, 'Chibiabos's Song' from Longfellow's *Hiawatha*, where an extract seems to me to make a self-sufficient poem. I have modernised spelling and punctuation and made things like initial capitals conform to present-day usage, though, again, I have left undisturbed some poems like no. **41**, Blake's 'Auguries of Innocence', where I feel such matters are part of the style and not mere conformity with the habits of the time. No. **38** (Gray's 'Elegy') is a difficult one because the poet's rule for capitalisation is hard to ascertain.

The poems are arranged in rough chronological order. It is only rough because I have sometimes departed from it to get a better-looking page.

I am grateful to Anthony Thwaite for much generously given advice in the compiling of this anthology. But the responsibility for all texts, facts and opinions remains mine.

THE AMIS
ANTHOLOGY

JOHN LYDGATE

1   Lyarde

Lyarde is an old horse and cannot well draw;
He shall be put into the park holly for to gnaw.
Barefoot withouten shoon there shall he go,
For he is an old horse and cannot more do.
While that Lyarde could draw, the while was he loved;
They put him to provender, and therewith he throve.
Now he cannot do his deed as he could beforn,
They lay before him peas-straw, and bear away the corn.
They lead him to the smithy to pull off his shoon
And put him to greenwood, there for to gone.
Whoso cannot do his deed, he shall to park,
Barefoot withouten shoon, and go with Lyarde.

ANONYMOUS

2 Adam

Adam lay y-bounden,
  Bounden in a bond;
Four thousand winter
  Thought he not too long;
And all was for an apple,
  An apple that he took,
As clerks finden written
  In their book.

Ne had the apple taken been,
  The apple taken been,
Ne had never Our Lady
  A-been heaven's queen.
Blessèd be the time
  That apple taken was!
Therefor we may singen
  Deo Gracias!

3   To Mistress Margaret Hussey

> Merry Margaret,
> As midsummer flower,
> Gentle as falcon
> Or hawk of the tower:
> With solace and gladness,
> Much mirth and no madness,
> All good and no badness;
> So joyously,
> So maidenly,
> So womanly
> Her demeaning
> In everything,
> Far, far passing
> That I can indite,
> Or suffice to write
> Of Merry Margaret
> As midsummer flower,
> Gentle as falcon
> Or hawk of the tower.
> As patient and as still
> And as full of good will
> As fair Isaphill,
> Coriander,
> Sweet pomander,
> Good Cassander,
> Steadfast of thought,
> Well made, well wrought,
> Far may be sought
> Ere that ye can find
> So courteous, so kind,
> As Merry Margaret,
> This midsummer flower,
> Gentle as falcon
> Or hawk of the tower.

4   Women

These women all
Both great and small
    Are wavering to and fro,
Now here, now there,
Now everywhere;
    But I will not say so.

So they love to range,
Their minds doth change
    And make their friend their foe;
As lovers true
Each day they choose new;
    But I will not say so.

They laugh, they smile,
They do beguile,
    As dice that men doth throw.
Who useth them much
Shall never be rich;
    But I will not say so.

Some hot, some cold,
There is no hold
    But as the wind doth blow;
When all is done,
They change like the moon;
    But I will not say so.

So thus one and other
Taketh after their mother,
    As cock by kind doth crow.
My song is ended,
The best may be amended;
    But I will not say so.

ANONYMOUS

5   The Bailiff's Daughter of Islington

There was a youth, and a well-belovèd youth,
    And he was an esquire's son,
He loved the bailiff's daughter dear,
    That lived in Islington.

But she was coy, and she would not believe
    That he did love her so,
No, nor at any time she would
    Any countenance to him show.

But when his friends did understand
    His fond and foolish mind,
They sent him up to fair London,
    An apprentice for to bind.

And when he had been seven long years,
    And his love he did not see,
'Many a tear have I shed for her sake
    When she little thought of me.'

All the maids of Islington
    Went forth to sport and play;
All but the bailiff's daughter dear;
    She secretly stole away.

She put off her gown of grey,
    And put on her puggish attire;
She's up to fair London gone,
    Her true-love to require.

As she went along the road,
    The weather being hot and dry,
There was she aware of her true-love,
    At length came riding by.

She stepped to him, as red as a rose,
    And took him by the bridle-ring:
'I pray you, kind sir, give me one penny,
    To ease my weary limb.'

'I prithee, sweetheart, canst thou tell me
    Where that thou wast born?'
'At Islington, kind sir,' said she,
    'Where I have had many a scorn.'

'I prithee, sweetheart, canst thou tell me
    Whether thou dost know
The bailiff's daughter of Islington?'
    'She's dead, sir, long ago.'

'Then will I sell my goodly steed,
    My saddle and my bow;
I will into some far countrey,
    Where no man doth me know.'

'Oh stay, oh stay, thou goodly youth!
    She standeth by thy side,
See, she's alive, she is not dead,
    And is ready to be thy bride.'

'Oh farewell grief, and welcome joy,
    Ten thousand times and o'er!
For now I have seen my own true-love,
    That I thought to have seen no more.'

6   Sardanapalus

The Assyrians' king – in peace, with foul desire
And filthy lusts that stained his regal heart –
In war, that should set princely hearts afire,
Vanquished, did yield for want of martial art.
The dint of swords from kisses seemed strange,
And harder than his lady's side, his targe;
From glutton feasts to soldiers' fare, a change;
His helmet, far above a garland's charge.
Who scarce the name of manhood did retain
When he had lost his honour and his right –
Proud, time of wealth, in storms appalled with dread –
Feeble of spirit, impatient of pain,
Drenched in sloth and womanish delight,
Murdered himself to show some manful deed.

7   To His Son

Three things there be that prosper up apace
And flourish, whilst they grow asunder far,
But on a day they meet all in one place,
And when they meet they one another mar.
And they be these: the wood, the weed, the wag.
The wood is that which makes the gallows-tree;
The weed is that which strings the hangman's bag;
The wag, my pretty knave, betokens thee.
Mark well, dear boy, whilst these assemble not,
Green springs the tree, hemp grows, the wag is wild;
But when they meet, it makes the timber rot,
It frets the halter, and it chokes the child.
　　Then bless thee, and beware, and let us pray
　　We part not with thee at this meeting day.

8   Walsingham

'As you came from the holy land
　　Of Walsingham,
Met you not with my true love
　　By the way as you came?'

'How shall I know your true love,
　　That have met many one
As I went to the holy land,
　　That have come, that have gone?'

'She is neither white nor brown,
　　But as the heavens fair,
There is none hath a form so divine
　　In the earth or the air.'

'Such a one did I meet, good Sir,
    Such an angelic face,
Who like a queen, like a nymph did appear
    By her gait, by her grace.'

'She hath left me here all alone,
    All alone as unknown,
Who sometimes did me lead with herself,
    And me loved as her own.'

'What's the cause that she leaves you alone
    And a new way doth take,
Who loved you once as her own
    And her joy did you make?'

'I have loved her all my youth,
    But now old as you see,
Love likes not the falling fruit
    From the withered tree.

'Know that Love is a careless child,
    And forgets promise past;
He is blind, he is deaf when he list
    And in faith never fast.

'His desire is a dureless content
    And a trustless joy;
He is won with a world of despair
    And is lost with a toy.

'Of womenkind such indeed is the love
    Or the word love abused,
Under which many childish desires
    And conceits are excused.

'But true Love is a durable fire
    In the mind ever burning;
Never sick, never old, never dead,
    From itself never turning.'

9   Lacking My Love

Lacking my love I go from place to place
Like a young fawn that late hath lost the hind,
And seek each where, where last I saw her face
Whose image yet I carry fresh in mind.
I seek the fields with her late footing signed,
I seek her bower with her late presence decked,
Yet nor in field nor bower I her can find,
Yet field and bower are full of her aspect.
But when mine eyes I thereunto direct
They idly back return to me again,
And when I hope to see their true object
I find myself but fed with fancies vain.
   Cease then, mine eyes, to seek herself to see,
   And let my thoughts behold herself in me.

FULKE GREVILLE, LORD BROOKE

10   Myra

I with whose colours Myra dressed her head,
  I that wore posies of her own hand-making,
I that mine own name in the chimneys read
  By Myra finely wrought ere I was waking –
    Must I look on, in hope time coming may
    With change bring back my turn again to play?

I that on Sunday at the church-stile found
  A garland sweet, with true-love knots in flowers,
Which I to wear about mine arm was bound,
  That each of us might know that all was ours –
    Must I now lead an idle life in wishes,
    And follow Cupid for his loaves and fishes?

I that did wear the ring her mother left,
  I for whose love she gloried to be blamed,
I with whose eyes her eyes committed theft,
  I who did make her blush when I was named –
    Must I lose ring, flowers, blush, theft, and go naked,
    Watching with sighs, till dead love be awaked?

Was it for this that I might Myra see
  Washing the water with her beauty's white?
Yet would she never write her love to me.
  Thinks wit of change, while thoughts are in delight?
    Mad girls must safely love, as they may leave;
    No man can print a kiss; lines may deceive.

11   Elegy

My prime of youth is but a frost of cares,
  My feast of joy is but a dish of pain,
My crop of corn is but a field of tares,
  And all my good is but vain hope of gain;
    The day is past, and yet I saw no sun,
    And now I live, and now my life is done.

My tale was heard and yet it was not told,
  My fruit is fallen and yet my leaves are green,
My youth is spent and yet I am not old,
  I saw the world and yet I was not seen;
    My thread is cut and yet it is not spun,
    And now I live, and now my life is done.

I sought my death and found it in my womb,
  I looked for life and saw it was a shade,
I trod the earth and knew it was my tomb,
  And now I die, and now I was but made;
    My glass is full, and now my glass is run,
    And now I live, and now my life is done.

GEORGE PEELE

12   Song: 'Whenas the rye reach to the chin'

Whenas the rye reach to the chin,
And chopcherry, chopcherry ripe within,
Strawberries swimming in the cream,
And schoolboys playing in the stream;
   Then O, then O, then O my true love said,
     Till that time come again,
   She could not live a maid.

ANONYMOUS

13　Madrigal

My Love in her attire doth show her wit,
　　It doth so well become her:
For every season she hath dressings fit,
　　For winter, spring, and summer.
No beauty she doth miss,
　　When all her robes are on:
But Beauty's self she is,
　　When all her robes are gone.

ANONYMOUS

14　Phillida Flouts Me

O! what a plague is love,
　　How shall I bear it?
She will unconstant prove,
　　I greatly fear it.
It so torments my mind,
　　That my strength faileth.
She wavers with the wind,
　　As the ship saileth.
Please her the best you may,
She looks another way.
Alas and well a day!
　　Phillida flouts me.

At the fair yesterday,
   She did pass by me;
She looked another way,
   And would not spy me.
I woo'd her for to dine,
   I could not get her.
Dick had her to the wine,
   He might entreat her.
With Daniel she did dance,
On me she would not glance.
O thrice unhappy chance!
     Phillida flouts me.

Fair maid, be not so coy,
   Do not disdain me.
I am my mother's joy,
   Sweet, entertain me.
She'll give me when she dies,
   All things that's fitting,
Her poultry and her bees
   And her geese sitting;
A pair of mallard's beds,
And barrel full of shreds;
And yet, for all these goods,
     Phillida flouts me.

Thou shalt eat curds and cream,
   All the year lasting;
And drink the crystal stream,
   Pleasant in tasting;
Whig and whey till thou burst
   And brambleberries
Pie-lid and pasty-crust,
   Pears, plums, and cherries.
Thy raiment shall be thin,
Made of a wether's skin;
All is not worth a pin,
     Phillida flouts me.

Cupid hath shot his dart,
    And hath me wounded;
It pricked my tender heart,
    And ne'er rebounded.
I was a fool to scorn
    His bow and quiver;
I am like one forlorn,
    Sick of a fever.
Now I may weep and mourn,
Whilst with Love's flames I burn;
Nothing will serve my turn;
        Phillida flouts me.

I am a lively lad,
    Howe'er she take me;
I am not half so bad
    As she would make me.
Whether she smile or frown,
    She may deceive me.
Ne'er a girl in the town,
    But fain would have me.
Since she doth from me fly,
Now I may sigh and die,
And never cease to cry
        Phillida flouts me.

In the last month of May
    I made her posies;
I heard her often say
    That she loved roses.
Cowslips and gilliflowers
    And the white lily,
I brought to deck the bowers
    For my sweet Philly.
But she did all disdain,
And threw them back again;
Therefore it's flat and plain
        Phillida flouts me.

Fair maiden, have a care,
    And in time take me;
I can have those as fair,
    If you forsake me.
For Doll the dairy-maid
    Laughed at me lately,
And wanton Winifred
    Favours me greatly.
One cast milk on my clothes,
T'other played with my nose;
What wanting signs are those?
        Phillida flouts me.

I cannot work and sleep
    All at a season;
Grief wounds my heart so deep,
    Without all reason.
I fade and pine away,
    With grief and sorrow;
I fall quite to decay
    Like any shadow.
I shall be dead, I fear,
Within a thousand year;
And for all that my dear
        Phillida flouts me.

15   Agincourt

Fair stood the wind for France,
When we our sails advance,
Nor now to prove our chance
   Longer will tarry;
But putting to the main,
At Caux, the mouth of Seine,
With all his martial train,
   Landed King Harry.

And taking many a fort
Furnished in warlike sort,
Marched towards Agincourt
   In happy hour,
Skirmishing day by day
With those that stopped his way,
Where the French general lay
   With all his power:

Who, in his height of pride,
King Henry to deride,
His ransom to provide
   To the king sending;
Which he neglects the while
As from a nation vile,
Yet with an angry smile
   Their fall portending.

And turning to his men,
Quoth our brave Henry then,
'Though they to one be ten,
   Be not amazèd.
Yet have we well begun,
Battles so bravely won
Have ever to the sun
   By fame been raisèd.

'And for myself,' quoth he,
'This my full rest shall be:
England ne'er mourn for me,
    Nor more esteem me;
Victor I will remain
Or on this earth lie slain;
Never shall she sustain
    Loss to redeem me.

'Poitiers and Crecy tell,
When most their pride did swell,
Under our swords they fell;
    No less our skill is
Than when our grandsire great,
Claiming the regal seat,
By many a warlike feat
    Lopped the French lilies.'

The Duke of York so dread
The eager vaward led;
With the main Henry sped,
    Amongst his henchmen;
Exeter had the rear,
A braver man not there:
O Lord, how hot they were
    On the false Frenchmen!

They now to fight are gone,
Armour on armour shone,
Drum now to drum did groan,
    To hear was wonder;
That with the cries they make
The very earth did shake,
Trumpet to trumpet spake,
    Thunder to thunder.

Well it thine age became,
O noble Erpingham,
Which did the signal aim
    To our hid forces!
When from a meadow by,
Like a storm suddenly,
The English archery
    Struck the French horses.

With Spanish yew so strong,
Arrows a cloth-yard long,
That like to serpents stung,
    Piercing the weather;
None from his fellow starts,
But playing manly parts,
And like true English hearts
    Stuck close together.

When down their bows they threw,
And forth their bilbos drew,
And on the French they flew,
    Not one was tardy;
Arms were from shoulders sent,
Scalps to the teeth were rent,
Down the French peasants went;
    Our men were hardy.

This while our noble king,
His broadsword brandishing,
Down the French host did ding
    As to o'erwhelm it,
And many a deep wound lent,
His arms with blood besprent,
And many a cruel dent
    Bruisèd his helmet.

Gloster, that duke so good,
Next of the royal blood,
For famous England stood,
   With his brave brother;
Clarence, in steel so bright,
Though but a maiden knight,
Yet in that furious fight
   Scarce such another!

Warwick in blood did wade,
Oxford the foe invade,
And cruel slaughter made,
   Still as they ran up;
Suffolk his axe did ply,
Beaumont and Willoughby
Bare them right doughtily,
   Ferrers and Fanhope.

Upon Saint Crispin's Day
Fought was this noble fray,
Which fame did not delay
   To England to carry.
O, when shall Englishmen
With such acts fill a pen,
Or England breed again
   Such a King Harry?

16   Laura

Rose-cheeked Laura, come;
Sing thou smoothly with thy beauty's
Silent music, either other
   Sweetly gracing.

Lovely forms do flow
From concent divinely framèd;
Heaven is music, and thy beauty's
   Birth is heavenly.

These dull notes we sing
Discords need for helps to grace them;
Only beauty purely loving
   Knows no discord;

But still moves delight,
Like clear springs renewed by flowing,
Ever perfect, ever in them-
   selves eternal.

THOMAS FORD

17   There is a Lady Sweet and Kind

There is a lady sweet and kind,
Was never face so pleased my mind;
I did but see her passing by,
And yet I love her till I die.

Her gesture, motion, and her smiles,
Her wit, her voice, my heart beguiles,
Beguiles my heart, I know not why,
And yet I love her till I die.

Her free behaviour, winning looks,
Would make a lawyer burn his books;
I touched her not, alas, not I,
And yet I love her till I die.

Had I her fast betwixt mine arms,
Judge you, that think such sports are harms,
Were it any harm? No no, fie fie!
For I will love her till I die.

Should I remain confinèd there
So long as Phoebus in his sphere,
I to request, she to deny,
Yet would I love her till I die.

Cupid is wingèd and doth range,
Her country so my love doth change;
But change she earth or change she sky,
Yet will I love her till I die.

18   Upon Kind and True Love

'Tis not how witty, nor how free,
Nor yet how beautiful she be,
But how much kind and true to me.
Freedom and wit none can confine
And beauty like the sun doth shine,
But kind and true are only mine.

Let others with attention sit
To listen, and admire her wit:
That is a rock where I'll not split.
Let others dote upon her eyes
And burn their hearts for sacrifice:
Beauty's a calm where danger lies.

But kind and true have been long tried:
A harbour where we may confide
And safely there at anchor ride.
From change of winds there we are free,
And need not fear storm's tyranny,
Nor pirate, though a prince he be.

HENRY KING

19   Such is Life

Like to the falling of a star,
Or as the flights of eagles are,
Or like the fresh spring's gaudy hue,
Or silver drops of morning dew,
Or like a wind that chafes the flood,
Or bubbles which on water stood;
Even such is Man, whose borrowed light
Is straight called in, and paid to night.

The wind blows out, the bubble dies,
The spring entombed in autumn lies,
The dew dries up, the star is shot,
The flight is past, and Man forgot.

GEORGE HERBERT

20   Redemption

Having been tenant long to a rich lord,
Not thriving, I resolvèd to be bold
And make a suit unto him, to afford
A new small-rented lease and cancel the old.
In heaven at his manor I him sought:
They told me there that he was lately gone
About some land which he had dearly bought
Long since on earth, to take possession.
I straight returned and, knowing his great birth,
Sought him accordingly in great resorts –
In cities, theatres, gardens, parks and courts:
At length I heard a ragged noise and mirth
    Of thieves and murderers; there I him espied,
    Who straight 'Your suit is granted' said, and died.

21   Prayer

Prayer, the Church's banquet, angels' age,
God's breath in man returning to his birth,
The soul in paraphrase, heart in pilgrimage,
The Christian plummet sounding heaven and earth;
Engine against the Almighty, sinner's tower,
Reversèd thunder, Christ-side-piercing spear,
The six-days-world transposing in an hour,
A kind of tune which all things hear and fear;
Softness, and peace, and joy, and love, and bliss,
Exalted manna, gladness of the best,
Heaven in ordinary, man well dressed,
The Milky Way, the bird of Paradise,
    Church-bells beyond the stars heard, the soul's blood,
    The land of spices, something understood.

22   Virtue

Sweet day, so cool, so calm, so bright,
The bridal of the earth and sky,
The dew shall weep thy fall tonight;
                 For thou must die.

Sweet rose, whose hue, angry and brave,
Bids the rash gazer wipe his eye,
Thy root is ever in its grave,
                 And thou must die.

Sweet spring, full of sweet days and roses,
A box where sweets compacted lie,
My music shows ye have your closes,
                 And all must die.

Only a sweet and virtuous soul,
Like seasoned timber, never gives,
But though the whole world turn to coal,
                 Then chiefly lives.

23   Love

Love bade me welcome, yet my soul drew back,
                 Guilty of dust and sin;
But quick-eyed Love, observing me grow slack
                 From my first entrance in,
Drew nearer to me, sweetly questioning
                 If I lacked anything.

'A guest,' I answered, 'worthy to be here.'
                 Love said, 'You shall be he.'
'I, the unkind, ungrateful? Ah, my dear,
                 I cannot look on thee.'
Love took my hand and smiling did reply,
                 'Who made the eyes but I?'

'Truth, Lord, but I have marred them; let my shame
      Go where it doth deserve.'
'And know you not,' says Love, 'who bore the blame?'
      'My dear, then I will serve.'
'You must sit down,' says Love, 'and taste my meat.'
      So I did sit and eat.

24   Song: 'I prithee spare me'

I prithee spare me, gentle boy,
Press me no more for that slight toy,
That foolish trifle of a heart;
I swear it will not do its part,
Though dost thine, employest thy power and art.

For through long custom it has known
The little secrets, and is grown
Sullen and wise, will have its will,
And like old hawks, pursues that still
That makes least sport, flies only where it can kill.

Some youth that has not made his story
Will think, perchance, the pain's the glory,
And mannerly sit out love's feast;
I shall be carving of the best,
Rudely call for the last course 'fore the rest.

And oh, when once that course is past,
How short a time the feast doth last!
Men rise away, and scarce say grace,
Or civilly once thank the face
That did invite, but seek another place.

25 Against Fruition

Fie upon hearts that burn with mutual fire!
I hate two minds that breathe but one desire.
Were I to curse the unhallowed sort of men
I'd wish them to love, and be loved again.
Love's a chameleon, that lives on mere air,
And surfeits when it comes to grosser fare.
'Tis petty jealousies and little fears,
Hopes joined with doubts and joys with April tears,
That crown our love with pleasure: these are gone
When once we come to full fruition,
Like waking in a morning, when all night
Our fancy hath been fed with true delight.
Oh, what a stroke 'twould be! sure I should die
Should I but hear my mistress once say Ay.
That monster expectation feeds too high
For any woman e'er to satisfy;
And no brave spirit ever cared for that
Which in down beds with ease he could come at.
She's but an honest whore that yields, although
She be as cold as ice, as pure as snow:
He that enjoys her hath no more to say
Than 'Keep us fasting, if you'll have us pray.'
Then, fairest mistress, hold the power you have
By still denying what we still do crave;
In keeping us in hopes strange things to see,
That never were, nor are, nor e'er shall be.

26   A Dialogue Between the Resolved Soul and
Created Pleasure

Courage, my soul: now learn to wield
The weight of thine immortal shield;
Close on thy head thy helmet bright;
Balance thy sword against the fight.
See where an army, strong as fair,
With silken banners spreads the air.
Now, if thou beëst that thing divine,
In this day's combat let it shine,
And show that Nature wants an art
To conquer one resolvèd heart.

Pleasure
Welcome, the creation's guest,
Lord of Earth, and heaven's heir.
Lay aside that warlike crest
And of Nature's banquet share,
Where the souls of fruits and flowers
Stand prepared to heighten yours.

Soul
I sup above, and cannot stay
To bait so long upon the way.

Pleasure
On these downy pillows lie
Whose soft plumes will thither fly;
On these roses strewed so plain
Lest one leaf thy side should strain.

Soul
My gentler rest is on a thought,
Conscious of doing what I ought.

Pleasure
If thou beëst with perfumes pleased,
Such as oft the gods appeased,
Thou in fragrant clouds shall show
Like another god below.

Soul
A soul that knows not to presume
Is heaven's and its own perfume.

Pleasure
Everything does seem to vie
Which should first attract thine eye:
But since none deserves that grace,
In this crystal view *thy* face.

Soul
When the Creator's skill is prized
The rest is all but earth disguised.

Pleasure
Hark how music then prepares
For thy stay these charming airs,
Which the posting winds recall
And suspend the rivers' fall.

Soul
Had I but any time to lose
On this I would it all dispose.
Cease, tempter: none can chain a mind
Whom this sweet chordage cannot bind.

Chorus
Earth cannot show so brave a sight
As where a single soul does fence
The batteries of alluring sense,
And heaven views it with delight.
Then persevere: for still new charges sound,
And if thou overcom'st thou shalt be crowned.

34

Pleasure
All this fair, and soft, and sweet,
Which scatteringly doth shine,
Shall within one beauty meet
And she be only thine.

Soul
If things of sight such heavens be,
What heavens are those we cannot see?

Pleasure
Wheresoe'er thy foot shall go
The minted gold shall lie,
Till thou purchase all below
And want new worlds to buy.

Soul
Were it not a price who'd value gold?
And that's worth naught that can be sold.

Pleasure
Wilt thou all the glory have
That war or peace commend?
Half the world shall be thy slave,
The other half thy friend.

Soul
What friends, if to myself untrue?
What slaves, unless I captive you?

Pleasure
Thou shalt know each hidden cause,
And see the future time:
Try what depth the centre draws,
And then to heaven climb.

Soul
None thither mounts by the degree
Of knowledge, but humility.

Chorus
Triumph, triumph, victorious soul,
The world has not one pleasure more;
The rest does lie beyond the pole
And is thine everlasting store.

27   To His Coy Mistress

Had we but world enough, and time,
This coyness, Lady, were no crime.
We would sit down and think which way
To walk, and pass our long love's day.
Thou by the Indian Ganges' side
Shouldst rubies find: I by the tide
Of Humber would complain. I would
Love you ten years before the Flood,
And you should, if you please, refuse
Till the conversion of the Jews.
My vegetable love should grow
Vaster than empires, and more slow;
An hundred years should go to praise
Thine eyes and on thy forehead gaze;
Two hundred to adore each breast;
But thirty thousand to the rest;
An age at least to every part,
And the last age should show your heart;
For, Lady, you deserve this state,
Nor would I love at lower rate.
   But at my back I always hear
Time's wingèd chariot hurrying near;
And yonder all before us lie
Deserts of vast eternity.
Thy beauty shall no more be found,
Nor, in thy marble vault, shall sound
My echoing song: then worms shall try
That long preserved virginity,
And your quaint honour turn to dust,
And into ashes all my lust:

The grave's a fine and private place,
But none, I think, do there embrace.
　Now therefore, while the youthful hue
Sits on thy skin like morning dew,
And while thy willing soul transpires
At every pore with instant fires,
Now let us sport us while we may,
And now, like amorous birds of prey,
Rather at once our time devour
Than languish in his slow-chapped power.
Let us roll all our strength and all
Our sweetness up into one ball,
And tear our pleasures with rough strife
Thorough the iron gates of life:
Thus, though we cannot make our sun
Stand still, yet we will make him run.

28　The Garden

How vainly men themselves amaze
To win the palm, the oak, or bays,
And their uncessant labours see
Crowned from some single herb or tree,
Whose short and narrow-vergèd shade
Does prudently their toils upbraid;
While all flowers and all trees do close
To weave the garlands of repose!

Fair Quiet, have I found thee here,
And Innocence, thy sister dear?
Mistaken long, I sought you then
In busy companies of men:
Your sacred plants, if here below,
Only among the plants will grow:
Society is all but rude
To this delicious solitude.

No white nor red was ever seen
So amorous as this lovely green.
Fond lovers, cruel as their flame,
Cut in these trees their mistress' name:
Little, alas! they know or heed
How far these beauties hers exceed!
Fair trees! wheresoe'er your barks I wound,
No name shall but your own be found.

When we have run our passions' heat,
Love hither makes his best retreat:
The gods, that mortal beauty chase,
Still in a tree did end their race;
Apollo hunted Daphne so,
Only that she might laurel grow;
And Pan did after Syrinx speed
Not as a nymph, but for a reed.

What wondrous life is this I lead!
Ripe apples drop about my head;
The luscious clusters of the vine
Upon my mouth do crush their wine;
The nectarine and curious peach
Into my hands themselves do reach;
Stumbling on melons, as I pass,
Ensnared with flowers, I fall on grass.

Meanwhile the mind from pleasure less
Withdraws into its happiness;
The mind, that ocean where each kind
Does straight its own resemblance find;
Yet it creates, transcending these,
Far other worlds, and other seas;
Annihilating all that's made
To a green thought in a green shade.

Here at the fountain's sliding foot,
Or at some fruit-tree's mossy root,
Casting the body's vest aside,
My soul into the boughs does glide;
There, like a bird, it sits and sings,
Then whets and combs its silver wings,
And, till prepared for longer flight,
Waves in its plumes the various light.

Such was that happy Garden-state
While man there walked without a mate:
After a place so pure and sweet,
What other help could yet be meet!
But 'twas beyond a mortal's share
To wander solitary there:
Two paradises 'twere in one,
To live in Paradise alone.

How well the skilful gardener drew
Of flowers and herbs this dial new!
Where, from above, the milder sun
Does through a fragrant zodiac run:
And, as it works, the industrious bee
Computes its time as well as we.
How could such sweet and wholesome hours
Be reckoned, but with herbs and flowers?

29   A Song of a Young Lady to Her Ancient Lover

Ancient person, for whom I
All the flattering youth defy,
Long be it ere thou grow old,
Aching, shaking, crazy cold,
But still continue as thou art,
Ancient person of my heart.

On thy withered lips and dry,
Which like barren furrows lie,
Brooding kisses I will pour
Shall thy youthful heart restore;
Such kind showers in autumn fall
And a second spring recall;
Nor from thee will ever part,
Ancient person of my heart.

Thy nobler parts, which but to name
In our sex would be counted shame,
By age's frozen grasp possessed,
From their ice shall be released,
And, soothed by my reviving hand,
In former warmth and vigour stand.
All a lover's wish can reach
For thy joy my love shall teach,
And for thy pleasure shall improve
All that art can add to love.
Yet still I love thee without art,
Ancient person of my heart.

Were I (who to my cost already am
One of those strange prodigious creatures, Man)
A spirit free to choose for my own share
What case of flesh and blood I pleased to wear,
I'd be a dog, a monkey or a bear
Or anything but that vain animal
Who is so proud of being rational.
The senses are too gross, and he'll contrive
A sixth, to contradict the other five,
And before certain instinct will prefer
Reason, which fifty times for one does err.
Reason, an ignis fatuus in the mind,
Which leaving light of nature, sense, behind,
Pathless and dangerous wandering ways it takes
Through errors, fenny bogs and thorny brakes –
Whilst the misguided fellow climbs with pain
Mountains of whimsies heaped in his own brain,
Stumbling from thought to thought falls headlong down
Into doubt's boundless sea, where like to drown,
Books bear him up a while – and makes him try
To swim with bladders of philosophy;
In hopes still to o'ertake the escaping light,
The vapour dances in his dazzled sight
Till, spent, it leaves him to eternal night.
Then old age and experience, hand in hand,
Lead him to death, and make him understand,
After a search so painful and so long,
That all his life he has been in the wrong.
Huddled in dirt the reasoning engine lies
Who was so proud, so witty, and so wise.
Pride drew him in, as cheats their cullies catch,
And made him venture, to be made a wretch.
His wisdom did his happiness destroy,
Aiming to know what world he should enjoy,
And wit was his vain frivolous pretence
Of pleasing others at his own expense,

For wits are treated just like common whores:
First they're enjoyed, and then kicked out of doors.
The pleasure past, a threatening doubt remains,
That frights the enjoyer with succeeding pains.
Women and men of wit are dangerous tools,
And ever fatal to admiring fools.
But most I hold man's reason in despite,
This supernatural gift, that makes a mite
Think he's the image of the infinite,
Comparing his short life, void of all rest,
To the eternal and the ever-blest;
This busy, puzzling stirrer-up of doubt,
That frames deep mysteries, then finds 'em out,
Filling with frantic crowds of thinking fools
Those reverend bedlams – colleges and schools,
Borne on whose wings each heavy sot can pierce
The limits of the boundless universe;
So charming ointments make an old witch fly
And bear a crippled carcass through the sky;
'Tis this exalted power whose business lies
In nonsense and impossibilities.
This made a whimsical philosopher
Before the spacious world his tub prefer,
And we have modern cloistered coxcombs who
Retire to think 'cause they have naught to do.
But thoughts are given for action's government;
Where action ceases, thought's impertinent:
Our sphere of action is life's happiness,
And he who thinks beyond thinks like an ass.
Thus, whilst against false reasoning I inveigh,
I own right reason, which I would obey,
That reason that distinguishes by sense,
And gives us rules of good and ill from thence,
That bounds desires with a reforming will
To keep 'em more in vigour, not to kill.
Your reason hinders, mine helps to enjoy,
Renewing appetites yours would destroy.
My reason is my friend, yours is a cheat;
Hunger calls out, my reason bids me eat:

Perversely yours your appetite does mock:
This asks for food, that answers What's o'clock?
Thus I think reason righted, but for man –
I'll ne'er recant, defend him if you can.
For all his pride and his philosophy,
'Tis evident beasts are in their degree
As wise at least, and better far than he.
Be judge yourself – I'll bring it to the test –
Which is the basest creature, man or beast?
Birds feed on birds, beasts on each other prey,
But savage man alone does man betray;
Pressed by necessity, they kill for food,
Man undoes man to do himself no good;
With teeth and claws, by nature armed, they hunt
Nature's allowances to supply their want,
But man, with smiles, embraces, friendships, praise,
Unhumanly his fellow's life betrays,
With voluntary pains works his distress,
Not through necessity, but wantonness;
For hunger, or for love, they fight or tear,
Whilst wretched man is still in arms for fear;
For fear he arms, and is of arms afraid,
By fear to fear successively betrayed,
Base fear, the source whence his best passions came,
His boasted honour and his dear-bought fame,
That lust of power to which he's such a slave
And for the which alone he dares be brave,
To which his various projects are designed,
Which makes him generous, affable and kind,
For which he takes such pains to be thought wise
And screws his actions in a forced disguise,
Leading a tedious life in misery,
Under laborious, mean hypocrisy.
Look to the bottom of his vast design,
Wherein man's wisdom, power and glory join:
The good he acts, the ill he does endure,
'Tis all for fear, to make himself secure.
Merely for safety after fame we thirst,
For all men would be cowards if they durst,

And honesty's against all common sense:
Men must be knaves, 'tis in their own defence.
Mankind's dishonest: if you think it fair,
Amongst known cheats, to play upon the square,
You'll be undone.
Nor can weak truth your reputation save:
The knaves will all agree to call you knave;
Wronged shall he live, insulted o'er, oppressed,
Who dares be less a villain than the rest.
Thus, sir, you see what human nature craves:
Most men are cowards, all men should be knaves;
The difference lies, as far as I can see,
Not in the thing itself but the degree,
And all the subject-matter of debate
Is only, who's a knave of the first rate.

31   Plain Dealing's Downfall

Long time Plain Dealing in the haughty town
Wandering about, although in threadbare gown,
At last unanimously was cried down.

When almost starved, she to the country fled
In hopes, though meanly she should be there fed,
And tumble nightly on a pea-straw bed.

But Knavery, knowing her intent, took post
And rumoured her approach through every coast,
Vowing his ruin that should be her host.

Frighted at this, each rustic shut his door,
Bid her be gone, and trouble him no more,
For he that entertained her must be poor.

At this, grief seized her, grief too great to tell,
When weeping, sighing, fainting, down she fell,
Whilst Knavery, laughing, rang her passing-bell.

ANONYMOUS

32 Hye Nonny Nonny Noe

Down lay the shepherd swain
   so sober and demure,
Wishing for his wench again
   so bonny and so pure,
With his head on hillock low
   and his arms akimbo,
And all was for the loss of his
   Hye nonny nonny noe.

His tears fell as thin
   as water from the still,
His hair upon his chin
   grew like thyme upon a hill,
His cherry cheeks pale as snow
   did testify his mickle woe,
And all was for the loss of his
   hye nonny nonny noe.

Sweet she was, as kind a love
   as ever fettered swain;
Never such a dainty one
   shall man enjoy again.
Set a thousand on a row,
   I forbid that any show
Ever the like of her
   hye nonny nonny noe.

Face she had of filbert hue
   and bosomed like a swan,
Back she had of bended ewe,
   and waisted by a span.
Hair she had as black as crow,
   from the head unto the toe,
Down down all over her
   hye nonny nonny noe.

With her mantle tucked up high
   she foddered her flock,
So buxom and alluringly
   her knee upheld her smock,
So nimbly did she use to go
   so smooth she danced on tip-toe,
That all the men were fond of her
   hye nonny nonny noe.

She smiled like a holy-day,
   she simpered like the spring,
She pranked it like a popinjay,
   and like a swallow sing:
She tripped it like a barren doe,
   She strutted like a gorcrow,
Which made the men so fond of her
   hye nonny nonny noe.

To sport it on the merry down
   to dance the lively hay;
To wrestle for a green gown
   in heat of all the day,
Never would she say me no,
   yet me thought I had though
Never enough of her
   hye nonny nonny noe.

But gone she is the prettiest lass
   that ever trod on plain.
Whatever hath betide of her
   blame not the shepherd swain,
For why she was her own foe,
   and gave herself the overthrow
By being so frank of her
   hye nonny nonny noe.

JONATHAN SWIFT

33 Daphne

Daphne knows, with equal ease,
How to vex and how to please,
But the folly of her sex
Makes her sole delight to vex.
Never woman more devised
Surer ways to be despised:
Paradoxes weakly wielding,
Always conquered, never yielding.
To dispute, her chief delight,
With not one opinion right:
Thick her arguments she lays on,
And with cavils combats reason:
Answers in decisive way,
Never hears what you can say:
Still her odd perverseness shows
Chiefly where she nothing knows.
And where she is most familiar,
Always peevisher and sillier:
All her spirits in a flame
When she knows she's most to blame.

 Send me hence ten thousand miles
From a face that always smiles:
None could ever act that part
But a Fury in her heart.

Ye who hate such inconsistence,
To be easy keep your distance;
Or in folly still befriend her,
But have no concern to mend her.
Lose not time to contradict her,
Nor endeavour to convict her.
Never take it in your thought
That she'll own or cure a fault.

Into contradiction warm her,
Then, perhaps, you may reform her:
Only take this rule along,
Always to advise her wrong;
And reprove her when she's right;
She may then grow wise for spite.

No – that scheme will ne'er succeed,
She has better learnt her creed:
She's too cunning and too skilful,
When to yield and when be wilful.
Nature holds her forth two mirrors,
One for truth and one for errors:
That looks hideous, fierce and frightful;
This is flattering and delightful;
That she throws away as foul;
Sits by this to dress her soul.

Thus you have the case in view,
Daphne, 'twixt the Dean and you,
Heaven forbid he should despise thee;
But will never more advise thee.

Twelve Articles
1. Lest it may more quarrels breed
    I will never hear you read.
2. By disputing I will never
    To convince you, once endeavour.
3. When a paradox you stick to,
    I will never contradict you.
4. When I talk, and you are heedless,
    I will show no anger needless.
5. When your speeches are absurd,
    I will ne'er object a word.
6. When you furious argue wrong,
    I will grieve, and hold my tongue.
7. Not a jest or humorous story
    Will I ever tell before ye:
    To be chidden for explaining
    When you quite mistake the meaning.

8. Never more will I suppose
   You can taste my verse or prose:
9. You no more at me shall fret,
   While I teach, and you forget;
10. You shall never hear me thunder,
    When you blunder on, and blunder.
11. Show your poverty of spirit,
    And in dress place all your merit;
    Give yourself ten thousand airs;
    That with me shall break no squares.
12. Never will I give advice
    Till you please to ask me thrice;
    Which if you in scorn reject,
    'Twill be just as I expect.

    Thus we both shall have our ends,
    And continue special friends.

34   Elegy to the Memory of an Unfortunate Lady

What beckoning ghost, along the moonlight shade
Invites my steps, and points to yonder glade?
'Tis she! – but why that bleeding bosom gored,
Why dimly gleams the visionary sword?
Oh, ever beauteous, ever friendly! tell,
Is it, in heaven, a crime to love too well?
To bear too tender or too firm a heart,
To act a lover's or a Roman's part?
Is there no bright reversion in the sky
For those who greatly think, or bravely die?
    Why bade ye else, ye powers! her soul aspire
Above the vulgar flight of low desire?
Ambition first sprung from your blest abodes,
The glorious fault of angels and of gods:
Thence to their images on earth it flows,
And in the breasts of kings and heroes glows!
Most souls, 'tis true, but peep out once an age,
Dull, sullen prisoners in the body's cage:
Dim lights of life that burn a length of years,
Useless, unseen, as lamps in sepulchres;
Like Eastern kings a lazy state they keep,
And close confined to their own palace sleep.
    From these perhaps (ere nature bade her die)
Fate snatched her early to the pitying sky.
As into air the purer spirits flow,
And separate from their kindred dregs below;
So flew the soul to its congenial place,
Nor left one virtue to redeem her race.
    But thou, false guardian of a charge too good,
Thou, mean deserter of thy brother's blood!
See on these ruby lips the trembling breath,
These cheeks now fading at the blast of death:
Cold is that breast which warmed the world before,
And those love-darting eyes must roll no more.

Thus, if eternal justice rules the ball,
Thus shall your wives, and thus your children fall:
On all the line a sudden vengeance waits,
And frequent hearses shall besiege your gates.
There passengers shall stand, and pointing say
(While the long funerals blacken all the way),
'Lo! these were they, whose souls the Furies steeled,
And cursed with hearts unknowing how to yield.'
Thus unlamented pass the proud away,
The gaze of fools, and pageant of a day!
So perish all, whose breast ne'er learned to glow
For others' good, or melt at others' woe.

What can atone (oh ever-injured shade!)
Thy fate unpitied, and thy rites unpaid?
No friend's complaint, no kind domestic tear
Pleased thy pale ghost, or graced thy mournful bier.
By foreign hands thy dying eyes were closed,
By foreign hands thy decent limbs composed,
By foreign hands thy humble grave adorned,
By strangers honoured, and by strangers mourned!
What though no friends in sable weeds appear,
Grieve for an hour, perhaps, then mourn a year,
And bear about the mockery of woe
To midnight dances, and the public show?
What though no weeping loves thy ashes grace,
Nor polished marble emulate thy face?
What though no sacred earth allow thee room,
Nor hallowed dirge be muttered o'er thy tomb?
Yet shall thy grave with rising flowers be dressed
And the green turf lie lightly on thy breast:
There shall the morn her earliest tears bestow,
There the first roses of the year shall blow;
While angels with their silver wings o'ershade
The ground now sacred by thy reliques made.

So peaceful rests, without a stone, a name,
What once had beauty, titles, wealth, and fame.
How loved, how honoured once, avails thee not,
To whom related, or by whom begot;
A heap of dust alone remains of thee;
'Tis all thou art, and all the proud shall be!

Poets themselves must fall, like those they sung;
Deaf the praised ear, and mute the tuneful tongue.
Even he, whose soul now melts in mournful lays,
Shall shortly want the generous tear he pays;
Then from his closing eyes thy form shall part,
And the last pang shall tear thee from his heart,
Life's idle business at one gasp be o'er,
The Muse forgot, and thou beloved no more!

35   Molly Moor

    Tully, the queen of beauty's boast,
Through all America the toast,
Does, that her face more eyes may catch,
Reform it with a negro-patch.
Venus for ever does delight
In thickest shade, and ebon night.
Observe the coal of purest jet
The fiercest flame does still beget.
As the most cloudy mysteries
The mussulmans devoutest prize,
So smartest beaux and wits adore
The gloomy grace of Molly Moor.
    The proudest snowy forms at last
Must in a sable pall be dressed:
E'en Dolly Dowglass' self must go
Down to the negro-shades below;
Into the pitchy kingdom, where
This raven lass shall queen appear;
And sit on Proserpina's throne,
When she is up to Ceres gone.

SAMUEL JOHNSON

36   Prologue to *A Word to the Wise*

This night presents a play which public rage,
Or right, or wrong, once hooted from the stage.
From zeal or malice, now no more we dread,
For English vengeance wars not with the dead.
A generous foe regards with pitying eye
The man whom fate has laid where all must lie.
To wit reviving from its author's dust,
Be kind, ye judges, or at least be just,
For no renewed hostilities invade
The oblivious grave's inviolable shade.
Let one great payment every claim appease,
And him, who cannot hurt, allow to please;
To please by scenes unconscious of offence,
By harmless merriment or useful sense.
Where aught of bright, or fair, the piece displays,
Approve it only – 'tis too late to praise.
If want of skill, or want of care appear,
Forbear to hiss – the poet cannot hear.
By all, like him, must praise and blame be found,
At best a fleeting gleam, or empty sound.
Yet then shall calm reflection bless the night
When liberal pity dignify'd delight;
When pleasure fired her torch at Virtue's flame,
And Mirth was Bounty with an humbler name.

THOMAS GRAY

37 Ode on the Spring

Lo! where the rosy-bosomed Hours,
Fair Venus' train, appear,
Disclose the long-expecting flowers,
And wake the purple year!
The Attic warbler pours her throat,
Responsive to the cuckoo's note,
The untaught harmony of spring:
While whispering pleasure as they fly,
Cool zephyrs through the clear blue sky
Their gathered fragrance fling.

Where'er the oak's thick branches stretch
A broader browner shade;
Where'er the rude and moss-grown beech
O'er-canopies the glade,
Beside some water's rushy brink
With me the Muse shall sit and think
(At ease reclined in rustic state)
How vain the ardour of the crowd,
How low, how little are the proud,
How indigent the great!

Still is the toiling hand of Care;
The panting herds repose.
Yet hark, how through the peopled air
The busy murmur glows!
The insect youth are on the wing,
Eager to taste the honeyed spring,
And float amid the liquid noon:
Some lightly o'er the current skim,
Some show their gaily-gilded trim
Quick-glancing to the sun.

To Contemplation's sober eye
Such is the race of man:
And they that creep, and they that fly,
Shall end where they began.
Alike the busy and the gay
But flutter through life's little day,
In fortune's varying colours dressed:
Brushed by the hand of rough Mischance,
Or chilled by age, their airy dance
They leave, in dust to rest.

Methinks I hear in accents low
The sportive kind reply:
'Poor moralist! and what art thou?
A solitary fly!
Thy joys no glittering female meets,
No hive hast thou of hoarded sweets,
No painted plumage to display:
On hasty wings thy youth is flown;
Thy sun is set, thy spring is gone –
We frolic, while 'tis May.'

38   Elegy Written in a Country Churchyard

The curfew tolls the knell of parting day,
The lowing herd wind slowly o'er the lea,
The ploughman homeward plods his weary way,
And leaves the world to darkness and to me.

Now fades the glimmering landscape on the sight,
And all the air a solemn stillness holds,
Save where the beetle wheels his droning flight,
And drowsy tinklings lull the distant folds;

Save that from yonder ivy-mantled tower
The moping owl does to the moon complain
Of such as, wandering near her secret bower,
Molest her ancient solitary reign.

Beneath those rugged elms, that yew-tree's shade,
Where heaves the turf in many a mouldering heap,
Each in his narrow cell for ever laid,
The rude forefathers of the hamlet sleep.

The breezy call of incense-breathing morn,
The swallow twittering from the straw-built shed,
The cock's shrill clarion or the echoing horn,
No more shall rouse them from their lowly bed.

For them no more the blazing hearth shall burn,
Or busy housewife ply her evening care:
No children run to lisp their sire's return,
Or climb his knees the envied kiss to share.

Oft did the harvest to their sickle yield,
Their furrow oft the stubborn glebe has broke;
How jocund did they drive their team afield!
How bowed the woods beneath their sturdy stroke!

Let not Ambition mock their useful toil,
Their homely joys and destiny obscure;
Nor Grandeur hear, with a disdainful smile,
The short and simple annals of the poor.

The boast of heraldry, the pomp of power,
And all that beauty, all that wealth e'er gave,
Awaits alike the inevitable hour.
The paths of glory lead but to the grave.

Nor you, ye proud, impute to these the fault,
If Memory o'er their tomb no trophies raise,
Where through the long-drawn aisle and fretted vault
The pealing anthem swells the note of praise.

Can storied urn or animated bust
Back to its mansion call the fleeting breath?
Can Honour's voice provoke the silent dust,
Or Flattery soothe the dull cold ear of Death?

Perhaps in this neglected spot is laid
Some heart once pregnant with celestial fire;
Hands that the rod of empire might have swayed,
Or waked to ecstasy the living lyre.

But Knowledge to their eyes her ample page
Rich with the spoils of time did ne'er unroll;
Chill Penury repressed their noble rage,
And froze the genial current of the soul.

Full many a gem of purest ray serene
The dark unfathomed caves of ocean bear:
Full many a flower is born to blush unseen
And waste its sweetness on the desert air.

Some village-Hampden that with dauntless breast
The little tyrant of his fields withstood;
Some mute inglorious Milton here may rest,
Some Cromwell guiltless of his country's blood.

Th' applause of listening senates to command,
The threats of pain and ruin to despise,
To scatter plenty o'er a smiling land,
And read their history in a nation's eyes,

Their lot forbade: nor circumscribed alone
Their growing virtues, but their crimes confined;
Forbade to wade through slaughter to a throne,
And shut the gates of mercy on mankind,

The struggling pangs of conscious truth to hide,
To quench the blushes of ingenuous shame,
Or heap the shrine of Luxury and Pride
With incense kindled at the Muse's flame.

Far from the madding crowd's ignoble strife
Their sober wishes never learned to stray;
Along the cool sequestered vale of life
They kept the noiseless tenor of their way.

Yet even these bones from insult to protect
Some frail memorial still erected nigh,
With uncouth rhymes and shapeless sculpture decked,
Implores the passing tribute of a sigh.

Their name, their years, spelt by the unlettered muse,
The place of fame and elegy supply:
And many a holy text around she strews,
That teach the rustic moralist to die.

For who to dumb Forgetfulness a prey,
This pleasing anxious being e'er resigned,
Left the warm precincts of the cheerful day,
Nor cast one longing lingering look behind?

On some fond breast the parting soul relies,
Some pious drops the closing eye requires;
Even from the tomb the voice of Nature cries,
Even in our ashes live their wonted fires.

For thee who, mindful of the unhonoured dead,
Dost in these lines their artless tale relate;
If chance, by lonely Contemplation led,
Some kindred spirit shall inquire thy fate,

Haply some hoary-headed swain may say,
'Oft have we seen him at the peep of dawn
Brushing with hasty steps the dews away
To meet the sun upon the upland lawn.

'There at the foot of yonder nodding beech
That wreathes its old fantastic roots so high,
His listless length at noontide would he stretch,
And pore upon the brook that babbles by.

'Hard by yon wood, now smiling as in scorn,
Muttering his wayward fancies he would rove,
Now drooping, woeful wan, like one forlorn,
Or crazed with care, or crossed in hopeless love.

'One morn I missed him on the customed hill,
Along the heath and near his favourite tree;
Another came; nor yet beside the rill,
Nor up the lawn, nor at the wood was he;

'The next with dirges due in sad array
Slow through the church-way path we saw him borne.
Approach and read (for thou canst read) the lay,
Graved on the stone beneath yon aged thorn.'

The Epitaph
Here rests his head upon the lap of earth
A youth to fortune and to fame unknown.
Fair Science frowned not on his humble birth,
And Melancholy marked him for her own.

Large was his bounty and his soul sincere,
Heaven did a recompense as largely send:
He gave to Misery all he had, a tear,
He gained from heaven ('twas all he wished) a friend.

No farther seek his merits to disclose,
Or draw his frailties from their dread abode
(There they alike in trembling hope repose),
The bosom of his Father and his God.

JEAN ELLIOT

39   Lament for Flodden

I've heard them lilting, at the ewe milking,
    Lasses a' lilting, before dawn of day;
But now they are moaning, on ilka green loaning;
    The flowers of the forest are a' wede away.

At boughts, in the morning, nae blithe lads are scorning;
    Lasses are lonely, and dowie, and wae;
Nae daffing, nae gabbing, but sighing and sabbing;
    Ilk ane lifts her leglen, and hies her away.

At har'st, at the shearing, nae youths now are jeering;
    Bandsters are runkled, and lyart or gray;
At fair, or at preaching, nae wooing, nae fleeching;
    The flowers of the forest are a' wede away.

At e'en, in the gloaming, nae younkers are roaming
    'Bout stacks, with the lasses at bogle to play;
But ilk maid sits dreary, lamenting her deary –
    The flowers of the forest are weded away.

Dool and wae for the order, sent our lads to the Border!
    The English, for ance, by guile wan the day;
The flowers of the forest, that fought aye the foremost,
    The prime of our land, are cauld in the clay.

We'll hear nae mair lilting, at the ewe milking;
    Women and bairns are heartless and wae:
Sighing and moaning, on ilka green loaning –
    The flowers of the forest are a' wede away.

WILLIAM COWPER

40   The Jackdaw

There is a bird who, by his coat,
And by the hoarseness of his note,
    Might be supposed a crow;
A great frequenter of the church,
Where, bishop-like, he finds a perch,
    And dormitory too.

Above the steeple shines a plate,
That turns and turns, to indicate
    From what point blows the weather.
Look up – your brains begin to swim,
'Tis in the clouds – that pleases him,
    He chooses it the rather.

Fond of the speculative height,
Thither he wings his airy flight,
    And thence securely sees
The bustle and the raree-show
That occupy mankind below,
    Secure and at his ease.

You think, no doubt, he sits and muses
On future broken bones and bruises,
    If he should chance to fall.
No; not a single thought like that
Employs his philosophic pate,
    Or troubles it at all.

He sees that this great roundabout –
The world, with all its motley rout,
    Church, army, physic, law,
Its customs, and its businesses –
Is no concern at all of his,
    And says – what says he? – Caw.

Thrice happy bird! I too have seen
Much of the vanities of men;
 And, sick of having seen 'em,
Would cheerfully these limbs resign
For such a pair of wings as thine,
 And such a head between 'em.

WILLIAM BLAKE

41   Auguries of Innocence

To see a World in a Grain of Sand
And a Heaven in a Wild Flower,
Hold Infinity in the palm of your hand
And Eternity in an hour.

A Robin Red breast in a Cage
Puts all Heaven in a Rage,
A dove house fill'd with doves & Pigeons
Shudders Hell thro' all its regions.
A dog starv'd at his Master's Gate
Predicts the ruin of the State.
A Horse misus'd upon the Road
Calls to Heaven for Human blood.
Each outcry of the hunted Hare
A fibre from the Brain does tear.
A Skylark wounded on the wing,
A Cherubim does cease to sing.
The Game Cock clip'd & arm'd for fight
Does the Rising Sun affright.
Every Wolf's & Lion's howl
Raises from Hell a Human Soul.
The wild deer, wand'ring here & there,
Keeps the Human Soul from Care.
The Lamb misus'd breeds Public strife
And yet forgives the Butcher's Knife.
The Bat that flits at close of Eve
Has left the Brain that won't Believe.
The Owl that calls upon the Night
Speaks the Unbeliever's fright.
He who shall hurt the little Wren
Shall never be belov'd by Men.
He who the Ox to wrath has mov'd
Shall never be by Woman lov'd.
The wanton Boy that kills the Fly
Shall feel the Spider's enmity.

He who torments the Chafer's sprite
Weaves a Bower in endless Night.
The Catterpiller on the Leaf
Repeats to thee thy Mother's grief.
Kill not the Moth nor Butterfly,
For the Last Judgment draweth nigh.
He who shall train the Horse to War
Shall never pass the Polar Bar.
The Beggar's Dog & Widow's Cat
Feed them & thou wilt grow fat.
The Gnat that sings his Summer's song
Poison gets from Slander's tongue.
The poison of the Snake & Newt
Is the sweat of Envy's Foot.
The Poison of the Honey Bee
Is the Artist's Jealousy.
The Prince's Robes & Beggar's Rags
Are Toadstools on the Miser's Bags.
A truth that's told with bad intent
Beats all the Lies you can invent.
It is right it should be so;
Man was made for Joy & Woe;
And when this we rightly know
Thro' the World we safely go.
Joy & Woe are woven fine,
A Clothing for the Soul divine;
Under every grief & pine
Runs a joy with silken twine.
The Babe is more than swadling Bands;
Throughout all these Human Lands
Tools were made, & Born were hands,
Every Farmer Understands.
Every Tear from Every Eye
Becomes a Babe in Eternity;
This is caught by Females bright
And return'd to its own delight.
The Bleat, the Bark, Bellow & Roar
Are Waves that Beat on Heaven's Shore.
The Babe that weeps the Rod beneath
Writes Revenge in realms of death.

The Beggar's Rags, fluttering in Air,
Does to Rags the Heaven tear.
The Soldier, arm'd with Sword & Gun,
Palsied strikes the Summer's Sun.
The poor Man's Farthing is worth more
Than all the Gold on Afric's Shore.
One Mite wrung from the Labrer's hands
Shall buy & sell the Miser's Lands:
Or, if protected from on high,
Does that whole Nation sell & buy.
He who mocks the Infant's Faith
Shall be mock'd in Age & Death.
He who shall teach the Child to Doubt
The rotting Grave shall ne'er get out.
He who respects the Infant's faith
Triumphs over Hell & Death.
The Child's Toys & the Old Man's Reasons
Are the Fruits of the Two seasons.
The Questioner, who sits so sly,
Shall never know how to Reply.
He who replies to words of Doubt
Doth put the Light of Knowledge out.
The Strongest Poison ever known
Came from Caesar's Laurel Crown.
Nought can deform the Human Race
Like to the Armour's iron brace.
When Gold & Gems adorn the Plow
To peaceful Arts shall Envy Bow.
A Riddle or the Cricket's Cry
Is to Doubt a fit Reply.
The Emmet's Inch & Eagle's Mile
Make Lame Philosophy to smile.
He who Doubts from what he sees
Will ne'er Believe, do what you Please.
If the Sun & Moon should doubt,
They'd immediately Go out.
To be in a Passion you Good may do,
But no Good if a Passion is in you.
The Whore & Gambler, by the State
Licenc'd, build that Nation's Fate.

The Harlot's cry from Street to Street
Shall weave Old England's winding Sheet.
The Winner's Shout, the Loser's Curse,
Dance before dead England's Hearse.
Every Night & every Morn
Some to Misery are Born.
Every Morn & Every Night
Some are Born to sweet delight.
Some are Born to sweet delight,
Some are Born to Endless Night.
We are led to Believe a Lie
When we see not Thro' the Eye
Which was Born in a Night to perish in a Night
When the Soul Slept in Beams of Light.
God Appears & God is Light
To those poor Souls who dwell in Night,
But does a Human Form Display
To those who Dwell in Realms of day.

42 London

I wander through each chartered street
Near where the chartered Thames does flow,
And mark in every face I meet
Marks of weakness, marks of woe.

In every cry of every man,
In every infant's cry of fear,
In every voice, in every ban,
The mind-forged manacles I hear.

How the chimney-sweeper's cry
Every blackening church appals,
And the hapless soldier's sigh
Runs in blood down palace walls;

But most through midnight streets I hear
How the youthful harlot's curse
Blasts the new-born infant's tear
And blights with plagues the marriage hearse.

43   John Anderson my Jo

John Anderson my jo, John,
    When we were first acquent,
Your locks were like the raven,
    Your bonnie brow was brent;
But now your brow is beld, John,
    Your locks are like the snow;
But blessings on your frosty pow,
    John Anderson, my jo.

John Anderson my jo, John,
    We clamb the hill thegither;
And mony a canty day, John,
    We've had wi' ane anither:
Now we maun totter down, John,
    But hand in hand we'll go,
And sleep thegither at the foot,
    John Anderson, my jo.

WILLIAM WORDSWORTH

44   She was a phantom of delight

She was a phantom of delight
When first she gleamed upon my sight;
A lovely apparition, sent
To be a moment's ornament;
Her eyes as stars of twilight fair;
Like twilight's, too, her dusky hair;
But all things else about her drawn
From Maytime and the cheerful dawn;
A dancing shape, an image gay,
To haunt, to startle, and waylay.

I saw her upon nearer view,
A spirit, yet a woman too!
Her household motions light and free,
And steps of virgin liberty;
A countenance in which did meet
Sweet records, promises as sweet;
A creature not too bright or good
For human nature's daily food;
For transient sorrows, simple wiles,
Praise, blame, love, kisses, tears and smiles.

And now I see with eye serene
The very pulse of the machine;
A being breathing thoughtful breath,
A traveller betwixt life and death;
The reason firm, the temperate will,
Endurance, foresight, strength and skill;
A perfect woman, nobly planned
To warn, to comfort, and command;
And yet a spirit still, and bright
With something of an angel light.

ROBERT SOUTHEY

45   After Blenheim

It was a summer evening,
  Old Kaspar's work was done,
And he before his cottage door
  Was sitting in the sun,
And by him sported on the green
His little grandchild Wilhelmine.

She saw her brother Peterkin
  Roll something large and round,
Which he beside the rivulet
  In playing there had found;
He came to ask what he had found,
That was so large, and smooth, and round.

Old Kaspar took it from the boy,
  Who stood expectant by;
And then the old man shook his head,
  And with a natural sigh,
'Tis some poor fellow's skull, said he,
Who fell in the great victory.

I find them in the garden,
  For there's many here about,
And often when I go to plough,
  The ploughshare turns them out;
For many thousand men, said he,
Were slain in the great victory.

Now tell us what 'twas all about,
  Young Peterkin, he cries,
And little Wilhelmine looks up
  With wonder-waiting eyes;
Now tell us all about the war,
And what they killed each other for.

It was the English, Kaspar cried,
    That put the French to rout;
But what they killed each other for,
    I could not well make out;
But everybody said, quoth he,
That 'twas a famous victory.

My father lived at Blenheim then,
    Yon little stream hard by;
They burnt his dwelling to the ground
    And he was forced to fly;
So with his wife and child he fled,
Nor had he where to rest his head.

With fire and sword the country round
    Was wasted far and wide,
And many a childing mother then,
    And new-born baby died.
But things like that, you know, must be
At every famous victory.

They say it was a shocking sight
    After the field was won,
For many thousand bodies here
    Lay rotting in the sun;
But things like that, you know, must be
After a famous victory.

Great praise the Duke of Marlbro' won,
    And our good Prince Eugene. –
Why 'twas a very wicked thing!
    Said little Wilhelmine.
Nay – nay – my little girl, quoth he,
It was a famous victory.

And everybody praised the Duke
    Who this great fight did win.
But what good came of it at last?
    Quoth little Peterkin.
Why that I cannot tell, said he,
But 'twas a famous victory.

THOMAS CAMPBELL

46   Lord Ullin's Daughter

A chieftain to the Highlands bound
   Cries 'Boatman, do not tarry!
And I'll give thee a silver pound
   To row us o'er the ferry.'

'Now who be ye would cross Lochgyle,
   This dark and stormy water?'
'O, I'm the chief of Ulva's isle,
   And this Lord Ullin's daughter.

'And fast before her father's men
   Three days we've fled together,
For, should he find us in the glen,
   My blood would stain the heather.

'His horsemen hard behind us ride;
   Should they our steps discover,
Then who will cheer my bonny bride
   When they have slain her lover?'

Outspoke the hardy Highland wight,
   'I'll go, my chief! I'm ready;
It is not for your silver bright,
   But for your winsome lady.

'And, by my word! the bonny bird
   In danger shall not tarry;
So, though the waves are raging white
   I'll row you o'er the ferry.'

By this the storm grew loud apace,
   The water-wraith was shrieking;
And in the scowl of heaven each face
   Grew dark as they were speaking.

But still, as wilder blew the wind,
  And as the night grew drearer,
Adown the glen rode armèd men –
  Their trampling sounded nearer.

'O haste thee, haste!' the lady cries,
  'Though tempests round us gather;
I'll meet the raging of the skies,
  But not an angry father.'

The boat has left a stormy land,
  A stormy sea before her, –
When, oh! too strong for human hand,
  The tempest gathered o'er her.

And still they rowed amidst the roar
  Of waters fast prevailing:
Lord Ullin reached that fatal shore, –
  His wrath was changed to wailing.

For sore dismayed, through storm and shade,
  His child he did discover:
One lovely hand she stretched for aid,
  And one was round her lover.

'Come back! come back!' he cried in grief
  Across the stormy water:
'And I'll forgive your Highland chief,
  My daughter! oh my daughter!'

'Twas vain: the loud waves lashed the shore,
  Return or aid preventing;
The waters wild went o'er his child,
  And he was left lamenting.

Of Nelson and the North
Sing the glorious day's renown,
When to battle fierce came forth
All the might of Denmark's crown,
And her arms along the deep proudly shone, –
By each gun the lighted brand
In a bold determined hand;
And the Prince of all the land
Led them on.

Like leviathans in view
Lay their bulwarks on the brine,
While the sign of battle flew
On the lofty British line:
It was ten of April morn by the chime:
As they drifted on their path
There was silence deep as death,
And the boldest held his breath
For a time.

But the might of England flushed
To anticipate the scene;
And her van the fleeter rushed
O'er the deadly space between.
'Hearts of oak!' our captain cried; when each gun
From its adamantine lips
Spread a death-shade round the ships,
Like the hurricane eclipse
Of the sun.

Again! again! again!
And the havoc did not slack,
Till a feeble cheer the Dane
To our cheering sent us back:
Their shots along the deep slowly boom;
Then ceased – and all is wail
As they strike the shattered sail,
Or in conflagration pale
Light the gloom.

Out spoke the victor then
As he hailed them o'er the wave,
'Ye are brothers! ye are men!
And we conquer but to save;
So peace instead of death let us bring:
But yield, proud foe, thy fleet
With the crews at England's feet,
And make submission meet
To our King.'

Then Denmark blessed our chief
That he gave her wounds repose;
And the sounds of joy and grief
From her people wildly rose,
As death withdrew his shades from the day;
While the sun looked smiling bright
O'er a wide and woeful sight,
Where the fires of funeral light
Died away.

Now joy, Old England, raise
For the tidings of thy might
By the festal cities' blaze,
While the wine-cup shines in light;
And yet, amidst that joy and uproar,
Let us think of them that sleep,
Full many a fathom deep,
By thy wild and stormy steep,
Elsinore!

Brave hearts! to Britain's pride
Once so faithful and so true,
On the deck of fame that died
With the gallant good Riou –
Soft sigh the winds of Heaven o'er their grave!
While the billow mournful rolls
And the mermaid's song condoles,
Singing glory to the souls
Of the brave!

48   Hohenlinden

On Linden, when the sun was low,
All bloodless lay the untrodden snow,
And dark as winter was the flow
  Of Iser, rolling rapidly.

But Linden saw another sight
When the drum beat at dead of night,
Commanding fires of death to light
  The darkness of her scenery.

By torch and trumpet fast arrayed,
Each horseman drew his battle blade,
And furious every charger neighed
  To join the dreadful revelry.

Then shook the hills with thunder riven,
Then rushed the steed to battle driven,
And louder than the bolts of heaven
  Far flashed the red artillery.

But redder yet that light shall glow
On Linden's hills of stainèd snow,
And bloodier yet the torrent flow
  Of Iser, rolling rapidly.

'Tis morn, but scarce yon level sun
Can pierce the war-clouds, rolling dun,
Where furious Frank and fiery Hun
  Shout in their sulphurous canopy.

The combat deepens. On, ye brave,
Who rush to glory, or the grave!
Wave, Munich! all thy banners wave,
  And charge with all thy chivalry!

Few, few shall part where many meet!
The snow shall be their winding-sheet,
And every turf beneath their feet
  Shall be a soldier's sepulchre.

49   The Soldier's Dream

Our bugles sang truce – for the night-cloud had lowered,
   And the sentinel stars set their watch in the sky;
And thousands had sunk on the ground overpowered,
   The weary to sleep, and the wounded to die.

When reposing that night on my pallet of straw,
   By the wolf-scaring faggot that guarded the slain,
At the dead of the night a sweet vision I saw,
   And thrice ere the morning I dreamt it again.

Methought from the battle-field's dreadful array
   Far, far I had roamed on a desolate track:
'Twas autumn, – and sunshine arose on the way
   To the home of my fathers, that welcomed me back.

I flew to the pleasant fields, traversed so oft
   In life's morning march when my bosom was young;
I heard my own mountain-goats bleating aloft,
   And knew the sweet strain that the corn-reapers sung.

Then pledged we the wine-cup, and fondly I swore
   From my home and my weeping friends never to part;
My little ones kissed me a thousand times o'er,
   And my wife sobbed aloud in her fulness of heart.

'Stay, stay with us, – rest, thou art weary and worn!'
   And fain was their war-broken soldier to stay;
But sorrow returned with the dawning of morn,
   And the voice in my dreaming ear melted away.

REGINALD HEBER

50   From Greenland's Icy Mountains

From Greenland's icy mountains,
    From India's coral strand,
Where Afric's sunny fountains
    Roll down their golden sand,
From many an ancient river,
    From many a palmy plain,
They call us to deliver
    Their land from error's chain.

What though the spicy breezes
    Blow soft o'er Java's isle,
Though every prospect pleases
    And only man is vile,
In vain with lavish kindness
    The gifts of God are strown,
The heathen in his blindness
    Bows down to wood and stone.

Can we, whose souls are lighted
    With wisdom from on high,
Can we to men benighted
    The lamp of life deny?
Salvation! oh, salvation!
    The joyful sound proclaim,
Till each remotest nation
    Has learned Messiah's name.

Waft, waft, ye winds, his story,
    And you, ye waters, roll,
Till, like a sea of glory,
    It spreads from pole to pole;
Till o'er our ransomed nature
    The Lamb for sinners slain,
Redeemer, King, Creator,
    In bliss returns to reign.

LEIGH HUNT

51   Three Sonnets

(i) To a Fish
You strange, astonished-looking, angle-faced,
Dreary-mouthed, gaping wretches of the sea,
Gulping salt water everlastingly,
Cold-blooded, though with red your blood be graced,
And mute, though dwellers in the roaring waste;
And you, all shapes beside, that fishy be –
Some round, some flat, some long, all devilry,
Legless, unloving, infamously chaste:

O scaly, slippery, wet, swift, staring wights,
What is't ye do? What life lead? eh, dull goggles?
How do ye vary your vile days and nights?
How pass your Sundays? Are ye still but joggles
In ceaseless wash? Still nought but gapes, and bites,
And drinks, and stares, diversified with boggles?

(ii) A Fish replies
Amazing monster! that, for aught I know,
With the first sight of thee didst make our race
For ever stare! O flat and shocking face,
Grimly divided from the breast below!
Thou that on dry land horribly dost go
With a split body and most ridiculous pace,
Prong after prong, disgracer of all grace,
Long-useless-finned, haired, upright, unwet, slow!

O breather of unbreathable, sword-sharp air,
How canst exist? How bear thyself, thou dry
And dreary sloth? What particle canst share
Of the only blessed life, the watery?
I sometimes see of ye an actual *pair*
Go by, linked fin by fin, most odiously.

(iii) The Fish turns into a Man, and then into a Spirit,
    and again speaks
Indulge thy smiling scorn, if smiling still,
O man! and loathe, but with a sort of love;
For difference must its use by difference prove,
And, in sweet clang, the spheres with music fill.
One of the spirits am I, that at his will
Live in whate'er has life – fish, eagle, dove –
No hate, no pride, beneath naught, nor above,
A visitor of the rounds of God's sweet skill.

Man's life is warm, glad, sad, 'twixt loves and graves,
Boundless in hope, honoured with pangs austere,
Heaven-gazing; and his angel-wings he craves:
The fish is swift, small-needing, vague yet clear,
A cold, sweet, silver life, wrapped in round waves,
Quickened with touches of transporting fear.

52 Newark Abbey

August 1842, with a reminiscence of August 1807

I gaze where August's sunbeam falls
Along these grey and lonely walls,
Till in its light absorbed appears
The lapse of five-and-thirty years.
    If change there be, I trace it not
In all this consecrated spot:
No new imprint of Ruin's march
On roofless wall and frameless arch:
The woods, the hills, the fields, the stream,
Are basking in the selfsame beam:
The fall, that turns the unseen mill,
As then it murmured, murmurs still.
It seems as if in one were cast
The present and the imaged past;
Spanning, as with a bridge sublime,
That fearful lapse of human time;
That gulf, unfathomably spread
Between the living and the dead.
    For all too well my spirit feels
The only change this scene reveals.
The sunbeams play, the breezes stir,
Unseen, unfelt, unheard by her,
Who, on that long-past August day,
Beheld with me these ruins grey.
    Whatever span the fates allow,
Ere I shall be as she is now,
Still, in my bosom's inmost cell,
Shall that deep-treasured memory dwell;
That, more than language can express,
Pure miracle of loveliness,
Whose voice so sweet, whose eyes so bright,
Were my soul's music, and its light,
In those blest days when life was new,
And hope was false, but love was true.

CHARLES WOLFE

53   The Burial of Sir John Moore after Corunna

Not a drum was heard, not a funeral note,
  As his corpse to the rampart we hurried;
Not a soldier discharged his farewell shot
  O'er the grave where our hero we buried.

We buried him darkly at dead of night,
  The sods with our bayonets turning,
By the struggling moonbeam's misty light
  And the lanthorn dimly burning.

No useless coffin enclosed his breast,
  Not in sheet or in shroud we wound him;
But he lay like a warrior taking his rest
  With his martial cloak around him.

Few and short were the prayers we said,
  And we spoke not a word of sorrow;
But we steadfastly gazed on the face that was dead,
  And we bitterly thought of the morrow.

We thought, as we hollowed his narrow bed
  And smoothed down his lonely pillow,
That the foe and the stranger would tread o'er his head,
  And we far away on the billow!

Lightly they'll talk of the spirit that's gone,
  And o'er his cold ashes upbraid him –
But little he'll reck, if they let him sleep on
  In the grave where a Briton has laid him.

But half of our heavy task was done
  When the clock struck the hour for retiring;
And we heard the distant and random gun
  That the foe was sullenly firing.

Slowly and sadly we laid him down,
  From the field of his fame fresh and gory;
We carved not a line, and we raised not a stone,
  But we left him alone with his glory.

54   The Graves of a Household

They grew in beauty side by side,
    They filled one home with glee; –
Their graves are scattered far and wide,
    By mount, and stream, and sea.

The same fond mother bent at night.
    O'er each fair sleeping brow:
She had each folded flower in sight –
    Where are those dreamers now?

One, 'midst the forest of the West,
    By a dark stream is laid –
The Indian knows his place of rest,
    Far in the cedar shade.

The sea, the blue lone sea, hath one –
    He lies where pearls lie deep,
He was the loved of all, yet none
    O'er his low bed may weep.

One sleeps where southern vines are drest
    Above the noble slain:
He wrapped his colours round his breast
    On a blood-red field of Spain.

And one – o'er *her* the myrtle showers
    Its leaves, by soft winds fanned;
She faded 'midst Italian flowers –
    The last of that bright band.

And parted thus they rest, who played
    Beneath the same green tree;
Whose voices mingled as they prayed
    Around one parent knee!

They that with smiles lit up the hall,
   And cheered with song the hearth! –
Alas, for love! if *thou* wert all,
   And nought beyond, O Earth!

H. F. LYTE

55   Abide With Me

Abide with me; fast falls the eventide;
The darkness deepens; Lord, with me abide.
When other helpers fail, and comforts flee,
Help of the helpless, O abide with me!

Swift to its close ebbs out life's little day;
Earth's joys grow dim, its glories pass away:
Change and decay in all around I see,
O Thou who changest not, abide with me.

Not a brief glance I beg, a passing word;
But as Thou dweltst with Thy disciples, Lord,
Familiar, condescending, patient, free, –
Come, not to sojourn, but abide with me.

Come not in terrors, as the King of kings;
But kind and good, with healing in Thy wings,
Tears for all woes, a heart for every plea,
Come, Friend of sinners, and thus bide with me.

Thou on my head in early youth didst smile,
And, though rebellious and perverse meanwhile,
Thou hast not left me, oft as I left Thee,
On to the close, O Lord, abide with me!

I need Thy presence every passing hour;
What but Thy grace can foil the tempter's power?
Who like Thyself my guide and stay can be?
Through cloud and sunshine, Lord, abide with me.

I fear no foe with Thee at hand to bless;
Ills have no weight and tears no bitterness;
Where is death's sting? Where, grave, thy victory?
I triumph still if Thou abide with me.

Hold Thou Thy cross before my closing eyes;
Shine through the gloom and point me to the skies!
Heaven's morning breaks and earth's vain shadows flee;
In life, in death, O Lord, abide with me.

JOHN KEATS

56   Ode on Melancholy

No, no! go not to Lethe, neither twist
  Wolf's-bane, tight-rooted, for its poisonous wine;
Nor suffer thy pale forehead to be kissed
  By nightshade, ruby grape of Proserpine;
Make not your rosary of yew-berries,
    Nor let the beetle, nor the death-moth be
      Your mournful Psyche, nor the downy owl
A partner in your sorrow's mysteries;
    For shade to shade will come too drowsily,
      And drown the wakeful anguish of the soul.

But when the melancholy fit shall fall
  Sudden from heaven like a weeping cloud,
That fosters the droop-headed flowers all,
  And hides the green hill in an April shroud;
Then glut thy sorrow on a morning rose,
    Or on the rainbow of the salt sand-wave,
      Or on the wealth of globèd peonies;
Or if thy mistress some rich anger shows,
    Emprison her soft hand, and let her rave,
      And feed deep, deep upon her peerless eyes.

She dwells with Beauty – Beauty that must die;
  And Joy, whose hand is ever at his lips
Bidding adieu; and aching Pleasure nigh,
  Turning to poison while the bee-mouth sips:
Ay, in the very temple of Delight
    Veiled Melancholy has her sovran shrine,
      Though seen of none save him whose strenuous tongue
Can burst Joy's grape against his palate fine;
    His soul shall taste the sadness of her might,
      And be among her cloudy trophies hung.

57   La Belle Dame Sans Merci

'O what can ail thee, knight-at-arms,
   Alone and palely loitering?
The sedge has withered from the lake,
   And no birds sing.

'O what can ail thee, knight-at-arms,
   So haggard and so woe-begone?
The squirrel's granary is full,
   And the harvest's done.

'I see a lily on thy brow
   With anguish moist and fever dew;
And on thy cheek a fading rose
   Fast withereth too.'

'I met a lady in the meads,
   Full beautiful – a faery's child,
Her hair was long, her foot was light,
   And her eyes were wild.

'I made a garland for her head,
   And bracelets too, and fragrant zone;
She looked at me as she did love,
   And made sweet moan.

'I set her on my pacing steed
   And nothing else saw all day long,
For sideways would she lean, and sing
   A faery's song.

'She found me roots of relish sweet,
   And honey wild and manna dew,
And sure in language strange she said,
   "I love thee true!"

'She took me to her elfin grot,
    And there she wept and sighed full sore;
And there I shut her wild, wild eyes
        With kisses four.

'And there she lullèd me asleep,
    And there I dreamed – Ah! woe betide!
The latest dream I ever dreamed
        On the cold hill's side.

'I saw pale kings and princes too,
    Pale warriors, death-pale were they all;
Who cried – "La belle Dame sans Merci
        Hath thee in thrall!"

'I saw their starved lips in the gloam
    With horrid warning gapèd wide,
And I awoke and found me here
        On the cold hill's side.

'And this is why I sojourn here
    Alone and palely loitering,
Though the sedge is withered from the lake,
        And no birds sing.'

58   Sonnet: November

The mellow year is hasting to its close;
The little birds have almost sung their last,
Their small notes twitter in the dreary blast –
That shrill-piped harbinger of early snows:
The patient beauty of the scentless rose,
Oft with the Morn's hoar crystal quaintly glass'd,
Hangs, a pale mourner for the summer past,
And makes a little summer where it grows:
In the chill sunbeam of the faint brief day
The dusky waters shudder as they shine,
The russet leaves obstruct the straggling way
Of oozy brooks, which no deep banks define,
And the gaunt woods, in ragged, scant array,
Wrap their old limbs with sombre ivy twine.

THOMAS HOOD

59   Ruth

She stood breast-high amid the corn,
Clasped by the golden light of morn,
Like the sweetheart of the sun,
Who many a glowing kiss had won.

On her cheek an autumn flush
Deeply ripened; – such a blush
In the midst of brown was born,
Like red poppies grown with corn.

Round her eyes her tresses fell,
Which were blackest none could tell,
But long lashes veiled a light,
That had else been all too bright.

And her hat, with shady brim,
Made her tressy forehead dim; –
Thus she stood amid the stooks,
Praising God with sweetest looks: –

Sure, I said, heav'n did not mean,
Where I reap thou shouldst but glean;
Lay thy sheaf adown and come,
Share my harvest and my home.

60   A Winter's Night

It was a chilly winter's night;
    And frost was glittering on the ground,
And evening stars were twinkling bright;
    And from the gloomy plain around
        Came no sound,
But where, within the wood-girt tower,
The churchbell slowly struck the hour;

As if that all of human birth
    Had risen to the final day,
And soaring from the wornout earth
    Were called in hurry and dismay,
        Far away;
And I alone of all mankind
Were left in loneliness behind.

61   Chibiabos's Song

'Onaway! Awake, beloved!
Thou the wild flower of the forest!
Thou the wild bird of the prairie!
Thou with eyes so soft and fawn-like!
    'If thou only lookest on me,
I am happy, I am happy,
As the lilies of the prairie,
When they feel the dew upon them!
    'Sweet thy breath is as the fragrance
Of the wild flowers in the morning,
As their fragrance is at evening,
In the Moon when leaves are falling.
    'Does not all the blood within me,
Leap to meet thee, leap to meet thee,
As the springs to meet the sunshine,
In the Moon when nights are brightest?
    'Onaway! my heart sings to thee,
Sings with joy when thou art near me,
As the sighing, singing branches
In the pleasant Moon of Strawberries!
    'When thou art not pleased, beloved,
Then my heart is sad and darkened,
As the shining river darkens
When the clouds drop shadows on it!
    'When thou smilest, my beloved,
Then my troubled heart is brightened,
As in sunshine gleam the ripples
That the cold wind makes in rivers.
    'Smiles the earth, and smile the waters,
Smile the cloudless skies above us,
But I lose the way of smiling
When thou art no longer near me!
    'I myself, myself! behold me!
Blood of my beating heart, behold me!
O awake, awake, beloved!
Onaway! awake, beloved!'

62 The Slave's Dream

Beside the ungathered rice he lay,
  His sickle in his hand;
His breast was bare, his matted hair
  Was buried in the sand.
Again, in the mist and shadow of sleep,
  He saw his Native Land.

Wide through the landscape of his dreams
  The lordly Niger flowed;
Beneath the palm-trees on the plain
  Once more a king he strode;
And heard the tinkling caravans
  Descend the mountain-road.

He saw once more his dark-eyed queen
  Among her children stand;
They clasped his neck, they kissed his cheeks,
  They held him by the hand! –
A tear burst from the sleeper's lids
  And fell into the sand.

And then at furious speed he rode
  Along the Niger's bank;
His bridle-reins were golden chains,
  And, with a martial clank,
At each leap he could feel his scabbard of steel
  Smiting his stallion's flank.

Before him, like a blood-red flag,
  The bright flamingoes flew;
From morn till night he followed their flight,
  O'er plains where the tamarind grew,
Till he saw the roofs of Caffre huts,
  And the ocean rose to view.

At night he heard the lion roar,
　And the hyena scream,
And the river-horse, as he crushed the reeds
　Beside some hidden stream;
And it passed, like a glorious roll of drums,
　Through the triumph of his dream.

The forests, with their myriad tongues,
　Shouted of liberty;
And the blast of the desert cried aloud,
　With a voice so wild and free,
That he started in his sleep and smiled
　At their tempestuous glee.

He did not feel the driver's whip,
　Nor the burning heat of day;
For Death had illumined the Land of Sleep,
　And his lifeless body lay
A worn-out fetter, that the soul
　Had broken and thrown away!

ALFRED, LORD TENNYSON

63   Mariana

Mariana in the moated grange (Measure for Measure)

With blackest moss the flower-plots
   Were thickly crusted, one and all:
The rusted nails fell from the knots
   That held the pear to the gable-wall.
The broken sheds looked sad and strange:
   Unlifted was the clinking latch;
   Weeded and worn the ancient thatch
Upon the lonely moated grange.
     She only said, 'My life is dreary,
       He cometh not,' she said;
     She said, 'I am aweary, aweary,
       I would that I were dead!'

Her tears fell with the dews at even;
   Her tears fell ere the dews were dried;
She could not look on the sweet heaven,
   Either at morn or eventide.
After the flitting of the bats,
   When thickest dark did trance the sky,
   She drew her casement-curtain by,
And glanced athwart the glooming flats.
     She only said, 'The night is dreary,
       He cometh not,' she said;
     She said, 'I am aweary, aweary,
       I would that I were dead!'

Upon the middle of the night,
   Waking she heard the night-fowl crow:
The cock sung out an hour ere light:
   From the dark fen the oxen's low
Came to her: without hope of change,
   In sleep she seemed to walk forlorn,
   Till cold winds woke the grey-eyed morn

About the lonely moated grange.
    She only said, 'The day is dreary,
      He cometh not,' she said;
    She said, 'I am aweary, aweary,
      I would that I were dead!'

About a stone-cast from the wall
    A sluice with blackened waters slept,
And o'er it many, round and small,
    The clustered marish-mosses crept.
Hard by a poplar shook alway,
    All silver-green with gnarlèd bark:
    For leagues no other tree did mark
The level waste, the rounding grey.
    She only said, 'My life is dreary,
      He cometh not,' she said;
    She said, 'I am aweary, aweary,
      I would that I were dead!'

And ever when the moon was low,
    And the shrill winds were up and away,
In the white curtain, to and fro,
    She saw the gusty shadow sway.
But when the moon was very low,
    And wild winds bound within their cell,
    The shadow of the poplar fell
Upon her bed, across her brow
    She only said, 'The night is dreary,
      He cometh not,' she said;
    She said, 'I am aweary, aweary,
      I would that I were dead!'

All day within the dreamy house,
    The doors upon their hinges creaked;
The blue fly sung in the pane; the mouse
    Behind the mouldering wainscot shrieked,
Or from the crevice peered about.
    Old faces glimmered through the doors,
    Old footsteps trod the upper floors,
Old voices called her from without.

She only said, 'My life is dreary,
  He cometh not,' she said;
She said, 'I am aweary, aweary,
  I would that I were dead!'

The sparrow's chirrup on the roof,
  The slow clock ticking, and the sound
Which to the wooing wind aloof
  The poplar made, did all confound
Her sense; but most she loathed the hour
  When the thick-moted sunbeam lay
  Athwart the chambers, and the day
Was sloping toward his western bower.
  Then, said she, 'I am very dreary,
    He will not come,' she said;
  She wept, 'I am aweary, aweary,
    Oh God, that I were dead!'

64 O Swallow, Swallow

  'O Swallow, Swallow, flying, flying South,
Fly to her, and fall upon her gilded eaves,
And tell her, tell her, what I tell to thee.

  'O tell her, Swallow, thou that knowest each,
That bright and fierce and fickle is the South,
And dark and true and tender is the North.

  'O Swallow, Swallow, if I could follow, and light
Upon her lattice, I would pipe and trill,
And cheep and twitter twenty million loves.

  'O were I thou that she might take me in,
And lay me on her bosom, and her heart
Would rock the snowy cradle till I died.

'Why lingereth she to clothe her heart with love,
Delaying as the tender ash delays
To clothe herself, when all the woods are green?

'O tell her, Swallow, that thy brood is flown:
Say to her, I do but wanton in the South,
But in the North long since my nest is made.

'O tell her, brief is life but love is long,
And brief the sun of summer in the North,
And brief the moon of beauty in the South.

'O Swallow, flying from the golden woods,
Fly to her, and pipe and woo her, and make her mine,
And tell her, tell her, that I follow thee.'

65   Come Down, O Maid

'Come down, O maid, from yonder mountain height:
What pleasure lives in height (the shepherd sang)
In height and cold, the splendour of the hills?
But cease to move so near the heavens, and cease
To glide a sunbeam by the blasted pine,
To sit a star upon the sparkling spire;
And come, for Love is of the valley, come,
For Love is of the valley, come thou down
And find him; by the happy threshold, he,
Or hand in hand with Plenty in the maize,
Or red with spirted purple of the vats,
Or foxlike in the vine; nor cares to walk
With Death and Morning on the silver horns,
Nor wilt thou snare him in the white ravine,
Nor find him dropped upon the firths of ice,
That huddling slant in furrow-cloven falls
To roll the torrent out of dusky doors:
But follow; let the torrent dance thee down
To find him in the valley; let the wild
Lean-headed eagles yelp alone, and leave
The monstrous ledges there to slope, and spill

Their thousand wreaths of dangling water-smoke,
That like a broken purpose waste in air:
So waste not thou; but come; for all the vales
Await thee; azure pillars of the hearth
Arise to thee; the children call, and I
Thy shepherd pipe, and sweet is every sound,
Sweeter thy voice, but every sound is sweet;
Myriads of rivulets hurrying through the lawn,
The moan of doves in immemorial elms,
And murmuring of innumerable bees.'

66   Tithonus

The woods decay, the woods decay and fall,
The vapours weep their burthen to the ground,
Man comes and tills the field and lies beneath,
And after many a summer dies the swan.
Me only cruel immortality
Consumes: I wither slowly in thine arms,
Here at the quiet limit of the world,
A white-haired shadow roaming like a dream
The ever-silent spaces of the East,
Far-folded mists, and gleaming halls of morn.

   Alas! for this grey shadow, once a man –
So glorious in his beauty and thy choice,
Who madest him thy chosen, that he seemed
To his great heart none other than a God!
I asked thee, 'Give me immortality.'
Then didst thou grant mine asking with a smile,
Like wealthy men who care not how they give.
But thy strong Hours indignant worked their wills,
And beat me down and marred and wasted me,
And though they could not end me, left me maimed
To dwell in presence of immortal youth,
Immortal age beside immortal youth,
And all I was, in ashes. Can thy love,
Thy beauty, make amends, though even now,

Close over us, the silver star, thy guide,
Shines in those tremulous eyes that fill with tears
To hear me? Let me go: take back thy gift:
Why should a man desire in any way
To vary from the kindly race of men,
Or pass beyond the goal of ordinance
Where all should pause, as is most meet for all?

A soft air fans the cloud apart; there comes
A glimpse of that dark world where I was born.
Once more the old mysterious glimmer steals
From thy pure brows, and from thy shoulders pure,
And bosom beating with a heart renewed.
Thy cheek begins to redden through the gloom,
Thy sweet eyes brighten slowly close to mine,
Ere yet they blind the stars, and the wild team
Which love thee, yearning for thy yoke, arise,
And shake the darkness from their loosened manes,
And beat the twilight into flakes of fire.

Lo! ever thus thou growest beautiful
In silence, then before thine answer given
Departest, and thy tears are on my cheek.

Why wilt thou ever scare me with thy tears,
And make me tremble lest a saying learnt,
In days far-off, on that dark earth, be true?
'The Gods themselves cannot recall their gifts.'

Ay me! ay me! with what another heart
In days far-off, and with what other eyes
I used to watch – if I be he that watched –
The lucid outline forming round thee; saw
The dim curls kindle into sunny rings;
Changed with thy mystic change, and felt my blood
Glow with the glow that slowly crimsoned all
Thy presence and thy portals, while I lay,
Mouth, forehead, eyelids, growing dewy-warm
With kisses balmier than half-opening buds
Of April, and could hear the lips that kissed

Whispering I knew not what of wild and sweet,
Like that strange song I heard Apollo sing,
While Ilion like a mist rose into towers.

Yet hold me not for ever in thine East:
How can my nature longer mix with thine?
Coldly thy rosy shadows bathe me, cold
Are all thy lights, and cold my wrinkled feet
Upon thy glimmering thresholds, when the stream
Floats up from those dim fields about the homes
Of happy men that have the power to die,
And grassy barrows of the happier dead.
Release me, and restore me to the ground;
Thou seëst all things, thou wilt see my grave:
Thou wilt renew thy beauty morn by morn;
I earth in earth forget these empty courts,
And thee returning on thy silver wheels.

67   Milton

Alcaics

O mighty-mouthed inventor of harmonies,
O skilled to sing of Time or Eternity,
   God-gifted organ-voice of England,
     Milton, a name to resound for ages;
Whose Titan angels, Gabriel, Abdiel,
Starred from Jehovah's gorgeous armouries,
   Tower, as the deep-domed empyrëan
     Rings to the roar of an angel onset –
Me rather all that bowery loneliness,
The brooks of Eden mazily murmuring,
   And bloom profuse and cedar arches
     Charm, as a wanderer out in ocean,
Where some refulgent sunset of India
Streams o'er a rich ambrosial ocean isle,
   And crimson-hued the stately palm-woods
     Whisper in odorous heights of even.

68   The Confessional

SPAIN

It is a lie – their Priests, their Pope,
Their Saints, their . . . all they fear or hope
Are lies, and lies – there! through my door
And ceiling, there! and walls and floor,
There, lies, they lie – shall still be hurled
Till spite of them I reach the world!

You think Priests just and holy men!
Before they put me in this den
I was a human creature too,
With flesh and blood like one of you,
A girl that laughed in beauty's pride
Like lilies in your world outside.

I had a lover – shame avaunt!
This poor wrenched body, grim and gaunt,
Was kissed all over till it burned,
By lips the truest, love e'er turned
His heart's own tint: one night they kissed
My soul out in a burning mist.

So, next day when the accustomed train
Of things grew round my sense again,
'That is a sin,' I said: and slow
With downcast eyes to church I go,
And pass to the confession-chair,
And tell the old mild father there.

But when I falter Beltran's name,
'Ha?' quoth the father; 'much I blame
The sin; yet wherefore idly grieve?
Despair not – strenuously retrieve!
Nay, I will turn this love of thine
To lawful love, almost divine;

'For he is young, and led astray,
This Beltran, and he schemes, men say,
To change the laws of church and state;
So, thine shall be an angel's fate,
Who, ere the thunder breaks, should roll
Its cloud away and save his soul.

'For, when he lies upon thy breast,
Thou mayst demand and be possessed
Of all his plans, and next day steal
To me, and all those plans reveal,
That I and every priest, to purge
His soul, may fast and use the scourge.'

That father's beard was long and white,
With love and truth his brow seemed bright;
I went back, all on fire with joy,
And, that same evening, bade the boy
Tell me, as lovers should, heart-free,
Something to prove his love of me.

He told me what he would not tell
For hope of heaven or fear of hell;
And I lay listening in such pride!
And, soon as he had left my side,
Tripped to the church by morning-light
To save his soul in his despite.

I told the father all his schemes,
Who were his comrades, what their dreams;
'And now make haste,' I said, 'to pray
The one spot from his soul away;
Tonight he comes, but not the same
Will look!' At night he never came.

Nor next night: on the after-morn,
I went forth with a strength new-born.
The church was empty; something drew
My steps into the street; I knew
It led me to the market-place:
Where, lo, on high, the father's face!

That horrible black scaffold dressed,
That stapled block . . . God sink the rest!
That head strapped back, that blinding vest,
Those knotted hands and naked breast,
Till near one busy hangman pressed,
And, on the neck these arms caressed . . .

No part in aught they hope or fear!
No heaven with them, no hell! – and here,
No earth, not so much space as pens
My body in their worst of dens
But shall bear God and man my cry,
Lies – lies, again – and still, they lie!

69 A Toccata of Galuppi's

Oh Galuppi, Baldassaro, this is very sad to find!
I can hardly misconceive you; it would prove me deaf and
    blind;
But although I take your meaning, 'tis with such a heavy
    mind!

Here you come with your old music, and here's all the good
    it brings.
What, they lived once thus at Venice where the merchants
    were the kings,
Where Saint Mark's is, where the Doges used to wed the sea
    with rings?

Ay, because the sea's the street there; and 'tis arched by . . .
  what you call
. . . Shylock's bridge with houses on it, where they kept the
  carnival:
I was never out of England – it's as if I saw it all.

Did young people take their pleasure when the sea was
  warm in May?
Balls and masks begun at midnight, burning ever to midday,
When they made up fresh adventures for the morrow, do
  you say?

Was a lady such a lady, cheeks so round and lips so red, –
On her neck the small face buoyant, like a bell-flower on its
  bed,
O'er the breast's superb abundance where a man might base
  his head?

Well, and it was graceful of them – they'd break talk off and
  afford
– She, to bite her mask's black velvet – he, to finger on his
  sword,
While you sat and played Toccatas, stately at the clavichord?

What? Those lesser thirds so plaintive, sixths diminished,
  sigh on sigh,
Told them something? Those suspensions, those solutions –
  'Must we die?'
Those commiserating sevenths – 'Life might last! we can but
  try!'

'Were you happy?' – 'Yes.' – 'And are you still as happy?' –
  'Yes. And you?'
– 'Then, more kisses!' – 'Did I stop them, when a million
  seemed so few?'
Hark, the dominant's persistence till it must be answered to!

So, an octave struck the answer. Oh, they praised you, I
 dare say!
'Brave Galuppi! that was music! good alike at grave and gay!
I can always leave off talking when I hear a master play!'

Then they left you for their pleasure: till in due time, one by
 one,
Some with lives that came to nothing, some with deeds as
 well undone,
Death stepped tacitly and took them where they never see
 the sun.

But when I sit down to reason, think to take my stand nor
 swerve,
While I triumph o'er a secret wrung from nature's close
 reserve,
In you come with your cold music till I creep through every
 nerve.

Yes, you, like a ghostly cricket, creaking where a house was
 burned:
'Dust and ashes, dead and done with, Venice spent what
 Venice earned.
The soul, doubtless, is immortal – where a soul can be
 discerned.

'Yours for instance: you know physics, something of
 geology,
Mathematics are your pastime; souls shall rise in their
 degree;
Butterflies may dread extinction, – you'll not die, it cannot
 be!

'As for Venice and her people, merely born to bloom and
 drop,
Here on earth they bore their fruitage, mirth and folly were
 the crop:
What of soul was left, I wonder, when the kissing had to
 stop?

'Dust and ashes!' So you creak it, and I want the heart to
    scold.
Dear dead women, with such hair, too – what's become of all
    the gold
Used to hang and brush their bosoms? I feel chilly and
    grown old.

70   'De Gustibus –'

I

Your ghost will walk, you lover of trees,
   (If our loves remain)
   In an English lane,
By a cornfield-side a-flutter with poppies.
Hark, those two in the hazel coppice –
A boy and a girl, if the good fates please,
   Making love, say, –
   The happier they!
Draw yourself up from the light of the moon,
And let them pass, as they will too soon,
   With the bean-flowers' boon,
   And the blackbird's tune,
   And May, and June!

II

What I love best in all the world
Is a castle, precipice-encurled,
In a gash of the wind-grieved Apennine.
Or look for me, old fellow of mine,
(If I get my head from out the mouth
O' the grave, and loose my spirit's bands,
And come again to the land of lands) –
In a sea-side house to the farther South,
Where the baked cicala dies of drouth,
And one sharp tree – 'tis a cypress – stands,
By the many hundred years red-rusted,
Rough iron-spiked, ripe fruit-o'ercrusted,
My sentinel to guard the sands
To the water's edge. For, what expands

Before the house, but the great opaque
Blue breadth of sea without a break?
While, in the house, for ever crumbles
Some fragment of the frescoed walls,
From blisters where a scorpion sprawls.
A girl bare-footed brings, and tumbles
Down on the pavement, green-flesh melons,
And says there's news today – the king
Was shot at, touched in the liver-wing,
Goes with his Bourbon arm in a sling:
– She hopes they have not caught the felons.
Italy, my Italy!
Queen Mary's saying serves for me –
    (When fortune's malice
    Lost her – Calais) –
Open my heart and you will see
Graved inside of it, 'Italy.'
Such lovers old are I and she:
So it always was, so shall ever be!

ANONYMOUS

71   The Key of the Kingdom

This is the key of the kingdom:
In that kingdom there is a city.
In that city there is a town.
In that town there is a street.
In that street there is a lane.
In that lane there is a yard.
In that yard there is a house.
In that house there is a room.
In that room there is a bed.
On that bed there is a basket.
In that basket there are some flowers.

Flowers in a basket.
Basket on the bed.
Bed in the room.
Room in the house.
House in the yard.
Yard in the lane.
Lane in the street.
Street in the town.
Town in the city.
City in the kingdom.
Of the kingdom this is the key.

CHARLES KINGSLEY

72   Song: When I was a greenhorn and young

When I was a greenhorn and young,
And wanted to be and to do,
I puzzled my brains about choosing my line,
Till I found out the way that things go.

The same piece of clay makes a tile,
A pitcher, a taw, or a brick.
Dan Horace knew life; you may cut out a saint,
Or a bench, from the self-same stick.

The urchin who squalls in a gaol,
By circumstance turns out a rogue;
While the castle-born brat is a senator born,
Or a saint, if religion's in vogue.

We fall on our legs in this world,
Blind kittens, tossed in neck and heels;
'Tis Dame Circumstance licks Nature's cubs into shape –
She's the mill-head, if we are the wheels.

Then why puzzle and fret, plot and dream?
He that's wise will just follow his nose;
Contentedly fish, while he swims with the stream;
'Tis no business of his where it goes.

Welcome, wild North-easter!
  Shame it is to see
Odes to every zephyr;
  Ne'er a verse to thee.
Welcome, black North-easter!
  O'er the German foam;
O'er the Danish moorlands,
  From thy frozen home.
Tired we are of summer,
  Tired of gaudy glare,
Showers soft and streaming,
  Hot and breathless air.
Tired of listless dreaming,
  Through the lazy day:
Jovial wind of winter,
  Turn us out to play!
Sweep the golden reed-beds;
  Crisp the lazy dyke;
Hunger into madness
  Every plunging pike.
Fill the lake with wild-fowl;
  Fill the marsh with snipe;
While on dreary moorlands
  Lonely curlew pipe.
Through the black fir-forest
  Thunder harsh and dry,
Shattering down the snow-flakes
  Off the curdled sky.
Hark! The brave North-easter!
  Breast-high lies the scent,
On by holt and headland,
  Over heath and bent.
Chime, ye dappled darlings,
  Through the sleet and snow.
Who can over-ride you?
  Let the horses go!
Chime, ye dappled darlings,
  Down the roaring blast;

You shall see a fox die
   Ere an hour be past.
Go! and rest to-morrow,
   Hunting in your dreams,
While our skates are ringing
   O'er the frozen streams.
Let the luscious South-wind
   Breathe in lovers' sighs,
While the lazy gallants
   Bask in ladies' eyes.
What does he but soften
   Heart alike and pen?
'Tis the hard grey weather
   Breeds hard English men.
What's the soft South-wester?
   'Tis the ladies' breeze,
Bringing home their true-loves
   Out of all the seas:
But the black North-easter,
   Through the snowstorm hurled,
Drives our English hearts of oak
   Seaward round the world.
Come, as came our fathers,
   Heralded by thee,
Conquering from the eastward,
   Lords by land and sea.
Come; and strong within us
   Stir the Viking's blood;
Bracing brain and sinew;
   Blow, thou wind of God!

Three fishers went sailing away to the West,
   Away to the West as the sun went down;
Each thought on the woman who loved him the best,
   And the children stood watching them out of the town;
   For men must work, and women must weep,
   And there's little to earn, and many to keep,
      Though the harbour bar be moaning.

Three wives sat up in the lighthouse tower,
   And they trimmed the lamps as the sun went down;
They looked at the squall, and they looked at the shower,
   And the night-rack came rolling up ragged and brown.
   But men must work, and women must weep,
   Though storms be sudden, and waters deep,
      And the harbour bar be moaning.

Three corpses lay out on the shining sands
   In the morning gleam as the tide went down,
And the women are weeping and wringing their hands
   For those who will never come home to the town;
   For men must work, and women must weep,
   And the sooner it's over, the sooner to sleep;
      And good-bye to the bar and its moaning.

75   The Forsaken Merman

Come, dear children, let us away;
Down and away below.
Now my brothers call from the bay;
Now the great winds shorewards blow;
Now the salt tides seawards flow;
Now the wild white horses play,
Champ and chafe and toss in the spray.
Children dear, let us away.
This way, this way.

Call her once before you go.
Call once yet.
In a voice that she will know:
'Margaret! Margaret!'
Children's voices should be dear
(Call once more) to a mother's ear:
Children's voices, wild with pain.
Surely she will come again.
Call her once and come away.
This way, this way.
'Mother dear, we cannot stay.'
The wild white horses foam and fret.
Margaret! Margaret!

Come, dear children, come away down.
Call no more.
One last look at the white-walled town,
And the little grey church on the windy shore.
Then come down.
She will not come though you call all day.
Come away, come away.

Children dear, was it yesterday
We heard the sweet bells over the bay?
In the caverns where we lay,

Through the surf and through the swell,
The far-off sound of a silver bell?
Sand-strewn caverns, cool and deep,
Where the winds are all asleep;
Where the spent lights quiver and gleam;
Where the salt weed sways in the stream;
Where the sea-beasts ranged all round
Feed in the ooze of their pasture-ground;
Where the sea-snakes coil and twine,
Dry their mail and bask in the brine;
Where great whales come sailing by,
Sail and sail, with unshut eye,
Round the world for ever and aye?
When did music come this way?
Children dear, was it yesterday?

Children dear, was it yesterday
(Call yet once) that she went away?
Once she sate with you and me,
On a red gold throne in the heart of the sea,
And the youngest sate on her knee.
She combed its bright hair, and she tended it well,
When down swung the sound of the far-off bell.
She sighed, she looked up through the clear green sea.
She said; 'I must go, for my kinsfolk pray
In the little grey church on the shore to-day.
'Twill be Easter-time in the world – ah me!
And I lose my poor soul, Merman, here with thee.'
I said; 'Go up, dear heart, through the waves;
Say thy prayer, and come back to the kind sea-caves.'
She smiled, she went up through the surf in the bay.
Children dear, was it yesterday?

    Children dear, were we long alone?
'The sea grows stormy, the little ones moan.
Long prayers,' I said, 'in the world they say.
Come,' I said, and we rose through the surf in the bay.
We went up the beach, by the sandy down
Where the sea-stocks bloom, to the white-walled town.

Through the narrow paved streets, where all was still,
To the little grey church on the windy hill.
From the church came a murmur of folk at their prayers,
But we stood without in the cold blowing airs.
We climbed on the graves, on the stones, worn with rains,
And we gazed up the aisle through the small leaded panes.
She sate by the pillar; we saw her clear:
'Margaret, hist! come quick, we are here.
Dear heart,' I said, 'we are long alone.
The sea grows stormy, the little ones moan.'
But, ah, she gave me never a look,
For her eyes were sealed to the holy book.
'Loud prays the priest; shut stands the door.'
Come away, children, call no more.
Come away, come down, call no more.

  Down, down, down.
Down to the depths of the sea.
She sits at her wheel in the humming town,
Singing most joyfully.
Hark, what she sings; 'O joy, O joy,
For the humming street, and the child with its toy.
For the priest, and the bell, and the holy well.
For the wheel where I spun,
And the blessed light of the sun.'
And so she sings her fill,
Singing most joyfully,
Till the shuttle falls from her hand,
And the whizzing wheel stands still.
She steals to the window, and looks at the sand;
And over the sand at the sea;
And her eyes are set in a stare;
And anon there breaks a sigh,
And anon there drops a tear,
From a sorrow-clouded eye,
And a heart sorrow-laden,
A long, long sigh,
For the cold strange eyes of a little Mermaiden,
And the gleam of her golden hair.

Come away, away children.
Come children, come down.
The hoarse wind blows colder;
Lights shine in the town.
She will start from her slumber
When gusts shake the door;
She will hear the winds howling,
Will hear the waves roar.
We shall see, while above us
The waves roar and whirl,
A ceiling of amber,
A pavement of pearl.
Singing, 'Here came a mortal,
But faithless was she.
And alone dwell for ever
The kings of the sea.'

But, children, at midnight,
When soft the winds blow;
When clear falls the moonlight;
When spring-tides are low:
When sweet airs come seaward
From heaths starred with broom;
And high rocks throw mildly
On the blanched sands a gloom:
Up the still, glistening beaches,
Up the creeks we will hie;
Over banks of bright seaweed
The ebb-tide leaves dry.
We will gaze, from the sand-hills,
At the white, sleeping town;
At the church on the hill-side –
And then come back down.
Singing, 'There dwells a loved one,
But cruel is she.
She left lonely for ever
The kings of the sea.'

Coldly, sadly descends
The autumn evening. The Field
Strewn with its dank yellow drifts
Of withered leaves, and the elms,
Fade into dimness apace,
Silent; – hardly a shout
From a few boys late at their play!
The lights come out in the street,
In the school-room windows; but cold,
Solemn, unlighted, austere,
Through the gathering darkness, arise
The Chapel walls, in whose bound
Thou, my father! art laid.

There thou dost lie, in the gloom
Of the autumn evening. But ah!
That word, *gloom*, to my mind
Brings thee back in the light
Of thy radiant vigour again!
In the gloom of November we passed
Days not of gloom at thy side;
Seasons impaired not the ray
Of thine even cheerfulness clear.
Such thou wast; and I stand
In the autumn evening, and think
Of bygone autumns with thee.

Fifteen years have gone round
Since thou arosest to tread,
In the summer morning, the road
Of death, at a call unforeseen,
Sudden. For fifteen years,
We who till then in thy shade
Rested as under the boughs
Of a mighty oak, have endured
Sunshine and rain as we might,
Bare, unshaded, alone,
Lacking the shelter of thee.

O strong soul, by what shore
Tarriest thou now? For that force,
Surely, has not been left vain!
Somewhere, surely, afar,
In the sounding labour-house vast
Of being, is practised that strength,
Zealous, beneficent, firm!

Yes, in some far-shining sphere,
Conscious or not of the past,
Still thou performest the word
Of the Spirit in whom thou dost live,
Prompt, unwearied, as here!
Still thou upraisest with zeal
The humble good from the ground,
Sternly repressest the bad.
Still, like a trumpet, dost rouse
Those who with half-open eyes
Tread the border-land dim
'Twixt vice and virtue; reviv'st,
Succourest; – this was thy work,
This was thy life upon earth.

What is the course of the life
Of mortal men on the earth? –
Most men eddy about
Here and there – eat and drink,
Chatter and love and hate,
Gather and squander, are raised
Aloft, are hurled in the dust,
Striving blindly, achieving
Nothing; and, then they die –
Perish; and no one asks
Who or what they have been,
More than he asks what waves
In the moonlit solitudes mild
Of the midmost Ocean, have swelled,
Foamed for a moment, and gone.

And there are some, whom a thirst
Ardent, unquenchable, fires,
Not with the crowd to be spent,
Not without aim to go round
In an eddy of purposeless dust,
Effort unmeaning and vain.
Ah yes, some of us strive
Not without action to die
Fruitless, but something to snatch
From dull oblivion, nor all
Glut the devouring grave!
We, we have chosen our path –
Path to a clear-purposed goal,
Path of advance! but it leads
A long, steep journey, through sunk
Gorges, o'er mountains in snow!
Cheerful, with friends, we set forth;
Then, on the height, comes the storm!
Thunder crashes from rock
To rock, the cataracts reply;
Lightnings dazzle our eyes;
Roaring torrents have breached
The track, the stream-bed descends
In the place where the wayfarer once
Planted his footstep – the spray
Boils o'er its borders; aloft,
The unseen snow-beds dislodge
Their hanging ruin; – alas,
Havoc is made in our train!
Friends who set forth at our side
Falter, are lost in the storm!
We, we only, are left!
With frowning foreheads, with lips
Sternly compressed, we strain on,
On – and at nightfall, at last,
Come to the end of our way,
To the lonely inn 'mid the rocks;
Where the gaunt and taciturn Host
Stands on the threshold, the wind

Shaking his thin white hairs –
Holds his lantern to scan
Our storm-beat figures, and asks:
Whom in our party we bring?
Whom we have left in the snow?

Sadly we answer: We bring
Only ourselves; we lost
Sight of the rest in the storm.
Hardly ourselves we fought through,
Stripped, without friends, as we are.
Friends, companions, and train
The avalanche swept from our side.

But thou would'st not *alone*
Be saved, my father! *alone*
Conquer and come to thy goal,
Leaving the rest in the wild.
We were weary, and we
Fearful, and we, in our march,
Fain to drop down and to die.
Still thou turnedst, and still
Beckonedst the trembler, and still
Gavest the weary thy hand!
If, in the paths of the world,
Stones might have wounded thy feet,
Toil or dejection have tried
Thy spirit, of that we saw
Nothing! to us thou wert still
Cheerful, and helpful, and firm.
Therefore to thee it was given
Many to save with thyself;
And, at the end of thy day,
O faithful shepherd! to come,
Bringing thy sheep in thy hand.

And through thee I believe
In the noble and great who are gone;
Pure souls honoured and blest
By former ages, who else –
Such, so soulless, so poor,
Is the race of men whom I see –
Seemed but a dream of the heart,
Seemed but a cry of desire.
Yes! I believe that there lived
Others like thee in the past,
Not like the men of the crowd
Who all round me to-day
Bluster or cringe, and make life
Hideous, and arid, and vile;
But souls tempered with fire,
Fervent, heroic, and good,
Helpers and friends of mankind.

Servants of God! – or sons
Shall I not call you? because
Not as servants ye knew
Your Father's innermost mind,
His, who unwillingly sees
One of his little ones lost –
Yours is the praise, if mankind
Hath not as yet in its march
Fainted, and fallen, and died!

See! in the rocks of the world
Marches the host of mankind,
A feeble, wavering line.
Where are they tending? – A god
Marshalled them, gave them their goal. –
Ah, but the way is so long!
Years they have been in the wild!
Sore thirst plagues them; the rocks,
Rising all round, overawe.
Factions divide them; their host
Threatens to break, to dissolve.

Ah, keep, keep them combined!
Else, of the myriads who fill
That army, not one shall arrive!
Sole they shall stray; in the rocks
Labour for ever in vain,
Die one by one in the waste.

Then, in such hour of need
Of your fainting, dispirited race,
Ye, like angels, appear,
Radiant with ardour divine.
Beacons of hope, ye appear!
Languor is not in your heart,
Weakness is not in your word,
Weariness not on your brow.
Ye alight in our van; at your voice,
Panic, despair, flee away.
Ye move through the ranks, recall
The stragglers, refresh the outworn,
Praise, re-inspire the brave.
Order, courage, return.
Eyes rekindling, and prayers,
Follow your steps as ye go.
Ye fill up the gaps in our files,
Strengthen the wavering line,
Stablish, continue our march,
On, to the bound of the waste,
On, to the City of God.

W. J. CORY

77   Heraclitus

They told me, Heraclitus, they told me you were dead;
They brought me bitter news to hear and bitter tears to shed.
I wept as I remembered how often you and I
Had tired the sun with talking and sent him down the sky.

And now that thou art lying, my dear old Carian guest,
A handful of grey ashes, long long ago at rest,
Still are thy pleasant voices, thy nightingales, awake,
For Death, he taketh all away, but them he cannot take.

CHRISTINA ROSSETTI

78   Summer

Winter is cold-hearted,
  Spring is yea and nay,
Autumn is a weathercock
  Blown every way.
  Summer days for me
When every leaf is on its tree;

When Robin's not a beggar,
  And Jenny Wren's a bride,
And larks hang singing, singing, singing,
  Over the wheat-fields wide,
  And anchored lilies ride,
  And the pendulum spider
  Swings from side to side;

And blue-black beetles transact business,
  And gnats fly in a host,
And furry caterpillars hasten
  That no time be lost,
  And moths grow fat and thrive,
  And ladybirds arrive.

Before green apples blush,
Before green nuts embrown,
Why one day in the country
  Is worth a month in town;
  Is worth a day and a year
Of the dusty, musty, lag-last fashion
  That days drone elsewhere

In the bleak mid-winter
   Frosty wind made moan,
Earth stood hard as iron,
   Water like a stone;
Snow had fallen, snow on snow,
   Snow on snow,
In the bleak mid-winter
   Long ago.

Our God, Heaven cannot hold Him
   Nor earth sustain;
Heaven and earth shall flee away
   When He comes to reign:
In the bleak mid-winter
   A stable-place sufficed
The Lord God Almighty
   Jesus Christ.

Enough for Him, whom cherubim
   Worship night and day,
A breastful of milk
   And a mangerful of hay;
Enough for Him, whom angels
   Fall down before,
The ox and ass and camel
   Which adore.

Angels and archangels
   May have gathered there,
Cherubim and seraphim
   Thronged the air;

But only His mother
　　In her maiden bliss
Worshipped the Beloved
　　With a kiss.

What can I give Him,
　　Poor as I am?
If I were a shepherd
　　I would bring a lamb,
If I were a Wise Man
　　I would do my part, –
Yet what I can I give Him,
　　Give my heart.

WILLIAM MORRIS

80   A Garden by the Sea

I know a little garden-close,
Set thick with lily and red rose,
Where I would wander if I might
From dewy morn to dewy night,
And have one with me wandering.

And though within it no birds sing,
And though no pillared house is there,
And though the apple-boughs are bare
Of fruit and blossom, would to God
Her feet upon the green grass trod,
And I beheld them as before.

There comes a murmur from the shore,
And in the close two fair streams are,
Drawn from the purple hills afar,
Drawn down unto the restless sea:
Dark hills whose heath-bloom feeds no bee,
Dark shore no ship has ever seen,
Tormented by the billows green
Whose murmur comes unceasingly
Unto the place for which I cry,
For which I cry both day and night,
For which I let slip all delight,
Whereby I grow both deaf and blind,
Careless to win, unskilled to find,
And quick to lose what all men seek.

Yet tottering as I am and weak,
Still have I left a little breath
To seek within the jaws of death
An entrance to that happy place,
To seek the unforgotten face,
Once seen, once kissed, once reft from me
Anigh the murmuring of the sea.

81   The Garden of Proserpine

Here, where the world is quiet;
   Here, where all trouble seems
Dead winds' and spent waves' riot
   In doubtful dreams of dreams;
I watch the green field growing
For reaping folk and sowing,
For harvest-time and mowing,
   A sleepy world of streams.

I am tired of tears and laughter,
   And men that laugh and weep;
Of what may come hereafter
   For men that sow to reap:
I am weary of days and hours,
Blown buds of barren flowers,
Desires and dreams and powers
   And everything but sleep.

Here life has death for neighbour,
   And far from eye or ear
Wan waves and wet winds labour,
   Weak ships and spirits steer;
They drive adrift, and whither
They wot not who make thither;
But no such winds blow hither,
   And no such things grow here.

No growth of moor or coppice,
   No heather-flower or vine,
But bloomless buds of poppies,
   Green grapes of Proserpine,
Pale beds of blowing rushes
Where no leaf blooms or blushes
Save this whereout she crushes
   For dead men deadly wine.

Pale, without name or number,
    In fruitless fields of corn,
They bow themselves and slumber
    All night till light is born;
And like a soul belated,
In hell and heaven unmated,
By cloud and mist abated
    Comes out of darkness morn.

Though one were strong as seven,
    He too with death shall dwell,
Nor wake with wings in heaven,
    Nor weep for pains in hell;
Though one were fair as roses,
His beauty clouds and closes;
And well though love reposes,
    In the end it is not well.

Pale, beyond porch and portal,
    Crowned with calm leaves, she stands
Who gathers all things mortal
    With cold immortal hands;
Her languid lips are sweeter
Than love's who fears to greet her
To men that mix and meet her
    From many times and lands.

She waits for each and other,
    She waits for all men born;
Forgets the earth her mother,
    The life of fruits and corn;
And spring and seed and swallow
Take wing for her and follow
Where summer song rings hollow
    And flowers are put to scorn.

There go the loves that wither,
    The old loves with wearier wings;
And all dead years draw thither,
    And all disastrous things;
Dead dreams of days forsaken,
Blind buds that snows have shaken,
Wild leaves that winds have taken,
    Red strays of ruined springs.

We are not sure of sorrow,
    And joy was never sure;
To-day will die to-morrow;
    Time stoops to no man's lure;
And love, grown faint and fretful,
With lips but half regretful
Sighs, and with eyes forgetful
    Weeps that no loves endure.

From too much love of living,
    From hope and fear set free,
We thank with brief thanksgiving
    Whatever gods may be
That no life lives for ever;
That dead men rise up never;
That even the weariest river
    Winds somewhere safe to sea.

Then star nor sun shall waken,
    Nor any change of light:
Nor sound of waters shaken,
    Nor any sound or sight:
Nor wintry leaves nor vernal,
Nor days nor things diurnal;
Only the sleep eternal
    In an eternal night.

GERARD MANLEY HOPKINS

82   In the Valley of the Elwy

I remember a house where all were good
   To me, God knows, deserving no such thing:
   Comforting smell breathed at very entering,
Fetched fresh, as I suppose, off some sweet wood.

That cordial air made those kind people a hood
   All over, as a bevy of eggs the mothering wing
   Will, or mild nights the new morsels of Spring:
Why, it seemed of course; seemed of right it should.

Lovely the woods, waters, meadows, combes, vales,
All the air things wear that build this world of Wales;
   Only the inmate does not correspond:

God, lover of souls, swaying considerate scales,
Complete thy creature dear O where it fails,
   Being mighty a master, being a father and fond.

83   Parted

Farewell to one now silenced quite,
Sent out of hearing, out of sight, –
    My friend of friends, whom I shall miss.
    He is not banished, though, for this, –
Nor he, nor sadness, nor delight.

Though I shall walk with him no more,
A low voice sounds upon the shore.
    He must not watch my resting-place
    But who shall drive a mournful face
From the sad winds about my door?

I shall not hear his voice complain
But who shall stop the patient rain?
    His tears must not disturb my heart,
    But who shall change the years, and part
The world from every thought of pain?

Although my life is left so dim,
The morning crowns the mountain-rim;
    Joy is not gone from summer skies,
    Nor innocence from children's eyes,
And all these things are part of him.

He is not banished, for the showers
Yet wake this green warm earth of ours.
    How can the summer but be sweet?
    I shall not have him at my feet,
And yet my feet are on the flowers.

84   Margaritæ Sorori, I. M.

A late lark twitters from the quiet skies;
And from the west,
Where the sun, his day's work ended,
Lingers as in content,
There falls on the old, grey city
An influence luminous and serene,
A shining peace.

The smoke ascends
In a rosy-and-golden haze. The spires
Shine, and are changed. In the valley
Shadows rise. The lark sings on. The sun,
Closing his benediction,
Sinks, and the darkening air
Thrills with a sense of the triumphing night –
Night, with her train of stars
And her great gift of sleep.

So be my passing!
My task accomplished and the long day done,
My wages taken, and in my heart
Some late lark singing,
Let me be gathered to the quiet west,
The sundown splendid and serene,
Death.

85   On the Way to Kew

On the way to Kew,
By the river old and grey,
Where in the Long Ago
We laughed and loitered so,
I met a ghost to-day,
A ghost that told of you,
A ghost of low replies
And sweet inscrutable eyes,
    Coming up from Richmond,
As you used to do.

By the river old and grey,
The enchanted Long Ago
Murmured and smiled anew.
On the way to Kew,
March had the laugh of May,
The bare boughs looked aglow,
And old immortal words
Sang in my breast like birds,
    Coming up from Richmond,
As I used with you.

With the life of Long Ago
Lived my thought of you.
By the river old and grey
Flowing his appointed way,
As I watched, I knew
What is so good to know:
Not in vain, not in vain,
I shall look for you again,
    Coming up from Richmond,
On the way to Kew.

Madam Life's a piece in bloom
    Death goes dogging everywhere:
She's the tenant of the room,
    He's the ruffian on the stair.

You shall see her as a friend,
    You shall bilk him once or twice;
But he'll trap you in the end,
    And he'll stick you for her price.

With his kneebones at your chest,
    And his knuckles in your throat,
You would reason – plead – protest!
    Clutching at her petticoat;

But she's heard it all before,
    Well she knows you've had your fun,
Gingerly she gains the door,
    And your little job is done.

87   Requiem

Under the wide and starry sky,
Dig the grave and let me lie.
Glad did I live and gladly die,
    And I laid me down with a will.

This be the verse you grave for me:
Here he lies where he longed to be;
Home is the sailor, home from sea,
    And the hunter home from the hill.

88   The Harlot's House

We caught the tread of dancing feet,
We loitered down the moonlit street,
And stopped beneath the harlot's house.

Inside, above the din and fray,
We heard the loud musicians play
The 'Treues Liebes Herz' of Strauss.

Like strange mechanical grotesques,
Making fantastic arabesques,
The shadows raced across the blind.

We watched the ghostly dancers spin
To sound of horn and violin,
Like black leaves wheeling in the wind.

Like wire-pulling automatons,
Slim silhouetted skeletons
Went sidling through the slow quadrille.

They took each other by the hand,
And danced a stately saraband;
Their laughter echoed thin and shrill.

Sometimes a clockwork puppet pressed
A phantom lover to her breast,
Sometimes they seemed to try to sing.

Sometimes a horrible marionette
Came out, and smoked its cigarette
Upon the steps like a live thing.

Then, turning to my love, I said,
'The dead are dancing with the dead,
The dust is whirling with the dust.'

But she – she heard the violin,
And left my side, and entered in:
Love passed into the house of lust.

Then suddenly the tune went false,
The dancers wearied of the waltz,
The shadows ceased to wheel and whirl.

And down the long and silent street,
The dawn, with silver-sandalled feet,
Crept like a frightened girl.

JOHN DAVIDSON

89   The Runnable Stag

When the pods went pop on the broom, green broom,
  And apples began to be golden-skinned,
We harboured a stag in the Priory coomb,
  And we feathered his trail up-wind, up-wind,
  We feathered his trail up-wind —
    A stag of warrant, a stag, a stag,
    A runnable stag, a kingly crop,
    Brow, bay and tray and three on top,
    A stag, a runnable stag.

Then the huntsman's horn rang yap, yap, yap,
  And 'Forwards' we heard the harbourer shout;
But 'twas only a brocket that broke a gap
  In the beechen underwood, driven out,
  From the underwood antlered out
    By warrant and might of the stag, the stag,
    The runnable stag, whose lordly mind
    Was bent on sleep, though beamed and tined
    He stood, a runnable stag.

So we tufted the covert till afternoon
  With Tinkerman's Pup and Bell-of-the-North;
And hunters were sulky and hounds out of tune
  Before we tufted the right stag forth,
  Before we tufted him forth,
    The stag of warrant, the wily stag,
    The runnable stag with his kingly crop,
    Brow, bay and tray and three on top,
    The royal and runnable stag.

It was Bell-of-the-North and Tinkerman's Pup
    That stuck to the scent till the copse was drawn.
'Tally ho! tally ho!' and the hunt was up,
    The tufters whipped and the pack laid on,
    The resolute pack laid on,
        And the stag of warrant away at last,
        The runnable stag, the same, the same,
        His hoofs on fire, his horns like flame,
        A stag, a runnable stag.

'Let your gelding be: if you check or chide
    He stumbles at once and you're out of the hunt;
For three hundred gentlemen, able to ride,
    On hunters accustomed to bear the brunt,
    Accustomed to bear the brunt,
        Are after the runnable stag, the stag,
        The runnable stag with his kingly crop,
        Brow, bay and tray and three on top,
        The right, the runnable stag.'

By perilous paths in coomb and dell,
    The heather, the rocks, and the river-bed,
The pace grew hot, for the scent lay well,
    And a runnable stag goes right ahead,
    The quarry went right ahead –
        Ahead, ahead, and fast and far;
        His antlered crest, his cloven hoof,
        Brow, bay and tray and three aloof,
        The stag, the runnable stag.

For a matter of twenty miles and more,
    By the densest hedge and the highest wall,
Through herds of bullocks he baffled the lore
    Of harbourer, huntsman, hounds and all,
    Of harbourer, hounds and all –
        The stag of warrant, the wily stag,
        For twenty miles, and five and five,
        He ran, and he never was caught alive,
        This stag, this runnable stag.

When he turned at bay in the leafy gloom,
  In the emerald gloom where the brook ran deep,
He heard in the distance the rollers boom,
  And he saw in a vision of peaceful sleep,
  In a wonderful vision of sleep,
    A stag of warrant, a stag, a stag,
    A runnable stag in a jewelled bed,
    Under the sheltering ocean dead,
    A stag, a runnable stag.

So a fateful hope lit up his eye,
  And he opened his nostrils wide again,
And he tossed his branching antlers high
  As he headed the hunt down the Charlock glen,
  As he raced down the echoing glen
    For five miles more, the stag, the stag,
    For twenty miles, and five and five,
    Not to be caught now, dead or alive,
    The stag, the runnable stag.

Three hundred gentlemen, able to ride,
  Three hundred horses as gallant and free,
Beheld him escape on the evening tide,
  Far out till he sank in the Severn Sea,
  Till he sank in the depths of the sea –
    The stag, the buoyant stag, the stag
    That slept at last in a jewelled bed
    Under the sheltering ocean spread,
    The stag, the runnable stag.

FRANCIS THOMPSON

90   The Kingdom of God

O world invisible, we view thee,
O world intangible, we touch thee,
O world unknowable, we know thee,
Inapprehensible, we clutch thee!

Does the fish soar to find the ocean,
The eagle plunge to find the air –
That we ask of the stars in motion
If they have rumour of thee there?

Not where the wheeling systems darken,
And our benumbed conceiving soars! –
The drift of pinions, would we hearken,
Beats at our own clay-shuttered doors.

The angels keep their ancient places; –
Turn but a stone, and start a wing!
'Tis ye, 'tis your estrangèd faces,
That miss the many-splendoured thing.

But (when so sad thou canst not sadder)
Cry; – and upon thy so sore loss
Shall shine the traffic of Jacob's ladder
Pitched betwixt Heaven and Charing Cross.

Yea, in the night, my Soul, my daughter,
Cry, – clinging Heaven by the hems;
And lo, Christ walking on the water,
Not of Gennesareth, but Thames!

A. E. HOUSMAN

91   1887

From Clee to heaven the beacon burns,
    The shires have seen it plain,
From north and south the sign returns
    And beacons burn again.

Look left, look right, the hills are bright,
    The dales are light between,
Because 'tis fifty years to-night
    That God has saved the Queen.

Now, when the flame they watch not towers
    About the soil they trod,
Lads, we'll remember friends of ours
    Who shared the work with God.

To skies that knit their heartstrings right,
    To fields that bred them brave,
The saviours come not home to-night:
    Themselves they could not save.

It dawns in Asia, tombstones show
    And Shropshire names are read;
And the Nile spills his overflow
    Beside the Severn's dead.

We pledge in peace by farm and town
    The Queen they served in war,
And fire the beacons up and down
    The land they perished for.

'God save the Queen' we living sing,
    From height to height 'tis heard;
And with the rest your voices ring,
    Lads of the Fifty-Third.

Oh, God will save her, fear you not:
  Be you the men you've been,
Get you the sons your fathers got,
  And God will save the Queen.

92   Bredon Hill

In summertime on Bredon
  The bells they sound so clear;
Round both the shires they ring them
  In steeples far and near,
  A happy noise to hear.

Here of a Sunday morning
  My love and I would lie,
And see the coloured counties,
  And hear the larks so high
  About us in the sky.

The bells would ring to call her
  In valleys miles away:
'Come all to church, good people;
  Good people, come and pray.'
  But here my love would stay.

And I would turn and answer
  Among the springing thyme,
'Oh, peal upon our wedding,
  And we will hear the chime,
  And come to church in time.'

But when the snows at Christmas
  On Bredon top were strown,
My love rose up so early
  And stole out unbeknown
  And went to church alone.

They tolled the one bell only,
    Groom there was none to see,
The mourners followed after,
    And so to church went she,
    And would not wait for me.

The bells they sound on Bredon,
    And still the steeples hum.
'Come all to church, good people,' –
    Oh, noisy bells, be dumb;
    I hear you, I will come.

93   The Lent Lily

'Tis spring; come out to ramble
    The hilly brakes around,
For under thorn and bramble
    About the hollow ground
    The primroses are found.

And there's the windflower chilly
    With all the winds at play,
And there's the Lenten lily
    That has not long to stay
    And dies on Easter day.

And since till girls go maying
    You find the primrose still,
And find the windflower playing
    With every wind at will,
    But not the daffodil,

Bring baskets now, and sally
    Upon the spring's array,
And bear from hill and valley
    The daffodil away
    That dies on Easter day.

94   'In my own shire'

In my own shire, if I was sad,
Homely comforters I had:
The earth, because my heart was sore,
Sorrowed for the son she bore;
And standing hills, long to remain,
Shared their short-lived comrade's pain.
And bound for the same bourn as I,
On every road I wandered by,
Trod beside me, close and dear,
The beautiful and death-struck year:
Whether in the woodland brown
I heard the beechnut rustle down,
And saw the purple crocus pale
Flower about the autumn dale;
Or littering far the fields of May
Lady-smocks a-bleaching lay,
And like a skylit water stood
The bluebells in the azured wood.

Yonder, lightening other loads,
The seasons range the country roads,
But here in London streets I ken
No such helpmates, only men;
And these are not in plight to bear,
If they would, another's care.
They have enough as 'tis: I see
In many an eye that measures me
The mortal sickness of a mind
Too unhappy to be kind.
Undone with misery, all they can
Is to hate their fellow man;
And till they drop they needs must still
Look at you and wish you ill.

95   'Be still, my soul'

Be still, my soul, be still; the arms you bear are brittle,
  Earth and high heaven are fixed of old and founded strong.
Think rather, – call to thought, if now you grieve a little,
  The days when we had rest, O soul, for they were long.

Men loved unkindness then, but lightless in the quarry
  I slept and saw not; tears fell down, I did not mourn;
Sweat ran and blood sprang out and I was never sorry:
  Then it was well with me, in days ere I was born.

Now, and I muse for why and never find the reason,
  I pace the earth, and drink the air, and feel the sun.
Be still, be still, my soul; it is but for a season:
  Let us endure an hour and see injustice done.

Ay, look: high heaven and earth ail from the prime
      foundation;
  All thoughts to rive the heart are here, and all are vain:
Horror and scorn and hate and fear and indignation –
  Oh why did I awake? when shall I sleep again?

96   'Terence, this is stupid stuff'

  'Terence, this is stupid stuff:
You eat your victuals fast enough;
There can't be much amiss, 'tis clear,
To see the rate you drink your beer.
But oh, good Lord, the verse you make,
It gives a chap the belly-ache.
The cow, the old cow, she is dead;
It sleeps well, the hornèd head:
We poor lads, 'tis our turn now
To hear such tunes as killed the cow.
Pretty friendship 'tis to rhyme
Your friends to death before their time
Moping melancholy mad:
Come, pipe a tune to dance to, lad.'

Why, if 'tis dancing you would be,
There's brisker pipes than poetry.
Say, for what were hop-yards meant,
Or why was Burton built on Trent?
Oh many a peer of England brews
Livelier liquor than the Muse,
And malt does more than Milton can
To justify God's ways to man.
Ale, man, ale's the stuff to drink
For fellows whom it hurts to think:
Look into the pewter pot
To see the world as the world's not.
And faith, 'tis pleasant till 'tis past:
The mischief is that 'twill not last.
Oh I have been to Ludlow fair
And left my necktie God knows where,
And carried half-way home, or near,
Pints and quarts of Ludlow beer:
Then the world seemed none so bad,
And I myself a sterling lad;
And down in lovely muck I've lain,
Happy till I woke again.
Then I saw the morning sky:
Heigho, the tale was all a lie;
The world, it was the old world yet,
I was I, my things were wet,
And nothing now remained to do
But begin the game anew.

Therefore, since the world has still
Much good, but much less good than ill,
And while the sun and moon endure
Luck's a chance, but trouble's sure,
I'd face it as a wise man would,
And train for ill and not for good.
'Tis true, the stuff I bring for sale
Is not so brisk a brew as ale:
Out of a stem that scored the hand
I wrung it in a weary land.
But take it: if the smack is sour,

The better for the embittered hour;
It should do good to heart and head
When your soul is in my soul's stead;
And I will friend you, if I may,
In the dark and cloudy day.

There was a king reigned in the East:
There, when kings will sit to feast,
They get their fill before they think
With poisoned meat and poisoned drink.
He gathered all that springs to birth
From the many-venomed earth;
First a little, thence to more,
He sampled all her killing store;
And easy, smiling, seasoned sound,
Sate the king when healths went round.
They put arsenic in his meat
And stared aghast to watch him eat;
They poured strychnine in his cup
And shook to see him drink it up:
They shook, they stared as white's their shirt:
Them it was their poison hurt.
– I tell the tale that I heard told.
Mithridates, he died old.

97   Epigraph to *Last Poems*

We'll to the woods no more,
The laurels all are cut,
The bowers are bare of bay
That once the Muses wore;
The year draws in the day
And soon will evening shut:
The laurels all are cut,
We'll to the woods no more.
Oh we'll no more, no more
To the leafy woods away,
To the high wild woods of laurel
And the bowers of bay no more.

98   Soldier from the wars returning

Soldier from the wars returning,
   Spoiler of the taken town,
Here is ease that asks not earning;
   Turn you in and sit you down.

Peace is come and wars are over,
   Welcome you and welcome all,
While the charger crops the clover
   And his bridle hangs in stall.

Now no more of winters biting,
   Filth in trench from fall to spring,
Summers full of sweat and fighting
   For the Kesar or the King.

Rest you, charger, rust you, bridle;
   Kings and kesars, keep your pay;
Soldier, sit you down and idle
   At the inn of night for aye.

99   The Oracles

'Tis mute, the word they went to hear on high Dodona
    mountain
   When winds were in the oakenshaws and all the
    cauldrons tolled,
And mute's the midland navel-stone beside the singing
    fountain,
   And echoes list to silence now where gods told lies of old.

I took my question to the shrine that has not ceased from
    speaking,
   The heart within, that tells the truth and tells it twice as
    plain;
And from the cave of oracles I heard the priestess shrieking
    That she and I should surely die and never live again.

Oh priestess, what you cry is clear, and sound good sense I
    think it;
  But let the screaming echoes rest, and froth your mouth
    no more.
'Tis true there's better boose than brine, but he that drowns
    must drink it;
  And oh, my lass, the news is news that men have heard
    before.

The King with half the East at heel is marched from lands of
    morning;
  Their fighters drink the rivers up, their shafts benight the air,
And he that stands will die for nought, and home there's no
    returning.
  The Spartans on the sea-wet rock sat down and combed
    their hair.

100   'Tell me not here'

Tell me not here, it needs not saying,
  What tune the enchantress plays
In aftermaths of soft September
  Or under blanching mays,
For she and I were long acquainted
  And I knew all her ways.

On russet floors, by waters idle,
  The pine lets fall its cone;
The cuckoo shouts all day at nothing
  In leafy dells alone;
And traveller's joy beguiles in autumn
  Hearts that have lost their own.

On acres of the seeded grasses
  The changing burnish heaves;
Or marshalled under moons of harvest
  Stand still all night the sheaves;
Or beeches strip in storms for winter
  And stain the wind with leaves.

Possess, as I possessed a season,
　　The countries I resign,
Where over elmy plains the highway
　　Would mount the hills and shine,
And full of shade the pillared forest
　　Would murmur and be mine.

For nature, heartless, witless nature,
　　Will neither care nor know
What stranger's feet may find the meadow
　　And trespass there and go,
Nor ask amid the dews of morning
　　If they are mine or no.

101　Fancy's Knell

When lads were home from labour
　　At Abdon under Clee,
A man would call his neighbour
　　And both would send for me.
And where the light in lances
　　Across the mead was laid,
There to the dances
　　I fetched my flute and played.

Ours were idle pleasures,
　　Yet oh, content we were,
The young to wind the measures,
　　The old to heed the air;
And I to lift with playing
　　From tree and tower and steep
The light delaying,
　　And flute the sun to sleep.

The youth toward his fancy
   Would turn his brow of tan,
And Tom would pair with Nancy
   And Dick step off with Fan;
The girl would lift her glances
   To his, and both be mute:
Well went the dances
   At evening to the flute.

Wenlock Edge was umbered,
   And bright was Abdon Burf,
And warm between them slumbered
   The smooth green miles of turf;
Until from grass and clover
   The upshot beam would fade,
And England over
   Advanced the lofty shade.

The lofty shade advances,
   I fetch my flute and play:
Come, lads, and learn the dances
   And praise the tune to-day.
To-morrow, more's the pity,
   Away we both must hie,
To air the ditty,
   And to earth I.

102   Diffugere Nives

Horace: Odes *iv* 7

The snows are fled away, leaves on the shaws
   And grasses in the mead renew their birth,
The river to the river-bed withdraws,
   And altered is the fashion of the earth.

The Nymphs and Graces three put off their fear
    And unapparelled in the woodland play.
The swift hour and the brief prime of the year
    Say to the soul, *Thou wast not born for aye.*

Thaw follows frost; hard on the heel of spring
    Treads summer sure to die, for hard on hers
Comes autumn, with his apples scattering;
    Then back to wintertide, when nothing stirs.

But oh, whate'er the sky-led seasons mar,
    Moon upon moon rebuilds it with her beams;
Come *we* where Tullus and where Ancus are,
    And good Aeneas, we are dust and dreams.

Torquatus, if the gods in heaven shall add
    The morrow to the day, what tongue has told?
Feast then thy heart, for what thy heart has had
    The fingers of no heir will ever hold.

When thou descendest once the shades among,
    The stern assize and equal judgment o'er,
Not thy long lineage nor thy golden tongue,
    No, nor thy righteousness, shall friend thee more.

Night holds Hippolytus the pure of stain,
    Diana steads him nothing, he must stay;
And Theseus leaves Pirithöus in the chain
    The love of comrades cannot take away.

103   Atys

'Lydians, lords of Hermus river,
    Sifters of the golden loam,
See you yet the lances quiver
    And the hunt returning home?'

'King, the star that shuts the even
  Calls the sheep from Tmolus down;
Home return the doves from heaven,
  And the prince to Sardis town.'

From the hunting heavy laden
  Up the Mysian road they ride;
And the star that mates the maiden
  Leads his son to Croesus' side.

'Lydians, under stream and fountain
  Finders of the golden vein,
Riding from Olympus mountain,
  Lydians, see you Atys plain?'

'King, I see the Phrygian stranger
  And the guards in hunter's trim,
Saviours of thy son from danger;
  Them I see. I see not him.'

'Lydians, as the troop advances,
  – It is eve and I am old –
Tell me why they trail their lances,
  Washers of the sands of gold.

'I am old and day is ending
  And the wildering night comes on;
Up the Mysian entry wending,
  Lydians, Lydians, what is yon?'

Hounds behind their master whining,
  Huntsmen pacing dumb beside,
On his breast the boar-spear shining,
  Home they bear his father's pride.

104   He Fell Among Thieves

'Ye have robbed', said he, 'ye have slaughtered and made an
     end,
   Take your ill-got plunder, and bury the dead:
What will ye more of your guest and sometime friend?'
   'Blood for our blood', they said.

He laughed: 'If one may settle the score for five,
   I am ready; but let the reckoning stand till day:
I have loved the sunlight as dearly as any alive.'
   'You shall die at dawn', said they.

He flung his empty revolver down the slope,
   He climbed alone to the Eastward edge of the trees;
All night long in a dream untroubled of hope
   He brooded, clasping his knees.

He did not hear the monotonous roar that fills
   The ravine where the Yassin river sullenly flows;
He did not see the starlight on the Laspur hills,
   Or the far Afghan snows.

He saw the April noon on his books aglow,
   The wistaria trailing in at the window wide;
He heard his father's voice from the terrace below
   Calling him down to ride.

He saw the grey little church across the park,
   The mounds that hide the loved and honoured dead;
The Norman arch, the chancel softly dark,
   The brasses black and red.

He saw the School Close, sunny and green,
   The runner beside him, the stand by the parapet wall,
The distant tape, and the crowd roaring between
   His own name over all.

He saw the dark wainscot and timbered roof,
　　The long tables, and the faces merry and keen;
The College Eight and their trainer dining aloof,
　　The Dons on the daïs serene.

He watched the liner's stem ploughing the foam,
　　He felt her trembling speed and the thrash of her screw;
He heard her passengers' voices talking of home,
　　He saw the flag she flew.

And now it was dawn. He rose strong on his feet,
　　And strode to his ruined camp below the wood;
He drank the breath of the morning cool and sweet;
　　His murderers round him stood.

Light on the Laspur hills was broadening fast,
　　The blood-red snow-peaks chilled to a dazzling white:
He turned, and saw the golden circle at last,
　　Cut by the Eastern height.

'O glorious Life, Who dwellest in earth and sun,
　　I have lived, I praise and adore Thee.'
　　　　　　　　　　　　　　　　A sword swept.
Over the pass the voices one by one
　　Faded, and the hill slept.

105 Ireland, Ireland

Down thy valleys, Ireland, Ireland,
    Down thy valleys green and sad,
Still thy spirit wanders wailing,
    Wanders wailing, wanders mad.

Long ago that anguish took thee,
    Ireland, Ireland, green and fair,
Spoilers strong in darkness took thee,
    Broke thy heart and left thee there.

Down thy valleys, Ireland, Ireland,
    Still thy spirit wanders mad;
All too late they love that wronged thee,
    Ireland, Ireland, green and sad.

106 The Viking's Song

When I thy lover first
    Shook out my canvas free
And like a pirate burst
    Into that dreaming sea,
The land knew no such thirst
    As then tormented me.

Now when at eve returned
    I near that shore divine,
Where once but watch-fires burned
    I see thy beacon shine,
And know the land hath learned
    Desire that welcomes mine.

107 The Nightjar

We loved our Nightjar, but she would not stay with us.
We had found her lying as dead, but soft and warm,
Under the apple tree beside the old thatched wall.
Two days we kept her in a basket by the fire,
Fed her, and thought she well might live – till suddenly
In the very moment of most confiding hope
She raised herself all tense, quivered and drooped and died.
Tears sprang into my eyes – why not? the heart of man
Soon sets itself to love a living companion,
The more so if by chance it asks some care of him.
And this one had the kind of loveliness that goes
Far deeper than the optic nerve – full fathom five
To the soul's ocean cave, where Wonder and Reason
Tell their alternate dreams of how the world was made.
So wonderful she was – her wings the wings of night
But powdered here and there with tiny golden clouds
And wave-line markings like sea-ripples on the sand.
O how I wish I might never forget that bird –
Never!
        But even now, like all beauty of earth,
She is fading from me into the dusk of Time.

108   For all we have and are

1914

For all we have and are,
For all our children's fate,
Stand up and take the war.
The Hun is at the gate!
Our world has passed away,
In wantonness o'erthrown.
There is nothing left to-day
But steel and fire and stone!
    Though all we knew depart,
    The old Commandments stand: –
    'In courage keep your heart,
    In strength lift up your hand.'

Once more we hear the word
That sickened earth of old: –
'No law except the Sword
Unsheathed and uncontrolled.'
Once more it knits mankind,
Once more the nations go
To meet and break and bind
A crazed and driven foe.

Comfort, content, delight,
The ages' slow-bought gain,
They shrivelled in a night.
Only ourselves remain
To face the naked days
In silent fortitude,
Through perils and dismays
Renewed and re-renewed.
    Though all we made depart,
    The old Commandments stand: –
    'In patience keep your heart,
    In strength lift up your hand.'

No easy hope or lies
Shall bring us to our goal,
But iron sacrifice
Of body, will, and soul.
There is but one task for all –
One life for each to give.
What stands if Freedom fall?
Who dies if England live?

109   Danny Deever

'What are the bugles blowin' for?' said Files-on-Parade.
'To turn you out, to turn you out,' the Colour-Sergeant said.
'What makes you look so white, so white?' said Files-on-
      Parade.
'I'm dreadin' what I've got to watch,' the Colour-Sergeant
      said.
      For they're hangin' Danny Deever, you can hear the Dead
         March play,
      The Regiment's in 'ollow square – they're hangin' him
         to-day;
      They've taken of his buttons off an' cut his stripes away,
      An' they're hangin' Danny Deever in the mornin'.

'What makes the rear-rank breathe so 'ard?' said Files-
      on-Parade.
'It's bitter cold, it's bitter cold,' the Colour-Sergeant said.
'What makes that front-rank man fall down?' said Files-
      on-Parade.
'A touch o' sun, a touch o' sun,' the Colour-Sergeant said.
      They are hangin' Danny Deever, they are marchin' of 'im
         round,
      They 'ave 'alted Danny Deever by 'is coffin on the ground;
      An' 'e'll swing in 'arf a minute for a sneakin' shootin'
         hound –
      O they're hangin' Danny Deever in the mornin'!

''Is cot was right-'and cot to mine,' said Files-on-Parade.
''E's sleepin' out an' far to-night,' the Colour-Sergeant said.
'I've drunk 'is beer a score o' times,' said Files-on-Parade.
''E's drinkin' bitter beer alone,' the Colour-Sergeant said.
    They are hangin' Danny Deever, you must mark 'im to 'is
        place,
    For 'e shot a comrade sleepin' – you must look 'im in the
        face;
    Nine 'undred of 'is county an' the Regiment's disgrace,
    While they're hangin' Danny Deever in the mornin'.

'What's that so black agin the sun?' said Files-on-Parade.
'It's Danny fightin' 'ard for life,' the Colour-Sergeant said.
'What's that that whimpers over'ead?' said Files-on-Parade.
'It's Danny's soul that's passin' now,' the Colour-Sergeant
    said.
    For they're done with Danny Deever, you can 'ear the
        quickstep play,
    The Regiment's in column, an' they're marchin' us away;
    Ho! the young recruits are shakin', an' they'll want their
        beer to-day,
    After hangin' Danny Deever in the mornin'!

110   Tommy

I went into a public-'ouse to get a pint o' beer,
The publican 'e up an' sez, 'We serve no red-coats here.'
The girls be'ind the bar they laughed an' giggled fit to die,
I outs into the street again an' to myself sez I:
    O it's Tommy this, an' Tommy that, an' 'Tommy, go
        away';
    But it's 'Thank you, Mister Atkins,' when the band
        begins to play –
    The band begins to play, my boys, the band begins to
        play,
    O it's 'Thank you, Mister Atkins,' when the band begins
        to play.

I went into a theatre as sober as could be,
They gave a drunk civilian room, but 'adn't none for me;
They sent me to the gallery or round the music-'alls,
But when it comes to fightin', Lord! they'll shove me in the
        stalls!
    For it's Tommy this, an' Tommy that, an' 'Tommy, wait
        outside';
    But it's 'Special train for Atkins' when the trooper's on
        the tide –
    The troopship's on the tide, my boys, the troopship's on
        the tide,
    O it's 'Special train for Atkins' when the trooper's on the
        tide.

Yes, makin' mock o' uniforms that guard you while you
        sleep
Is cheaper than them uniforms, an' they're starvation cheap;
An' hustlin' drunken soldiers when they're goin' large a bit
Is five times better business than paradin' in full kit.
    Then it's Tommy this, an' Tommy that, an' 'Tommy,
        'ow's yer soul?'
    But it's 'Thin red line of 'eroes' when the drums begin to
        roll –
    The drums begin to roll, my boys, the drums begin to
        roll,
    O it's 'Thin red line of 'eroes' when the drums begin to
        roll.

We aren't no thin red 'eroes, nor we aren't no blackguards
        too,
But single men in barricks, most remarkable like you;
An' if sometimes our conduck isn't all your fancy paints,
Why, single men in barricks don't grow into plaster saints;
    While it's Tommy this, an' Tommy that, an' 'Tommy,
        fall be'ind,'
    But it's 'Please to walk in front, sir,' when there's
        trouble in the wind –
    There's trouble in the wind, my boys, there's trouble in
        the wind,
    O it's 'Please to walk in front, sir,' when there's trouble
        in the wind.

You talk o' better food for us, an' schools, an' fires, an' all:
We'll wait for extry rations if you treat us rational.
Don't mess about the cook-room slops, but prove it to our
    face
The Widow's Uniform is not the soldier-man's disgrace.
    For it's Tommy this, an' Tommy that, an' 'Chuck him
      out, the brute!'
    But it's 'Saviour of 'is country' when the guns begin to
      shoot;
    An' it's Tommy this, an' Tommy that, an' anything you
      please;
    An' Tommy ain't a bloomin' fool – you bet that Tommy
      sees!

111   Mandalay

By the old Moulmein Pagoda, lookin' lazy at the sea,
There's a Burma girl a-settin', and I know she thinks o' me;
For the wind is in the palm-trees, and the temple-bells they
    say:
'Come you back, you British soldier; come you back to
    Mandalay!'
    Come you back to Mandalay,
    Where the old Flotilla lay:
    Can't you 'ear their paddles chunkin' from Rangoon
      to Mandalay?
    On the road to Mandalay,
    Where the flyin'-fishes play,
    An' the dawn comes up like thunder outer China
      'crost the Bay!

'Er petticoat was yaller an' 'er little cap was green,
An' 'er name was Supi-yaw-lat – jes' the same as Theebaw's
    Queen,
An' I seed her first a-smokin' of a whackin' white cheroot,
An' a-wastin' Christian kisses on an 'eathen idol's foot:
    Bloomin' idol made o' mud –
    Wot they called the Great Gawd Budd –
    Plucky lot she cared for idols when I kissed 'er where
    she stud!
    On the road to Mandalay . . .

When the mist was on the rice-fields an' the sun was
    droppin' slow,
She'd git 'er little banjo an' she'd sing '*Kulla-lo-lo!*'
With 'er arm upon my shoulder an' 'er cheek agin my cheek
We useter watch the steamer an' the *hathis* pilin' teak.
    Elephints a-pilin' teak
    In the sludgy, squdgy creek,
    Where the silence 'ung that 'eavy you was 'arf afraid
    to speak!
    On the road to Mandalay . . .

But that's all shove be'ind me – long ago an' fur away,
An' there ain't no buses runnin' from the Bank to Mandalay;
An' I'm learnin' 'ere in London what the ten-year soldier
    tells:
'If you've 'eard the East a-callin', you won't never 'eed
    naught else.'
    No! you won't 'eed nothin' else
    But them spicy garlic smells,
    An' the sunshine an' the palm-trees an' the tinkly
    temple-bells;
    On the road to Mandalay . . .

I am sick o' wastin' leather on these gritty pavin'-stones,
An' the blasted English drizzle wakes the fever in my bones;
Tho' I walks with fifty 'ousemaids outer Chelsea to the
    Strand,
An' they talks a lot o' lovin', but wot do they understand?
        Beefy face an' grubby 'and –
        Law! wot do they understand?
        I've a neater, sweeter maiden in a cleaner, greener
        land!
        On the road to Mandalay . . .

Ship me somewheres east of Suez, where the best is like the
    worst,
Where there aren't no Ten Commandments an' a man can
    raise a thirst;
For the temple-bells are callin', an' it's there that I would
    be –
By the old Moulmein Pagoda, looking lazy at the sea;
        On the road to Mandalay,
        Where the old Flotilla lay,
        With our sick beneath the awnings when we went to
        Mandalay!
        O the road to Mandalay,
        Where the flyin'-fishes play,
        An' the dawn comes up like thunder outer China
        'crost the Bay!

112   The Way Through the Woods

They shut the road through the woods
Seventy years ago.
Weather and rain have undone it again,
And now you would never know
There was once a road through the woods
Before they planted the trees.
It is underneath the coppice and heath
And the thin anemones.

Only the keeper sees
That, where the ring-dove broods,
And the badgers roll at ease,
There was once a road through the woods.

Yet, if you enter the woods
Of a summer evening late,
When the night-air cools on the trout-ringed pools
Where the otter whistles his mate,
(They fear not men in the woods,
Because they see so few)
You will hear the beat of a horse's feet,
And the swish of a skirt in the dew,
Steadily cantering through
The misty solitudes,
As though they perfectly knew
The old lost road through the woods . . .
But there is no road through the woods.

113   The Children

1914–18

These were our children who died for our lands: they were
      dear in our sight.
   We have only the memory left of their home-treasured
      sayings and laughter.
   The price of our loss shall be paid to our hands, not
      another's hereafter.
Neither the Alien nor Priest shall decide on it. That is our
      right.
         But who shall return us the children?

At the hour the Barbarian chose to disclose his pretences,
  And raged against Man, they engaged, on the breasts that
    they bared for us,
  The first felon-stroke of the sword he had long-time
    prepared for us –
Their bodies were all our defence while we wrought our
  defences.

They bought us anew with their blood, forbearing to blame
  us,
Those hours which we had not made good when the
  Judgment o'ercame us.
They believed us and perished for it. Our statecraft, our
  learning
Delivered them bound to the Pit and alive to the burning
Whither they mirthfully hastened as jostling for honour –
Not since her birth has our Earth seen such worth loosed
  upon her.

Nor was their agony brief, or once only imposed on them.
  The wounded, the war-spent, the sick received no
    exemption:
  Being cured they returned and endured and achieved our
    redemption,
Hopeless themselves of relief, till Death, marvelling, closed
  on them.

That flesh we had nursed from the first in all cleanness was
  given
To corruption unveiled and assailed by the malice of
  Heaven –
By the heart-shaking jests of Decay where it lolled on the
  wires –
To be blanched or gay-painted by fumes – to be cindered by
  fires –
To be senselessly tossed and retossed in stale mutilation
From crater to crater. For this we shall take expiation.
    But who shall return us our children?

As I pass through my incarnations in every age and race,
I make my proper prostrations to the Gods of the Market-
Place.
Peering through reverent fingers I watch them flourish and
fall,
And the Gods of the Copybook Headings, I notice, outlast
them all.

We were living in trees when they met us. They showed us
each in turn
That Water would certainly wet us, as Fire would certainly
burn:
But we found them lacking in Uplift, Vision and Breadth of
Mind,
So we left them to teach the Gorillas while we followed the
March of Mankind.

We moved as the Spirit listed. *They* never altered their pace,
Being neither cloud nor wind-borne like the Gods of the
Market-Place;
But they always caught up with our progress, and presently
word would come
That a tribe had been wiped off its icefield, or the lights had
gone out in Rome.

With the Hopes that our World is built on they were utterly
out of touch,
They denied that the Moon was Stilton; they denied she was
even Dutch.
They denied that Wishes were Horses; they denied that a Pig
had Wings.
So we worshipped the Gods of the Market Who promised
these beautiful things.

When the Cambrian measures were forming, They promised
    perpetual peace.
They swore, if we gave them our weapons, that the wars of
    the tribes would cease.
But when we disarmed They sold us and delivered us bound
    to our foe,
And the Gods of the Copybook Headings said: '*Stick to the
    Devil you know.*'

On the first Feminian Sandstones we were promised the
    Fuller Life
(Which started by loving our neighbour and ended by loving
    his wife)
Till our women had no more children and the men lost
    reason and faith,
And the Gods of the Copybook Headings said: '*The Wages of
    Sin is Death.*'

In the Carboniferous Epoch we were promised abundance
    for all,
By robbing selected Peter to pay for collective Paul;
But, though we had plenty of money, there was nothing our
    money could buy,
And the Gods of the Copybook Headings said: '*If you don't
    work you die.*'

Then the Gods of the Market tumbled, and their smooth-
    tongued wizards withdrew,
And the hearts of the meanest were humbled and began to
    believe it was true
That All is not Gold that Glitters, and Two and Two make
    Four –
And the Gods of the Copybook Headings limped up to
    explain it once more.
    .   .   .   .

As it will be in the future, it was at the birth of Man –
There are only four things certain since Social Progress
    began: –

That the Dog returns to his Vomit and the Sow returns to her
    Mire,
And the burnt Fool's bandaged finger goes wabbling back to
    the Fire;

And that after this is accomplished, and the brave new
    world begins
When all men are paid for existing and no man must pay for
    his sins,
As surely as Water will wet us, as surely as Fire will burn,
The Gods of the Copybook Headings with terror and
    slaughter return!

115   John Kinsella's Lament for Mrs Mary Moore

A bloody and a sudden end,
　　Gunshot or a noose,
For Death who takes what man would keep,
　　Leaves what man would lose.
He might have had my sister,
　　My cousins by the score,
But nothing satisfied the fool
　　But my dear Mary Moore,
None other knows what pleasures man
　　At table or in bed.
What shall I do for pretty girls
　　Now my old bawd is dead?

Though stiff to strike a bargain,
　　Like an old Jew man,
Her bargain struck we laughed and talked
　　And emptied many a can;
And O! but she had stories,
　　Though not for the priest's ear,
To keep the soul of man alive,
　　Banish age and care,
And being old she put a skin
　　On everything she said.
What shall I do for pretty girls
　　Now my old bawd is dead?

The priests have got a book that says
  But for Adam's sin
Eden's Garden would be there
  And I there within.
No expectation fails there,
  No pleasing habit ends,
No man grows old, no girl grows cold,
  But friends walk by friends.
Who quarrels over halfpennies
  That plucks the trees for bread?
What shall I do for pretty girls
  Now my old bawd is dead?

ERNEST DOWSON

116   Non Sum Qualis Eram Bonae sub Regno Cynarae

Last night, ah, yesternight, betwixt her lips and mine
There fell thy shadow, Cynara! thy breath was shed
Upon my soul between the kisses and the wine;
And I was desolate and sick of an old passion,
    Yea, I was desolate and bowed my head:
I have been faithful to thee, Cynara! in my fashion.

All night upon mine heart I felt her warm heart beat,
Night-long within mine arms in love and sleep she lay;
Surely the kisses of her bought red mouth were sweet;
But I was desolate and sick of an old passion,
    When I awoke and found the dawn was grey:
I have been faithful to thee, Cynara! in my fashion.

I have forgot much, Cynara! gone with the wind,
Flung roses, roses, riotously with the throng,
Dancing, to put thy pale lost lilies out of mind;
But I was desolate and sick of an old passion,
    Yea, all the time, because the dance was long:
I have been faithful to thee, Cynara! in my fashion.

I cried for madder music and for stronger wine,
But when the feast is finished and the lamps expire,
Then falls thy shadow, Cynara! the night is thine;
And I am desolate and sick of an old passion,
    Yea, hungry for the lips of my desire:
I have been faithful to thee, Cynara! in my fashion.

LAURENCE BINYON

117 The Burning of the Leaves

Now is the time for the burning of the leaves.
They go to the fire; the nostril pricks with smoke
Wandering slowly into a weeping mist.
Brittle and blotched, ragged and rotten sheaves!
A flame seizes the smouldering ruin and bites
On stubborn stalks that crackle as they resist.

The last hollyhock's fallen tower is dust;
All the spices of June are a bitter reek,
All the extravagant riches spent and mean.
All burns! The reddest rose is a ghost;
Sparks whirl up, to expire in the mist: the wild
Fingers of fire are making corruption clean.

Now is the time for stripping the spirit bare,
Time for the burning of days ended and done,
Idle solace of things that have gone before:
Rootless hopes and fruitless desire are there;
Let them go to the fire, with never a look behind.
The world that was ours is a world that is ours no more.

They will come again, the leaf and the flower, to arise
From squalor of rottenness into the old splendour,
And magical scents to a wondering memory bring;
The same glory, to shine upon different eyes.
Earth cares for her own ruins, naught for ours.
Nothing is certain, only the certain spring.

118   Ha'nacker Mill

Sally is gone that was so kindly
    Sally is gone from Ha'nacker Hill.
And the Briar grows ever since then so blindly
    And ever since then the clapper is still,
    And the sweeps have fallen from Ha'nacker Mill.

Ha'nacker Hill is in Desolation:
    Ruin a-top and a field unploughed.
And Spirits that call on a fallen nation
    Spirits that loved her calling aloud:
    Spirits abroad in a windy cloud.

Spirits that call and no one answers;
    Ha'nacker's down and England's done.
Wind and Thistle for pipe and dancers
    And never a ploughman under the Sun.
    Never a ploughman. Never a one.

RALPH HODGSON

119 Time, You Old Gipsy Man

Time, you old gipsy man,
   Will you not stay,
Put up your caravan
   Just for one day?

All things I'll give you
Will you be my guest,
Bells for your jennet
Of silver the best,
Goldsmiths shall beat you
A great golden ring,
Peacocks shall bow to you,
Little boys sing,
Oh, and sweet girls will
Festoon you with may,
Time, you old gipsy,
Why hasten away?

Last week in Babylon,
Last night in Rome,
Morning, and in the crush
Under Paul's dome;
Under Paul's dial
You tighten your rein –
Only a moment,
And off once again;
Off to some city
Now blind in the womb,
Off to another
Ere that's in the tomb.

Time, you old gipsy man,
   Will you not stay,
Put up your caravan
   Just for one day?

120   The Song of the Mad Prince

Who said, 'Peacock Pie'?
The old King to the sparrow:
Who said, 'Crops are ripe'?
Rust to the harrow:
Who said, 'Where sleeps she now?
Where rests she now her head,
Bathed in eve's loveliness'? –
That's what I said.

Who said, 'Ay, mum's the word'?
Sexton to willow:
Who said, 'Green dusk for dreams,
Moss for a pillow'?
Who said, 'All Time's delight
Hath she for narrow bed;
Life's troubled bubble broken'?
That's what I said.

121   The Railway Junction

From here through tunnelled gloom the track
Forks into two; and one of these
Wheels onward into darkening hills,
And one toward distant seas.

How still it is; the signal light
At set of sun shines palely green;
A thrush sings; other sound there's none,
Nor traveller to be seen –

Where late there was a throng. And now,
In peace awhile, I sit alone;
Though soon, at the appointed hour,
I shall myself be gone.

But not their way: the bow-legged groom,
The parson in black, the widow and son,
The sailor with his cage, the gaunt
Gamekeeper with his gun,

That fair one, too, discreetly veiled –
All, who so mutely came, and went,
Will reach those far nocturnal hills,
Or shores, ere night is spent.

I nothing know why thus we met –
Their thoughts, their longings, hopes, their fate:
And what shall I remember, except –
The evening growing late –

That here through tunnelled gloom the track
Forks into two; of these
One into darkening hills leads on,
And one toward distant seas?

122 Nod

Softly along the road of evening,
    In a twilight dim with rose,
Wrinkled with age, and drenched with dew,
    Old Nod, the shepherd, goes.

His drowsy flock streams on before him,
    Their fleeces charged with gold,
To where the sun's last beam leans low
    On Nod the shepherd's fold.

The hedge is quick and green with brier,
　From their sand the conies creep;
And all the birds that fly in heaven
　Flock singing home to sleep.

His lambs outnumber a noon's roses,
　Yet, when night's shadows fall,
His blind old sheep-dog, Slumber-soon,
　Misses not one of all.

His are the quiet steeps of dreamland,
　The waters of no-more-pain,
His ram's bell rings 'neath an arch of stars,
　'Rest, rest, and rest again.'

123　All That's Past

Very old are the woods;
　And the buds that break
Out of the brier's boughs,
　When March winds wake,
So old with their beauty are –
　Oh, no man knows
Through what wild centuries
　Roves back the rose.

Very old are the brooks;
　And the rills that rise
Where snow sleeps cold beneath
　The azure skies
Sing such a history
　Of come and gone,
Their every drop is as wise
　As Solomon.

Very old are we men;
  Our dreams are tales
Told in dim Eden
  By Eve's nightingales;
We wake and whisper awhile,
  But, the day gone by,
Silence and sleep like fields
  Of amaranth lie.

124   The Scribe

What lovely things
  Thy hand hath made:
The smooth-plumed bird
  In its emerald shade,
The seed of the grass,
  The speck of stone
Which the wayfaring ant
  Stirs – and hastes on!

Though I should sit
  By some tarn in thy hills,
Using its ink
  As the spirit wills
To write of Earth's wonders,
  Its live, willed things,
Flit would the ages
  On soundless wings
Ere unto Z
  My pen drew nigh;
Leviathan told,
  And the honey-fly:
And still would remain
  My wit to try –
My worn reeds broken,
  The dark tarn dry,
All words forgotten –
  Thou, Lord, and I.

125   The Old Summerhouse

This blue-washed, old, thatched summerhouse –
Paint scaling, and fading from its walls –
How often from its hingeless door
I have watched – dead leaf, like the ghost of a mouse,
Rasping the worn brick floor –
The snows of the weir descending below,
And their thunderous waterfall.

Fall – fall: dark, garrulous rumour,
Until I could listen no more.
Could listen no more – for beauty with sorrow
Is a burden hard to be borne:
The evening light on the foam, and the swans, there;
That music, remote, forlorn.

126   Arabia

Far are the shades of Arabia,
    Where the Princes ride at noon,
'Mid the verdurous vales and thickets,
    Under the ghost of the moon;
And so dark is that vaulted purple
    Flowers in the forest rise
And toss into blossom 'gainst the phantom stars
    Pale in the noonday skies.

Sweet is the music of Arabia
    In my heart, when out of dreams
I still in the thin clear mirk of dawn
    Descry her gliding streams;
Hear her strange lutes on the green banks
    Ring loud with the grief and delight
Of the dim-silked, dark-haired Musicians
    In the brooding silence of night.

They haunt me – her lutes and her forests;
   No beauty on earth I see
But shadowed with that dream recalls
   Her loveliness to me:
Still eyes look coldly upon me,
   Cold voices whisper and say –
'He is crazed with the spell of far Arabia,
   They have stolen his wits away.'

G. K. CHESTERTON

127   The Rolling English Road

Before the Roman came to Rye or out to Severn strode,
The rolling English drunkard made the rolling English road.
A reeling road, a rolling road, that rambles round the shire,
And after him the parson ran, the sexton and the squire;
A merry road, a mazy road, and such as we did tread
That night we went to Birmingham by way of Beachy Head.

I knew no harm of Bonaparte and plenty of the Squire,
And for to fight the Frenchmen I did not much desire;
But I did bash their baggonets because they came arrayed
To straighten out the crooked road an English drunkard
    made,
Where you and I went down the lane with ale-mugs in our
    hands,
The night we went to Glastonbury by way of Goodwin
    Sands.

His sins they were forgiven him; or why do flowers run
Behind him; and the hedges all strengthening in the sun?
The wild thing went from left to right and knew not which
    was which,
But the wild rose was above him when they found him in the
    ditch.
God pardon us, nor harden us; we did not see so clear
The night we went to Bannockburn by way of Brighton Pier.

My friends, we will not go again or ape an ancient rage,
Or stretch the folly of our youth to be the shame of age,
But walk with clearer eyes and ears this path that
    wandereth,
And see undrugged in evening light the decent inn of death;
For there is good news yet to hear and fine things to be seen,
Before we go to Paradise by way of Kensal Green.

White founts falling in the courts of the sun,
And the Soldan of Byzantium is smiling as they run;
There is laughter like the fountains in that face of all men
    feared,
It stirs the forest darkness, the darkness of his beard,
It curls the blood-red crescent, the crescent of his lips,
For the inmost sea of all the earth is shaken with his ships.
They have dared the white republics up the capes of Italy,
They have dashed the Adriatic round the Lion of the Sea,
And the Pope has cast his arms abroad for agony and loss,
And called the kings of Christendom for swords about the
    Cross,
The cold queen of England is looking in the glass;
The shadow of the Valois is yawning at the Mass;
From evening isles fantastical rings faint the Spanish gun,
And the Lord upon the Golden Horn is laughing in the sun.

Dim drums throbbing, in the hills half heard,
Where only on a nameless throne a crownless prince has
    stirred,
Where, risen from a doubtful seat and half-attainted stall,
The last knight of Europe takes weapons from the wall,
The last and lingering troubadour to whom the bird has sung,
That once went singing southward when all the world was
    young,
In that enormous silence, tiny and unafraid,
Comes up along a winding road the noise of the Crusade.
Strong gongs groaning as the guns boom far,
Don John of Austria is going to the war,
Stiff flags straining in the night-blasts cold
In the gloom black-purple, in the glint old-gold,
Torchlight crimson on the copper kettle-drums,
Then the tuckets, then the trumpets, then the cannon, and
    he comes.
Don John laughing in the brave beard curled,
Spurning of his stirrups like the thrones of all the world,
Holding his head up for a flag of all the free.

Love-light of Spain – hurrah!
Death-light of Africa!
Don John of Austria
Is riding to the sea.

Mahound is in his paradise above the evening star.
(*Don John of Austria is going to the war*.)
He moves a mighty turban on the timeless houri's knees,
His turban that is woven of the sunset and the seas.
He shakes the peacock gardens as he rises from his ease,
And he strides among the tree-tops and is taller than the
    trees,
And his voice through all the garden is a thunder sent to
    bring
Black Azrael and Ariel and Ammon on the wing.
Giants and the Genii,
Multiplex of wing and eye,
Whose strong obedience broke the sky
When Solomon was king.

They rush in red and purple from the red clouds of the
    morn,
From temples where the yellow gods shut up their eyes in
    scorn;
They rise in green robes roaring from the green hells of the
    sea
Where fallen skies and evil hues and eyeless creatures be;
On them the sea-valves cluster and the grey sea-forests curl,
Splashed with a splendid sickness, the sickness of the pearl;
They swell in sapphire smoke out of the blue cracks of the
    ground, –
They gather and they wonder and give worship to
    Mahound.
And he saith, 'Break up the mountains where the
    hermit-folk may hide,
And sift the red and silver sands lest bone of saint abide,
And chase the Giaours flying night and day, not giving rest,
For that which was our trouble comes again out of the west.
We have set the seal of Solomon on all things under sun,
Of knowledge and of sorrow and endurance of things done,

But a noise is in the mountains, in the mountains, and I
know
The voice that shook our palaces – four hundred years ago:
It is he that saith not "Kismet"; it is he that knows not Fate;
It is Richard, it is Raymond, it is Godfrey in the gate!
It is he whose loss is laughter when he counts the wager
worth,
Put down your feet upon him, that our peace be on the
earth.'
For he heard drums groaning and he heard guns jar,
(*Don John of Austria is going to the war.*)
Sudden and still – hurrah!
Bolt from Iberia!
Don John of Austria
Is gone by Alcalar.

St Michael's on his Mountain in the sea-roads of the north
(*Don John of Austria is girt and going forth.*)
Where the grey seas glitter and the sharp tides shift
And the sea folk labour and the red sails lift.
He shakes his lance of iron and he claps his wings of stone;
The noise is gone through Normandy; the noise is gone
alone;
The North is full of tangled things and texts and aching eyes
And dead is all the innocence of anger and surprise,
And Christian killeth Christian in a narrow dusty room,
And Christian dreadeth Christ that hath a newer face of
doom,
And Christian hateth Mary that God kissed in Galilee,
But Don John of Austria is riding to the sea.
Don John calling through the blast and the eclipse,
Crying with the trumpet, with the trumpet of his lips,
Trumpet that sayeth ha!
Domino gloria!
Don John of Austria
Is shouting to the ships.

King Philip's in his closet with the Fleece about his neck.
(*Don John of Austria is armed upon the deck.*)
The walls are hung with velvet that is black and soft as sin,

And little dwarfs creep out of it and little dwarfs creep in.
He holds a crystal phial that has colours like the moon,
He touches, and it tingles, and he trembles very soon,
And his face is as a fungus of a leprous white and grey,
Like plants in the high houses that are shuttered from the
    day,
And death is in the phial, and the end of noble work,
But Don John of Austria has fired upon the Turk.
Don John's hunting, and his hounds have bayed –
Booms away past Italy the rumour of his raid.
Gun upon gun, ha! ha!
Gun upon gun, hurrah!
Don John of Austria
Has loosed the cannonade.

The Pope was in his chapel before day or battle broke,
(*Don John of Austria is hidden in the smoke.*)
The hidden room in a man's house where God sits all the
    year,
The secret window whence the world looks small and very
    dear.
He sees as in a mirror on the monstrous twilight sea
The crescent of his cruel ships whose name is mystery;
They fling great shadows foe-wards, making Cross and
    Castle dark,
They veil the plumèd lions on the galleys of St Mark;
And above the ships are palaces of brown, black-bearded
    chiefs,
And below the ships are prisons, where the multitudinous
    griefs,
Christian captives sick and sunless, all a labouring race
    repines
Like a race in sunken cities, like a nation in the mines.
They are lost like slaves that swat, and in the skies of
    morning hung
The stairways of the tallest gods when tyranny was young.
They are countless, voiceless, hopeless as those fallen or
    fleeing on
Before the high Kings' horses in the granite of Babylon.
And many a one grows witless in his quiet room in hell

Where a yellow face looks inward through the lattice of his
  cell,
And he finds his God forgotten, and he seeks no more a
  sign –
(*But Don John of Austria has burst the battle-line!*)
Don John pounding from the slaughter-painted poop,
Purpling all the ocean like a bloody pirate's sloop,
Scarlet running over on the silvers and the golds,
Breaking of the hatches up and bursting of the holds,
Thronging of the thousands up that labour under sea
White for bliss and blind for sun and stunned for liberty.
Vivat Hispania!
Domino Gloria!
Don John of Austria
Has set his people free!

Cervantes on his galley sets the sword back in the sheath,
(*Don John of Austria rides homeward with a wreath.*)
And he sees across a weary land a straggling road in Spain,
Up which a lean and foolish knight forever rides in vain,
And he smiles, but not as Sultans smile, and settles back the
  blade . . .
(*But Don John of Austria rides home from the Crusade.*)

129   Elegy in a Country Churchyard

The men that worked for England
They have their graves at home:
And bees and birds of England
About the cross can roam.

But they that fought for England,
Following a falling star,
Alas, alas for England
They have their graves afar.

And they that rule in England,
In stately conclave met,
Alas, alas for England
They have no graves as yet.

130 The Owl

Downhill I came, hungry, and yet not starved;
Cold, yet had heat within me that was proof
Against the North wind; tired, yet so that rest
Had seemed the sweetest thing under a roof.

Then at the inn I had food, fire, and rest,
Knowing how hungry, cold, and tired was I.
All of the night was quite barred out except
An owl's cry, a most melancholy cry

Shaken out long and clear upon the hill,
No merry note, nor cause of merriment,
But one telling me plain what I escaped
And others could not, that night, as in I went.

And salted was my food, and my repose,
Salted and sobered, too, by the bird's voice
Speaking for all who lay under the stars,
Soldiers and poor, unable to rejoice.

131 Thaw

Over the land freckled with snow half-thawed
The speculating rooks at their nests cawed
And saw from elm-tops, delicate as flower of grass,
What we below could not see, Winter pass.

132 Women He Liked

Women he liked, did shovel-bearded Bob,
Old Farmer Hayward of the Heath, but he
Loved horses. He himself was like a cob,
And leather-coloured. Also he loved a tree.

For the life in them he loved most living things,
But a tree chiefly. All along the lane
He planted elms where now the stormcock sings
That travellers hear from the slow-climbing train.

Till then the track had never had a name
For all its thicket and the nightingales
That should have earned it. No one was to blame.
To name a thing beloved man sometimes fails.

Many years since, Bob Hayward died, and now
None passes there because the mist and the rain
Out of the elms have turned the lane to slough
And gloom, the name alone survives, Bob's Lane.

133   It Rains

It rains, and nothing stirs within the fence
Anywhere through the orchard's untrodden, dense
Forest of parsley. The great diamonds
Of rain on the grassblades there is none to break,
Or the fallen petals further down to shake.

And I am nearly as happy as possible
To search the wilderness in vain though well,
To think of two walking, kissing there,
Drenched, yet forgetting the kisses of the rain:
Sad, too, to think that never, never again,

Unless alone, so happy shall I walk
In the rain. When I turn away, on its fine stalk
Twilight has fined to naught, the parsley flower
Figures, suspended still and ghostly white,
The past hovering as it revisits the light.

134   Adlestrop

Yes. I remember Adlestrop –
The name, because one afternoon
Of heat the express-train drew up there
Unwontedly. It was late June.

The steam hissed. Someone cleared his throat.
No one left and no one came
On the bare platform. What I saw
Was Adlestrop – only the name

And willows, willow-herb, and grass,
And meadowsweet, and haycocks dry,
No whit less still and lonely fair
Than the high cloudlets in the sky.

And for that minute a blackbird sang
Close by, and round him, mistier,
Farther and farther, all the birds
Of Oxfordshire and Gloucestershire.

135   Tall Nettles

Tall nettles cover up, as they have done
These many springs, the rusty harrow, the plough
Long worn out, and the roller made of stone:
Only the elm butt tops the nettles now.

This corner of the farmyard I like most:
As well as any bloom upon a flower
I like the dust on the nettles, never lost
Except to prove the sweetness of a shower.

136   November

November's days are thirty:
November's earth is dirty,
Those thirty days, from first to last;
And the prettiest things on ground are the paths
With morning and evening hobnails dinted,
With foot and wing-tip overprinted
Or separately charactered,
Of little beast and little bird.
The fields are mashed by sheep, the roads
Make the worst going, the best the woods
Where dead leaves upward and downward scatter.
Few care for the mixture of earth and water,
Twig, leaf, flint, thorn,
Straw, feather, all that men scorn,
Pounded up and sodden by flood,
Condemned as mud.

But of all the months when earth is greener
Not one has clean skies that are cleaner.
Clean and clear and sweet and cold,
They shine above the earth so old,
While the after-tempest cloud
Sails over in silence though winds are loud,
Till the full moon in the east
Looks at the planet in the west
And earth is silent as it is black,
Yet not unhappy for its lack.
Up from the dirty earth men stare:
One imagines a refuge there
Above the mud, in the pure bright
Of the cloudless heavenly light:
Another loves earth and November more dearly
Because without them, he sees clearly,
The sky would be nothing more to his eye
Than he, in any case, is to the sky;
He loves even the mud whose dyes
Renounce all brightness to the skies.

137   The Long Small Room

The long small room that showed willows in the west
Narrowed up to the end the fireplace filled,
Although not wide. I liked it. No one guessed
What need or accident made them so build.

Only the moon, the mouse and the sparrow peeped
In from the ivy round the casement thick.
Of all they saw and heard there they shall keep
The tale for the old ivy and older brick.

When I look back I am like moon, sparrow, and mouse
That witnessed what they could never understand
Or alter or prevent in the dark house.
One thing remains the same – this my right hand

Crawling crab-like over the clean white page,
Resting awhile each morning on the pillow,
Then once more starting to crawl on towards age.
The hundred last leaves stream upon the willow.

138   Cock-Crow

Out of the wood of thoughts that grows by night
To be cut down by the sharp axe of light, –
Out of the night, two cocks together crow,
Cleaving the darkness with a silver blow:
And bright before my eyes twin trumpeters stand,
Heralds of splendour, one at either hand,
Each facing each as in a coat of arms:
The milkers lace their boots up at the farms.

139 Rain

Rain, midnight rain, nothing but the wild rain
On this bleak hut, and solitude, and me
Remembering again that I shall die
And neither hear the rain nor give it thanks
For washing me cleaner than I have been
Since I was born into this solitude.
Blessed are the dead that the rain rains upon:
But here I pray that none whom once I loved
Is dying to-night or lying still awake
Solitary, listening to the rain,
Either in pain or thus in sympathy
Helpless among the living and the dead,
Like a cold water among broken reeds,
Myriads of broken reeds all still and stiff,
Like me who have no love which this wild rain
Has not dissolved except the love of death,
If love it be for what is perfect and
Cannot, the tempest tells me, disappoint.

I have come to the borders of sleep,
The unfathomable deep
Forest where all must lose
Their way, however straight,
Or winding, soon or late;
They cannot choose.

Many a road and track
That, since the dawn's first crack,
Up to the forest brink,
Deceived the travellers,
Suddenly now blurs,
And in they sink.

Here love ends,
Despair, ambition ends;
All pleasure and all trouble,
Although most sweet or bitter,
Here ends in sleep that is sweeter
Than tasks most noble.

There is not any book
Or face of dearest look
That I would not turn from now
To go into the unknown
I must enter, and leave, alone,
I know not how.
The tall forest towers;
Its cloudy foliage lowers
Ahead, shelf above shelf;
Its silence I hear and obey
That I may lose my way
And myself.

141 Lollingdon Downs

Up on the downs the red-eyed kestrels hover,
Eyeing the grass.
The field-mouse flits like a shadow into cover
As their shadows pass.

Men are burning the gorse on the down's shoulder;
A drift of smoke
Glitters with fire and hangs, and the skies smoulder,
And the lungs choke.

Once the tribe did thus on the downs, on these downs,
    burning
Men in the frame,
Crying to the gods of the downs till their brains were turning
And the gods came.

And to-day on the downs, in the wind, the hawks, the
    grasses,
In blood and air,
Something passes me and cries as it passes,
On the chalk downland bare.

142 C.L.M.

In the dark womb where I began
My mother's life made me a man.
Through all the months of human birth
Her beauty fed my common earth.
I cannot see, nor breathe, nor stir,
But through the death of some of her.

Down in the darkness of the grave
She cannot see the life she gave.
For all her love, she cannot tell
Whether I use it ill or well,
Nor knock at dusty doors to find
Her beauty dusty in the mind.

If the grave's gates could be undone,
She would not know her little son,
I am so grown. If we should meet
She would pass by me in the street,
Unless my soul's face let her see
My sense of what she did for me.

What have I done to keep in mind
My debt to her and womankind?
What woman's happier life repays
Her for those months of wretched days?
For all my mouthless body leeched
Ere Birth's releasing hell was reached?

What have I done, or tried, or said
In thanks to that dear woman dead?
Men triumph over women still,
Men trample women's rights at will,
And man's lust roves the world untamed.

O grave, keep shut lest I be shamed.

143   An Epilogue

I have seen flowers come in stony places
And kind things done by men with ugly faces,
And the gold cup won by the worst horse at the races,
So I trust, too.

144   Aspidistra Street

Go along that road, and look at sorrow.
Every window grumbles.
All day long the drizzle fills the puddles,
Trickles in the runnels and the gutters,
Drips and drops and dripples, drops and dribbles,
While the melancholy aspidistra
Frowns between the parlour curtains.

Uniformity, dull Master! –
Birth and marriage, middle-age and death;
Rain and gossip: Sunday, Monday, Tuesday . . .

Sure, the lovely fools who made Utopia
Planned it without any aspidistra.
There will be a heaven on earth, but first
We must banish from the parlour
Plush and poker-work and paper flowers,
Brackets, staring photographs and what-nots,
Serviettes, frills and étagères,
Anti-macassars, vases, chiffonniers;

And the gloomy aspidistra
Glowering through the window-pane,
Meditating heavy maxims,
Moralising to the rain.

ALFRED NOYES

145 The Highwayman

I

The wind was a torrent of darkness among the gusty trees,
The moon was a ghostly galleon tossed upon cloudy seas,
The road was a ribbon of moonlight over the purple moor,
And the highwayman came riding –
        Riding – riding –
The highwayman came riding, up to the old inn-door.

He'd a French cocked-hat on his forehead, a bunch of lace at
    his chin,
A coat of claret velvet, and breeches of brown doe-skin;
They fitted with never a wrinkle: his boots were up to the
    thigh!
And he rode with a jewelled twinkle,
        His pistol butts a-twinkle,
His rapier hilt a-twinkle, under the jewelled sky.

Over the cobbles he clattered and clashed in the dark
    inn-yard,
And he tapped with his whip on the shutters, but all was
    locked and barred;
He whistled a tune to the window, and who should be
    waiting there
But the landlord's black-eyed daughter,
        Bess, the landlord's daughter,
Plaiting a dark red love-knot into her long black hair.

And dark in the old inn-yard a stable-wicket creaked
Where Tim the ostler listened; his face was white and
    peaked;
His eyes were hollows of madness, his hair like mouldy hay,
But he loved the landlord's daughter,
        The landlord's red-lipped daughter;
Dumb as a dog he listened, and he heard the robber say –

'One kiss, my bonny sweetheart, I'm after a prize to-night,
But I shall be back with the yellow gold before the morning
    light;
Yet, if they press me sharply, and harry me through the day,
Then look for me by moonlight,
            Watch for me by moonlight,
I'll come to thee by moonlight, though hell should bar the
    way.'

He rose upright in the stirrups; he scarce could reach her
    hand,
But she loosened her hair i' the casement! His face burnt like
    a brand
As the black cascade of perfume came tumbling over his
    breast;
And he kissed its waves in the moonlight,
            (Oh, sweet black waves in the moonlight!)
Then he tugged at his rein in the moonlight, and galloped
    away to the west.

II

He did not come in the dawning; he did not come at noon;
And out o' the tawny sunset, before the rise o' the moon,
When the road was a gipsy's ribbon, looping the purple
    moor,
A red-coat troop came marching –
            Marching – marching –
King George's men came marching, up to the old inn-door.

They said no word to the landlord, they drank his ale
    instead,
But they gagged his daughter and bound her to the foot of
    her narrow bed;
Two of them knelt at her casement, with muskets at their
    side!
There was death at every window;
            And hell at one dark window;
For Bess could see, through her casement, the road that *he*
    would ride.

They had tied her up to attention, with many a sniggering jest;
They had bound a musket beside her, with the barrel beneath her breast!
'Now keep good watch!' and they kissed her.
        She heard the dead man say –
Look for me by moonlight;
        Watch for me by moonlight;
I'll come to thee by moonlight, though hell should bar the way!

She twisted her hands behind her; but all the knots held good!
She writhed her hands till her fingers were wet with sweat or blood!
They stretched and strained in the darkness, and the hours crawled by like years,
Till, now, on the stroke of midnight,
        Cold, on the stroke of midnight,
The tip of one finger touched it! The trigger at least was hers!

The tip of one finger touched it; she strove no more for the rest!
Up, she stood to attention, with the barrel beneath her breast,
She would not risk their hearing; she would not strive again;
For the road lay bare in the moonlight;
        Blank and bare in the moonlight;
And the blood of her veins in the moonlight throbbed to her love's refrain.

Tlot-tlot; tlot-tlot! Had they heard it? The horse-hoofs ringing clear;
Tlot-tlot, tlot-tlot, in the distance? Were they deaf that they did not hear?
Down the ribbon of moonlight, over the brow of the hill,
The highwayman came riding,
        Riding, riding!
The red-coats looked to their priming! She stood up, straight and still!

Tlot-tlot, in the frosty silence! *tlot-tlot*, in the echoing night!
Nearer he came and nearer! Her face was like a light!
Her eyes grew wide for a moment; she drew one last deep
    breath,
Then her finger moved in the moonlight,
            Her musket shattered the moonlight,
Shattered her breast in the moonlight and warned him –
    with her death.

He turned; he spurred to the westward; he did not know
    who stood
Bowed, with her head o'er the musket, drenched with her
    own red blood!
Not till the dawn he heard it, and slowly blanched to hear
How Bess, the landlord's daughter,
            The landlord's black-eyed daughter,
Had watched for her love in the moonlight, and died in the
    darkness there.

Back, he spurred like a madman, shrieking a curse to the
    sky,
With the white road smoking behind him and his rapier
    brandished high!
Blood-red were his spurs i' the golden noon; wine-red was
    his velvet coat;
When they shot him down on the highway,
            Down like a dog on the highway,
And he lay in his blood on the highway, with the bunch of
    lace at his throat.

And still of a winter's night, they say, when the wind is in the
    trees,
When the moon is a ghostly galleon tossed upon cloudy seas,
When the road is a ribbon of moonlight over the purple moor,
A highwayman comes riding –
            Riding – riding –
A highwayman comes riding, up to the old inn-door.

Over the cobbles he clatters and clangs in the dark inn-yard
And he taps with his whip on the shutters, but all is locked and
barred;
He whistles a tune to the window, and who should be waiting there
But the landlord's black-eyed daughter,
Bess, the landlord's daughter,
Plaiting a dark red love-knot into her long black hair.

T. E. HULME

146   Autumn

A touch of cold in the Autumn night –
I walked abroad,
And saw the ruddy moon lean over a hedge
Like a red-faced farmer.
I did not stop to speak, but nodded,
And round about were the wistful stars
With white faces like town children.

147   The Embankment

The fantasia of a fallen gentleman on a cold, bitter night

Once, in finesse of fiddles found I ecstasy,
In a flash of gold heels on the hard pavement.
Now see I
That warmth's the very stuff of poesy.
Oh, God, make small
The old star-eaten blanket of the sky,
That I may fold it round me and in comfort lie.

148   Image

Old houses were scaffolding once
                 and workmen whistling.

149   The Golden Journey to Samarkand

Prologue

We who with songs beguile your pilgrimage
   And swear that Beauty lives though lilies die,
We Poets of the proud old lineage
   Who sing to find your hearts, we know not why, –

What shall we tell you? Tales, marvellous tales
   Of ships and stars and isles where good men rest,
Where nevermore the rose of sunset pales,
   And winds and shadows fall toward the West:

And there the world's first huge white-bearded kings
   In dim glades sleeping, murmur in their sleep,
And closer round their breasts the ivy clings,
   Cutting its pathway slow and red and deep.

II

And how beguile you? Death has no repose
   Warmer and deeper than that Orient sand
Which hides the beauty and bright faith of those
   Who made the Golden Journey to Samarkand.

And now they wait and whiten peaceably,
   Those conquerors, those poets, those so fair:
They know time comes, not only you and I,
   But the whole world shall whiten, here or there;

When those long caravans that cross the plain
   With dauntless feet and sound of silver bells
Put forth no more for glory or for gain,
   Take no more solace from the palm-girt wells.

When the great markets by the sea shut fast
   All that calm Sunday that goes on and on:
When even lovers find their peace at last,
   And Earth is but a star, that once had shone.

150   A ship, an isle, a sickle moon

A ship, an isle, a sickle moon –
With few but with how splendid stars
The mirrors of the sea are strewn
Between their silver bars!

An isle beside an isle she lay,
The pale ship anchored in the bay,
While in the young moon's port of gold
A star-ship – as the mirrors told –
Put forth its great and lonely light
To the unreflecting Ocean, Night.
And still, a ship upon her seas,
The isle and the island cypresses
Went sailing on without the gale:
And still there moved the moon so pale,
A crescent ship without a sail!

151   Winter Nightfall

The old yellow stucco
Of the time of the Regent
Is flaking and peeling:
The rows of square windows
In the straight yellow building
    Are empty and still;
And the dusty dark evergreens
Guarding the wicket
Are draped with wet cobwebs,
And above this poor wilderness
Toneless and sombre
    Is the flat of the hill.

They said that a colonel
Who long ago died here
Was the last one to live here:
An old retired colonel,
Some Fraser or Murray,
    I don't know his name;
Death came here and summoned him,
And the shells of him vanished
Beyond all speculation;
And silence resumed here,
Silence and emptiness,
    And nobody came.

Was it wet when he lived here,
Were the skies dun and hurrying,
Was the rain so irresolute?
Did he watch the night coming,
Did he shiver at nightfall,
    Before he was dead?
Did the wind go so creepily,
Chilly and puffing,

With drops of cold rain in it?
Was the hill's lifted shoulder
So lowering and menacing,
    So dark and so dread?

Did he turn through his doorway
And go to his study,
And light many candles?
And fold in the shutters,
And heap up the fireplace
    To fight off the damps?
And muse on his boyhood,
And wonder if India
Ever was real?
And shut out the loneliness
With pig-sticking memoirs
    And collections of stamps?

Perhaps. But he's gone now,
He and his furniture
Dispersed now for ever;
And the last of his trophies,
Antlers and photographs,
    Heaven knows where.
And there's grass in his gateway,
Grass on his footpath,
Grass on his door-step;
The garden's grown over,
The well-chain is broken,
    The windows are bare.

And I leave him behind me,
For the straggling, discoloured
Rags of the daylight,
And hills and stone walls
And a rick long forgotten
    Of blackening hay:
The road pale and sticky,
And cart-ruts and nail-marks,
And wind-ruffled puddles,
And the slop of my footsteps
In this desolate country's
    Cadaverous clay.

152   The Ruined Chapel

From meadows with the sheep so shorn
They, not their lambs, seem newly born,
Through the graveyard I pass,
Where only blue plume-thistle waves
And headstones lie so deep in grass
They follow dead men to their graves,
And as I enter by no door
This chapel where the slow moss crawls
I wonder that so small a floor
Can have the sky for roof, mountains for walls.

153   The Stockdoves

They rose up in a twinkling cloud
And wheeled about and bowed
To settle on the trees
Perching like small clay images.

Then with a noise of sudden rain
They clattered off again
And over Ballard Down
They circled like a flying town.

Though one could sooner blast a rock
Than scatter that dense flock
That through the winter weather
Some iron rule has held together,

Yet in another month from now
Love like a spark will blow
Those birds the country over
To drop in trees, lover by lover.

154 The Shepherd's Hut

The smear of blue peat smoke
That staggered on the wind and broke,
The only sign of life,
Where was the shepherd's wife,
Who left those flapping clothes to dry,
Taking no thought for her family?
For, as they bellied out
And limbs took shape and waved about,
I thought, She little knows
That ghosts are trying on her children's clothes.

155   Attack

At dawn the ridge emerges massed and dun
In wild purple of the glowering sun,
Smouldering through spouts of drifting smoke that shroud
The menacing scarred slope; and, one by one,
Tanks creep and topple forward to the wire.
The barrage roars and lifts. Then, clumsily bowed
With bombs and guns and shovels and battle-gear,
Men jostle and climb to meet the bristling fire.
Lines of grey, muttering faces, masked with fear,
They leave their trenches, going over the top,
While time ticks blank and busy on their wrists,
And hope, with furtive eyes and grappling fists,
Flounders in mud. O Jesus, make it stop!

RUPERT BROOKE

156   The Soldier

If I should die, think only this of me:
    That there's some corner of a foreign field
That is for ever England. There shall be
    In that rich earth a richer dust concealed;
A dust whom England bore, shaped, made aware,
    Gave, once, her flowers to love, her ways to roam,
A body of England's, breathing English air,
    Washed by the rivers, blest by suns of home.

And think, this heart, all evil shed away,
    A pulse in the eternal mind, no less
        Gives somewhere back the thoughts by England
            given;
Her sights and sounds; dreams happy as her day;
    And laughter, learnt of friends; and gentleness,
        In hearts at peace, under an English heaven.

157   The Voice

Safe in the magic of my woods
    I lay, and watched the dying light.
Faint in the pale high solitudes,
    And washed with rain and veiled by night,

Silver and blue and green were showing.
    And the dark woods grew darker still;
And birds were hushed; and peace was growing;
    And quietness crept up the hill;

And no wind was blowing . . .

And I knew
That this was the hour of knowing,
And the night and the woods and you

Were one together, and I should find
Soon in the silence the hidden key
Of all that had hurt and puzzled me –
Why you were you, and the night was kind,
And the woods were part of the heart of me.

And there I waited breathlessly,
Alone; and slowly the holy three,
The three that I loved, together grew
One, in the hour of knowing,
Night, and the woods, and you –

And suddenly
There was an uproar in my woods,
The noise of a fool in mock distress,
Crashing and laughing and blindly going,
Of ignorant feet and a swishing dress,
And a Voice profaning the solitudes.

The spell was broken, the key denied me,
And at length your flat clear voice beside me
Mouthed cheerful clear flat platitudes.

You came and quacked beside me in the wood.
You said, 'The view from here is very good!'
You said, 'It's nice to be alone a bit!'
And, 'How the days are drawing out!' you said.
You said, 'The sunset's pretty, isn't it?'

By God! I wish – I wish that you were dead!

EDWIN MUIR

158   The Breaking

Peace in the western sky,
A ploughman follows the plough,
Children come home from school:
War is preparing now.

Great-grandfather on his farm
In eighteen hundred and ten
Heard of great victories
From wandering tinkermen,
Until the press-gang came,
Took son and servant away,
The fields were left forlorn
And there was nothing to say.
The farmer ploughed and reaped,
Led five lean harvests in,
The young men long away:
There was a great war then.

All things stand in their place
Till hatred beats them down,
Furies and fantasies
Strike flat the little town.
Then all rise up again,
But heart and blood and bone,
The very stones in the street,
Roof and foundation stone,
Remember and foreknow.
Memories, prophecies,
The song the ploughman sings,
The simple dream of peace,
Dark dreams in the dead of night
And on the reckless brow
Bent to let chaos in,
Tell that they shall come down,
Be broken, and rise again.

JOHN CROWE RANSOM

159   Captain Carpenter

Captain Carpenter rose up in his prime
Put on his pistols and went riding out
But had got well-nigh nowhere at that time
Till he fell in with ladies in a rout.

It was a pretty lady and all her train
That played with him so sweetly but before
An hour she'd taken a sword with all her main
And twined him of his nose for evermore.

Captain Carpenter mounted up one day
And rode straightway into a stranger rogue
That looked unchristian but be that as may
The Captain did not wait upon prologue

But drew upon him out of his great heart
The other swung against him with a club
And cracked his two legs at the shinny part
And let him roll and stick like any tub.

Captain Carpenter rode many a time
From male and female took he sundry harms
He met the wife of Satan crying 'I'm
The she-wolf bids you shall bear no more arms.'

Their strokes and counters whistled in the wind
I wish he had delivered half his blows
But where she should have made off like a hind
The bitch bit off his arms at the elbows.

And Captain Carpenter parted with his ears
To a black devil that used him in this wise
O Jesus ere his threescore and ten years
Another had plucked out his sweet blue eyes.

Captain Carpenter got up on his roan
And sallied from the gate in hell's despite
I heard him asking in the grimmest tone
If any enemy yet there was to fight?

'To any adversary it is fame
If he risk to be wounded by my tongue
Or burnt in two beneath my red heart's flame
Such are the perils he is cast among.

'But if he can he has a pretty choice
From an anatomy with little to lose
Whether he cut my tongue and take my voice
Or whether it be my round red heart he choose.'

It was the neatest knave that ever was seen
Stepping in perfume from his lady's bower
Who at this word put in his merry mien
And fell on Captain Carpenter like a tower.

I would not knock old fellows in the dust
But there lay Captain Carpenter on his back
His weapons were the old heart in his bust
And a blade shook between rotten teeth alack.

The rogue in scarlet and gray soon knew his mind
He wished to get his trophy and depart
With gentle apology and touch refined
He pierced him and produced the Captain's heart.

God's mercy rest on Captain Carpenter now
I thought him Sirs an honest gentleman
Citizen husband soldier and scholar enow
Let jangling kites eat of him if they can.

But God's deep curses follow after those
That shore him of his goodly nose and ears
His legs and strong arms at the two elbows
And eyes that had not watered seventy years.

The curse of hell upon the sleek upstart
Who got the Captain finally on his back
And took the red red vitals of his heart
And made the kites to whet their beaks clack clack.

W. J. TURNER

160   Romance

When I was but thirteen or so
  I went into a golden land,
Chimborazo, Cotopaxi
  Took me by the hand.

My father died, my brother too,
  They passed like fleeting dreams,
I stood where Popocatapetl
  In the sunlight gleams.

I dimly heard the master's voice
  And boys far off at play,
Chimborazo, Cotopaxi
  Had stolen me away.

I walked in a great golden dream
  To and fro from school –
Shining Popocatapetl
  The dusty streets did rule.

I walked home with a gold dark boy,
  And never a word I'd say,
Chimborazo, Cotopaxi
  Had taken my speech away:

I gazed entranced upon his face
  Fairer than any flower –
O shining Popocatapetl
  It was thy magic hour:

The houses, people, traffic seemed
  Thin fading dreams by day,
Chimborazo, Cotopaxi
  They had stolen my soul away!

RICHARD ALDINGTON

161   Evening

The chimneys, rank on rank,
Cut the clear sky;
The moon,
With a rag of gauze about her loins
Poses among them, an awkward Venus –

And here am I looking wantonly at her
Over the kitchen sink.

KENNETH ASHLEY

162   Goods Train at Night

The station is empty and desolate;
A sick lamp wanly glows;
Slowly puffs a goods engine,
Slow yet alive with great energy;
Drawing rumbling truck
After rumbling, rumbling truck;
Big, half-seen, insensate.
Yet each as it jolts through the glow
Responds to the questioning light
Dumbly revealing
Diverse personality:
'Neal & Co.'; 'John Bugsworth'; 'Norland Collieries Limited';
'Jolly & Sons'; 'Jolly & Sons'; 'Jolly & Sons';
Thrice repeated, percussive, insistent –
Each wet wall-side successively announcing
Names: badges and symbols of men,
Of men in their intricate trafficking –
But there quickens a deeper emotion,
Roused by the iterant names,
Beyond the mere intricate commerce,
The infinite wonder of life.
Effort and hope and love, the heart's desire,
Leap in the womb of the brain
As the trucks clang their way through the night.
Slides by the guard's van at the last,
With a last definite clatter of steel upon steel
And a glitter of ruby-red light.

So: silence recaptures the station;
The damp steam eddies out;
The drizzle weaves a silver pattern,
An endless shining silver pattern,
A silver woof in the lamplight.
And I find myself full of a grief –
A dull little grief for humanity.

227

163 The Realist

On the sandy downs beside the sea
She found a feather, silver and black –
Silver as salmon, black as jet,
Blown from a gull's or a magpie's back.
'Look!' she cried, with a swift delight,
'The loveliest thing this evening yet –
A plume of faery, sable and white,
A flutter of pierrot mystery,
Oh look!' He nodded a careless head –
'Just do to clean my pipe,' he said.

164   Insensibility

I

Happy are men who yet before they are killed
Can let their veins run cold.
Whom no compassion fleers
Or makes their feet
Sore on the alleys cobbled with their brothers.
The front line withers,
But they are troops who fade, not flowers
For poets' tearful fooling:
Men, gaps for filling:
Losses, who might have fought
Longer; but no one bothers.

II

And some cease feeling
Even themselves or for themselves.
Dullness best solves
The tease and doubt of shelling,
And Chance's strange arithmetic
Comes simpler than the reckoning of their shilling.
They keep no check on armies' decimation.

III

Happy are these who lose imagination:
They have enough to carry with ammunition.
Their spirit drags no pack,
Their old wounds, save with cold, can not more ache.
Having seen all things red,
Their eyes are rid
Of the hurt of the colour of blood for ever.
And terror's first constriction over,
Their hearts remain small-drawn.
Their senses in some scorching cautery of battle
Now long since ironed,
Can laugh among the dying, unconcerned.

IV

Happy the soldier home, with not a notion
How somewhere, every dawn, some men attack,
And many sighs are drained.
Happy the lad whose mind was never trained:
His days are worth forgetting more than not.
He sings along the march
Which we march taciturn, because of dusk,
The long, forlorn, relentless trend
From larger day to huger night.

V

We wise, who with a thought besmirch
Blood over all our soul,
How should we see our task
But through his blunt and lashless eyes?
Alive, he is not vital overmuch;
Dying, not mortal overmuch;
Nor sad, nor proud,
Nor curious at all.
He cannot tell
Old men's placidity from his.

VI

But cursed are dullards whom no cannon stuns,
That they should be as stones;
Wretched are they, and mean
With paucity that never was simplicity.
By choice they made themselves immune
To pity and whatever mourns in man
Before the last sea and the hapless stars;
Whatever moans when many leave these shores;
Whatever shares
The eternal reciprocity of tears.

165 Anthem for Doomed Youth

What passing-bells for these who die as cattle?
   Only the monstrous anger of the guns.
   Only the stuttering rifles' rapid rattle
Can patter out their hasty orisons.
No mockeries for them from prayers or bells,
   Nor any voice of mourning save the choirs, –
The shrill, demented choirs of wailing shells;
   And bugles calling for them from sad shires.

What candles may be held to speed them all?
   Not in the hands of boys, but in their eyes
Shall shine the holy glimmers of good-byes.
   The pallor of girls' brows shall be their pall;
Their flowers the tenderness of silent minds,
And each slow dusk a drawing-down of blinds.

166 Exposure

Our brains ache, in the merciless iced east winds that knive
   us . . .
Wearied we keep awake because the night is silent . . .
Low, drooping flares confuse our memory of the salient . . .
Worried by silence, sentries whisper, curious, nervous,
      But nothing happens.

Watching, we hear the mad gusts tugging on the wire,
Like twitching agonies of men among its brambles.
Northward, incessantly, the flickering gunnery rumbles,
Far off, like a dull rumour of some other war.
      What are we doing here?

The poignant misery of dawn begins to grow . . .
We only know war lasts, rain soaks, and clouds sag stormy.
Dawn massing in the east her melancholy army
Attacks once more in ranks on shivering ranks of grey,
      But nothing happens.

Sudden successive flights of bullets streak the silence.
Less deathly than the air that shudders black with snow,
With sidelong flowing flakes that flock, pause, and renew;
We watch them wandering up and down the wind's
    nonchalance,
        But nothing happens.

Pale flakes with fingering stealth come feeling for our faces –
We cringe in holes, back on forgotten dreams, and stare,
    snow-dazed,
Deep into grassier ditches. So we drowse, sun-dozed,
Littered with blossoms trickling where the blackbird fusses.
        Is it that we are dying?

Slowly our ghosts drag home: glimpsing the sunk fires,
    glazed
With crusted dark-red jewels; crickets jingle there;
For hours the innocent mice rejoice: the house is theirs;
Shutters and doors, all closed: on us the doors are closed, –
        We turn back to our dying.

Since we believe not otherwise can kind fires burn;
Nor ever suns smile true on child, or field, or fruit.
For God's invincible spring our love is made afraid;
Therefore, not loath, we lie out here; therefore were born,
        For love of God seems dying.

To-night, His frost will fasten on this mud and us,
Shrivelling many hands, puckering foreheads crisp.
The burying-party, picks and shovels in their shaking grasp,
Pause over half-known faces. All their eyes are ice,
        But nothing happens.

232

167 Futility

Move him into the sun –
Gently its touch awoke him once,
At home, whispering of fields unsown.
Always it woke him, even in France,
Until this morning and this snow.
If anything might rouse him now
The kind old sun will know.

Think how it wakes the seeds, –
Woke, once, the clays of a cold star.
Are limbs, so dear-achieved, are sides,
Full-nerved – still warm – too hard to stir?
Was it for this the clay grew tall?
– O what made fatuous sunbeams toil
To break earth's sleep at all?

168 Six O'Clock in Princes Street

In twos and threes, they have not far to roam,
  Crowds that thread eastward, gay of eyes;
Those seek no further than their quiet home,
  Wives, walking westward, slow and wise.

Neither should I go fooling over clouds,
  Following gleams unsafe, untrue,
And tiring after beauty through star-crowds,
  Dared I go side by side with you;

Or be you on the gutter where you stand,
  Pale rain-flawed phantom of the place,
With news of all the nations in your hand,
  And all their sorrows in your face.

169 The Roads Also

The roads also have their wistful rest,
When the weathercocks perch still and roost,
And the town is a candle-lit room –
The streets also dream their dream.

The old houses muse of the old days
And their fond trees leaning on them doze,
On their steps chatter and clatter stops,
On their doors a strange hand taps.

Men remember alien ardours
As the dusk unearths old mournful odours.
In the garden unborn child souls wail
And the dead scribble on walls.

Though their own child cry for them in tears,
Women weep but hear no sound upstairs.
They believe in loves they had not lived
And in passion past the reach of the stairs
    To the world's towers or stars.

170   Dead Cow Farm

An ancient saga tells us how
In the beginning the First Cow
(For nothing living yet had birth
But Elemental Cow on earth)
Began to lick cold stones and mud:
Under her warm tongue flesh and blood
Blossomed, a miracle to believe:
And so was Adam born, and Eve.
Here now is chaos once again,
Primeval mud, cold stones and rain.
Here flesh decays and blood drips red,
And the Cow's dead, the old Cow's dead.

171   Love Without Hope

Love without hope, as when the young bird-catcher
Swept off his tall hat to the Squire's own daughter,
So let the imprisoned larks escape and fly
Singing about her head, as she rode by.

172   Love in Barrenness

Below the ridge a raven flew
And we heard the lost curlew
Mourning out of sight below.
Mountain tops were touched with snow;
Even the long dividing plain
Showed no wealth of sheep or grain,
But fields of boulders lay like corn
And raven's croak was shepherd's horn
Where slow cloud-shadow strayed across
A pasture of thin heath and moss.

The North Wind rose: I saw him press
With lusty force against your dress,
Moulding your body's inward grace
And streaming off from your set face;
So now no longer flesh and blood
But poised in marble flight you stood.
O wingless Victory, loved of men,
Who could withstand your beauty then?

173   The Presence

Why say 'death'? Death is neither harsh nor kind:
Other pleasures or pains could hold the mind
If she were dead. For dead is gone indeed,
Lost beyond recovery and need,
Discarded, ended, rotted underground –
Of whom no personal feature could be found
To stand out from the soft blur evenly spread
On memory, if she were truly dead.

But living still, barred from accustomed use
Of body and dress and motion, with profuse
Reproaches (since this anguish of her grew
Do I still love her as I swear I do?)
She fills the house and garden terribly
With her bewilderment, accusing me,
Till every stone and flower, table and book,
Cries out her name, pierces me with her look,
'You are deaf, listen!
You are blind, see!'
                              How deaf or blind,
When horror of the grave maddens the mind
With those same pangs that lately choked her breath,
Altered her substance, and made sport of death?

174 Callow Captain

The sun beams jovial from an ancient sky,
  Flooding the round hills with heroic spate.
A callow captain, glaring, sword at thigh,
  Trots out his charger through the camp gate.
Soon comes the hour, his marriage hour, and soon
  He fathers children, reigns with ancestors
Who, likewise serving in the wars, won
  For a much-tattered flag renewed honours.

A wind ruffles the book, and he whose name
  Was mine vanishes; all is at an end.
Fortunate soldier: to be spared shame
  Of chapter-years unprofitable to spend,
To ride off into reticence, nor throw
  Before the story-sun a long shadow.

175 On Rising Early

Rising early and walking in the garden
Before the sun has properly climbed the hill –
His rays warming the roof, not yet the grass
That is white with dew still.

And not enough breeze to eddy a puff of smoke,
And out in the meadows a thick mist lying yet,
And nothing anywhere ill or noticeable –
Thanks indeed for that.

But was there ever a day with wit enough
To be always early, to draw the smoke up straight
Even at three o'clock of an afternoon,
To spare dullness or sweat?

Indeed, many such days I remember
That were dew-white and gracious to the last,
That ruled out meal-times, yet had no more hunger
Than was felt by rising a half-hour before breakfast,
Nor more fatigue – where was it that I went
So unencumbered, with my feet tramping
Like strangers on the past?

176   Recalling War

Entrance and exit wounds are silvered clean,
The track aches only when the rain reminds.
The one-legged man forgets his leg of wood,
The one-armed man his jointed wooden arm.
The blinded man sees with his ears and hands
As much or more than once with both his eyes.
Their war was fought these twenty years ago
And now assumes the nature-look of time,
As when the morning traveller turns and views
His wild night-stumbling carved into a hill.

What, then, was war? No mere discord of flags
But an infection of the common sky
That sagged ominously upon the earth
Even when the season was the airiest May.
Down pressed the sky, and we, oppressed, thrust out
Boastful tongue, clenched fist and valiant yard.
Natural infirmities were out of mode,
For Death was young again: patron alone
Of healthy dying, premature fate-spasm.

Fear made fine bed-fellows. Sick with delight
At life's discovered transitoriness,
Our youth became all-flesh and waived the mind.
Never was such antiqueness of romance,
Such tasty honey oozing from the heart.
And old importances came swimming back –
Wine, meat, log-fires, a roof over the head,
A weapon at the thigh, surgeons at call.

Even there was a use again for God –
A word of rage in lack of meat, wine, fire,
In ache of wounds beyond all surgeoning.

War was return of earth to ugly earth,
War was foundering of sublimities,
Extinction of each happy art and faith
By which the world had still kept head in air,
Protesting logic or protesting love,
Until the unendurable moment struck –
The inward scream, the duty to run mad.

And we recall the merry ways of guns –
Nibbling the walls of factory and church
Like a child, piecrust; felling groves of trees
Like a child, dandelions with a switch!
Machine-guns rattle toy-like from a hill,
Down in a row the brave tin-soldiers fall:
A sight to be recalled in elder days
When learnedly the future we devote
To yet more boastful visions of despair.

177   The Cuirassiers of the Frontier

Goths, Vandals, Huns, Isaurian mountaineers,
Made Roman by our Roman sacrament,
We can know little (as we care little)
Of the Metropolis: her candled churches,
Her white-gowned pederastic senators,
The cut-throat factions of her Hippodrome,
The eunuchs of her draped saloons.

Here is the frontier, here our camp and place –
Beans for the pot, fodder for horses,
And Roman arms. Enough. He who among us
At full gallop, the bowstring to his ear,
Lets drive his heavy arrows, to sink
Stinging through Persian corslets damascened,
Then follows with the lance – he has our love.

239

The Christ bade Holy Peter sheathe his sword,
Being outnumbered by the Temple guard.
And this was prudence, the cause not yet lost
While Peter might persuade the crowd to rescue.
Peter renegued, breaking his sacrament.
With us the penalty is death by stoning,
Not to be made a bishop.

In Peter's Church there is no faith nor truth,
Nor justice anywhere in palace or court.
That we continue watchful on the rampart
Concerns no priest. A gaping silken dragon,
Puffed by the wind, suffices us for God.
We, not the City, are the Empire's soul:
A rotten tree lives only in its rind.

178   Wigs and Beards

In the bad old days a bewigged country Squire
Would never pay his debts, unless at cards,
Shot, angled, urged his pack through standing grain,
Horsewhipped his tenantry, snorted at the arts,
Toped himself under the table every night,
Blasphemed God with a cropful of God-damns,
Aired whorehouse French or lame Italian,
Set fashions of pluperfect slovenliness
And claimed seigneurial rights over all women
Who slept, imprudently, under the same roof.

Taxes and wars long ago ploughed them under –
'And serve the bastards right' the Beards agree,
Hurling their empties through the café window
And belching loud as they proceed downstairs.
Latter-day bastards of that famous stock,
That never rode a nag, nor gaffed a trout,
Nor winged a pheasant, nor went soldiering,
But remain true to the same hell-fire code
In all available particulars

And scorn to pay their debts even at cards.
Moreunder (which is to subtract, not add),
Their ancestors called themselves gentlemen
As they, in the same sense, call themselves artists.

179   Cold Weather Proverb

Fearless approach and puffed feather
In birds, famine bespeak;
In man, belly filled full.

180   General Bloodstock's Lament for England

This image (seemingly animated) walks with them in the fields in broad
Day-light; and if they are employed in delving, harrowing, Seed-sowing
or any other Occupation, they are at the same time mimicked by the
ghostly Visitant. Men of the Second Sight . . . call this reflex-man a
Co-walker, every way like the Man, as his Twin-brother and Companion,
haunting as his Shadow.

(Kirk's *Secret Commonwealth*, 1691)

Alas, England, my own generous mother,
One gift I have from you I hate,
The second sight: I see your weird co-walker,
Silver-zoned Albion, stepping in your track,
Mimicking your sad and doubtful gait,
Your clasped hands, your head-shakings, your bent back.

The white hem of a winding sheet
Draws slowly upward from her feet;
Soon it will mount knee-high, then to the thigh.
It crackles like the parchment of the treaties,
Bonds, contracts and conveyances,
With which, beggared and faint and like to die,
You signed away your island sovereignty
To rogues who learned their primer at your knees.

181   The Person from Porlock

> . . . At that moment the Author was unfortunately called out by a
> person on business from Porlock and on his return found to his mortifi-
> cation that though he retained some vague recollection of his vision, yet
> with the exception of eight or ten scattered lines and images, all the rest
> had passed away.
>
> (Coleridge's preface to *Kubla Khan: a Fragment*)

Unkind fate sent the Porlock person
To collect fivepence from a poet's house;
Pocketing which old debt he drove away,
Heedless and gay, homeward bound for Porlock.

O Porlock person, habitual scapegoat
Should any masterpiece be marred or scotched,
I wish your burly fist on the front door
Had banged yet oftener in literature!

182   The Twin of Sleep

Death is the twin of Sleep, they say:
    For I shall rise renewed,
Free from the cramps of yesterday,
    Clear-eyed and supple-thewed.

But though this bland analogy
    Helps other folk to face
Decrepitude, senility,
    Madness, disease, disgrace,

I do not like Death's greedy looks:
    Give me his twin instead –
Sleep never auctions off my books,
    My boots, my shirts, my bed.

EDMUND BLUNDEN

183   Thames Gulls

  Beautiful it is to see
On London Bridge the bold-eyed seabirds wheel,
And hear them cry, and all for a light-flung crust
Fling us their wealth, their freedom, speed and gleam.
  And beautiful to see
Them that pass by lured by these birds to stay,
And smile and say 'how tame they are' – how tame!
Friendly as stars to steersmen in mid seas,
And as remote as midnight's darling stars,
Pleasant as voices heard from days long done,
As nigh the hand as windflowers in the woods,
And inaccessible as Dido's phantom.

184   Report on Experience

I have been young, and now am not too old;
And I have seen the righteous forsaken,
His health, his honour and his quality taken.
  This is not what we were formerly told.

I have seen a green country, useful to the race,
Knocked silly with guns and mines, its villages vanished,
Even the last rat and last kestrel banished –
  God bless us all, this was peculiar grace.

I knew Seraphina; Nature gave her hue,
Glance, sympathy, note, like one from Eden.
I saw her smile warp, heard her lyric deaden;
  She turned to harlotry; – this I took to be new.

Say what you will, our God sees how they run.
These disillusions are His curious proving
That He loves humanity and will go on loving;
  Over there are faith, life, virtue in the sun.

185   Jig

That winter love spoke and we raised no objection, at
Easter 'twas daisies all light and affectionate,
June sent us crazy for natural selection – not
Four traction-engines could tear us apart.
Autumn then coloured the map of our land,
Oaks shuddered and apples came ripe to the hand,
In the gap of the hills we played happily, happily,
Even the moon couldn't tell us apart.

Grave winter drew near and said, 'This will not do at all –
If you continue, I fear you will rue it all.'
So at the New Year we vowed to eschew it
Although we both knew it would break our heart.
But spring made hay of our good resolutions –
Lovers, you may be as wise as Confucians,
Yet once love betrays you he plays you and plays you
Like fishes for ever, so take it to heart.

186   Hornpipe

Now the peak of summer's past, the sky is overcast
And the love we swore would last for an age seems deceit:
Paler is the guelder since the day we first beheld her
In blush beside the elder drifting sweet, drifting sweet.

Oh quickly they fade – the sunny esplanade,
Speed-boats, wooden spades, and the dunes where we've
    lain:
Others will be lying amid the sea-pinks sighing
For love to be undying, and they'll sigh in vain.

244

It's hurrah for each night we have spent our love so lightly
And never dreamed there might be no more to spend at all.
It's goodbye to every lover who thinks he'll live in clover
All his life, for noon is over soon and night-dews fall.

If I could keep you there with the berries in your hair
And your lacy fingers fair as the may, sweet may,
I'd have no heart to do it, for to stay love is to rue it
And the harder we pursue it, the faster it's away.

JOHN BETJEMAN

187 Croydon

In a house like that
    Your Uncle Dick was born;
Satchel on back he walked to Whitgift
    Every weekday morn.

Boys together in Coulsdon woodlands,
    Bramble-berried and steep,
He and his pals would look for spadgers
    Hidden deep.

The laurels are speckled in Marchmont Avenue
    Just as they were before,
But the steps are dusty that still lead up to
    Your Uncle Dick's front door.

Pear and apple in Croydon gardens
    Bud and blossom and fall,
But your Uncle Dick has left his Croydon
    Once for all.

188 Myfanwy

Kind o'er the *kinderbank* leans my Myfanwy,
    White o'er the play-pen the sheen of her dress,
Fresh from the bathroom and soft in the nursery
    Soap-scented fingers I long to caress.

Were you a prefect and head of your dormit'ry?
    Were you a hockey girl, tennis or gym?
Who was your favourite? Who had a crush on you?
    Which were the baths where they taught you to swim?

Smooth down the Avenue glitters the bicycle,
　　Black-stockinged legs under navy-blue serge,
Home and Colonial, Star, International,
　　Balancing bicycle leant on the verge.

Trace me your wheel-tracks, you fortunate bicycle,
　　Out of the shopping and into the dark,
Back down the Avenue, back to the pottingshed,
　　Back to the house on the fringe of the park.

Golden the light on the locks of Myfanwy,
　　Golden the light on the book on her knee,
Finger-marked pages of Rackham's Hans Andersen,
　　Time for the children to come down to tea.

Oh! Fuller's angel-cake, Robertson's marmalade,
　　Liberty lampshade, come, shine on us all,
My! what a spread for the friends of Myfanwy
　　Some in the alcove and some in the hall.

Then what sardines in the half-lighted passages!
　　Locking of fingers in long hide-and-seek.
You will protect me, my silken Myfanwy,
　　Ringleader, tom-boy, and chum to the weak.

189　Christmas

The bells of waiting Advent ring,
　　The Tortoise stove is lit again
And lamp-oil light across the night
　　Has caught the streaks of winter rain
In many a stained-glass window sheen
From Crimson Lake to Hooker's Green.

The holly in the windy hedge
    And round the Manor House the yew
Will soon be stripped to deck the ledge,
    The altar, font and arch and pew,
So that the villagers can say
'The church looks nice' on Christmas Day.

Provincial public houses blaze
    And Corporation tramcars clang,
On lighted tenements I gaze
    Where paper decorations hang,
And bunting in the red Town Hall
Says 'Merry Christmas to you all.'

And London shops on Christmas Eve
    Are strung with silver bells and flowers
As hurrying clerks the City leave
    To pigeon-haunted classic towers,
And marbled clouds go scudding by
The many-steepled London sky.

And girls in slacks remember Dad,
    And oafish louts remember Mum,
And sleepless children's hearts are glad,
    And Christmas-morning bells say 'Come!'
Even to shining ones who dwell
Safe in the Dorchester Hotel.

And is it true? And is it true,
    This most tremendous tale of all,
Seen in a stained-glass window's hue,
    A Baby in an ox's stall?
The Maker of the stars and sea
Become a Child on earth for me?

And is it true? For if it is,
    No loving fingers tying strings
Around those tissued fripperies,
    The sweet and silly Christmas things,
Bath salts and inexpensive scent
And hideous tie so kindly meant,

No love that in a family dwells,
  No carolling in frosty air,
Nor all the steeple-shaking bells
  Can with this single Truth compare –
That God was Man in Palestine
And lives to-day in Bread and Wine.

190   Seaside Golf

How straight it flew, how long it flew.
  It clear'd the rutty track
And soaring, disappeared from view
  Beyond the bunker's back –
A glorious, sailing, bounding drive
That made me glad I was alive.

And down the fairway, far along
  It glowed a lonely white;
I played an iron sure and strong
  And clipp'd it out of sight,
And spite of grassy banks between
I knew I'd find it on the green.

And so I did. It lay content
  Two paces from the pin;
A steady putt and then it went
  Oh, most securely in.
The very turf rejoiced to see
That quite unprecedented three.

Ah! seaweed smells from sandy caves
  And thyme and mist in whiffs,
In-coming tide, Atlantic waves
  Slapping the sunny cliffs,
Lark song and sea sounds in the air
And splendour, splendour everywhere.

191   The Cottage Hospital

At the end of a long-walled garden
    in a red provincial town,
A brick path led to a mulberry –
    scanty grass at its feet.
I lay under blackening branches
    where the mulberry leaves hung down
Sheltering ruby fruit globes
    from a Sunday-tea-time heat.
Apple and plum espaliers
    basked upon bricks of brown;
The air was swimming with insects,
    and children played in the street.

Out of this bright intentness
    into the mulberry shade
Musca domestica (housefly)
    swung from the August light
Slap into slithery rigging
    by the waiting spider made
Which spun the lithe elastic
    till the fly was shrouded tight.
Down came the hairy talons
    and horrible poison blade
And none of the garden noticed
    that fizzing, hopeless fight.

Say in what Cottage Hospital
    whose pale green walls resound
With the tap upon polished parquet
    of inflexible nurses' feet
Shall I myself be lying
    when they range the screens around?
And say shall I groan in dying,
    as I twist the sweaty sheet?
Or gasp for breath uncrying,
    as I feel my senses drowned
While the air is swimming with insects
    and children play in the street?

192 Remorse

The lungs draw in the air and rattle it out again;
  The eyes revolve in their sockets and upwards stare;
No more worry and waiting and troublesome doubt again –
  She whom I loved and left is no longer there.

The nurse puts down her knitting and walks across to her,
  With quick professional eye she surveys the dead.
Just one patient the less and little the loss to her,
  Distantly tender she settles the shrunken head.

Protestant claims and Catholic, the wrong and the right of
    them,
  Unimportant they seem in the face of death –
But my neglect and unkindness – to lose the sight of them
  I would listen even again to that labouring breath.

193 A Lament for Moira McCavendish

Through the midlands of Ireland I journeyed by diesel
  And bright in the sun shone the emerald plain;
Though loud sang the birds on the thorn-bush and teasel
  They could not be heard for the sound of the train.

The roll of the railway made musing creative:
  I though of the colleen I soon was to see
With her wiry black hair and grey eyes of the native,
  Sweet Moira McCavendish, acushla machree.

Her brother's wee cabin stands distant from Tallow
  A league and a half, where the Blackwater flows,
And the musk and potato, the mint and the mallow
  Do grow there in beauty, along with the rose.

'Twas smoothly we raced through the open expansion
  Of rush-covered levels and gate-lodge and gate
And the ruined demesne and the windowless mansion
  Where once the oppressor had revelled in state.

At Castletownroche, as the prospect grew hillier,
  I saw the far mountains to Moira long known
Till I came to the valley and townland familiar
  With the Protestant church standing locked and alone.

O vein of my heart! upon Tallow Road Station
  No face was to greet me, so freckled and white;
As the diesel slid out, leaving still desolation,
  The McCavendish ass-cart was nowhere in sight.

For a league and half to the Blackwater river
  I tramped with my bundle her cabin to see
And herself by the fuchsias, her young lips a-quiver
  Half-smiling, half-weeping a welcome to me.

Och Moira McCavendish! the fangs of the creeper
  Have struck at the thatch and thrust open the door;
The couch in the garden grows ranker and deeper
  Than musk and potato which bloomed there before.

Flow on, you remorseless and salmon-full waters!
  What care I for prospects so silvery fair?
The heart in me's dead, like your sweetest of daughters,
  And I would that my spirit were lost on the air.

I like the way these old brick garden walls
Unevenly run down to Letcombe Brook.
I like the mist of green about the elms
In earliest leaf-time. More intensely green
The duck-weed undulates; a mud-grey trout
Hovers and darts away at my approach.

From rumpled beds on far-off new estates,
From houses over shops along the square,
From red-brick villas somewhat further out,
Ringers arrive, converging on the tower.
Third Sunday after Easter. Public ways
Reek faintly yet of last night's fish and chips.
The plumes of smoke from upright chimney-pots
Denote the death of last week's Sunday press,
While this week's waits on many a step and sill
Unopened, folded, supplements and all.

Suddenly on the unsuspecting air
The bells clash out. It seems a miracle
That leaf and flower should never even stir
In such great waves of medieval sound:
They ripple over roofs to fields and farms
So that 'the fellowship of Christ's religion'
Is roused to breakfast, church or sleep again.

From this wide vale, where all our married lives
We two have lived, we now are whirled away
Momently clinging to the things we knew –
Friends, footpaths, hedges, house and animals –
Till, borne along like twigs and bits of straw,
We sink below the sliding stream of time.

LOUIS MACNEICE

195 Sunday Morning

Down the road someone is practising scales,
The notes like little fishes vanish with a wink of tails,
Man's heart expands to tinker with his car
For this is Sunday morning, Fate's great bazaar;
Regard these means as ends, concentrate on this Now,
And you may grow to music or drive beyond Hindhead
    anyhow,
Take corners on two wheels until you go so fast
That you can clutch a fringe or two of the windy past,
That you can abstract this day and make it to the week of
    time
A small eternity, a sonnet self-contained in rhyme.

But listen, up the road, something gulps, the church spire
Opens its eight bells out, skulls' mouths which will not tire
To tell how there is no music or movement which secures
Escape from the weekday time. Which deadens and
    endures.

196 Wolves

I do not want to be reflective any more
Envying and despising unreflective things
Finding pathos in dogs and undeveloped handwriting
And young girls doing their hair and all the castles of sand
Flushed by the children's bedtime, level with the shore.

The tide comes in and goes out again, I do not want
To be always stressing either its flux or its permanence,
I do not want to be a tragic or philosophic chorus
But to keep my eye only on the nearer future
And after that let the sea flow over us.

Come then all of you, come closer, form a circle,
Join hands and make believe that joined
Hands will keep away the wolves of water
Who howl along our coast. And be it assumed
That no one hears them among the talk and laughter.

197   Valediction

Their verdure dare not show . . . their verdure dare not
   show . . .
Cant and randy – the seals' heads bobbing in the tide-flow
Between the islands, sleek and black and irrelevant
They cannot depose logically what they want:
Died by gunshot under borrowed pennons,
Sniped from the wet gorse and taken by the limp fins
And slung like a dead seal in a boghole, beaten up
By peasants with long lips and the whisky-drinker's cough.
Park your car in the city of Dublin, see Sackville Street
Without the sandbags in the old photos, meet
The statues of the patriots, history never dies,
At any rate in Ireland, arson and murder are legacies
Like old rings hollow-eyed without their stones
Dumb talismans.
See Belfast, devout and profane and hard,
Built on reclaimed mud, hammers playing in the shipyard,
Time punched with holes like a steel sheet, time
Hardening the faces, veneering with a grey and speckled
   rime
The faces under the shawls and caps:
This was my mother-city, these my paps.
Country of callous lava cooled to stone,
Of minute sodden haycocks, of ship-sirens' moan,
Of falling intonations – I would call you to book
I would say to you, Look;
I would say, This is what you have given me
Indifference and sentimentality

A metallic giggle, a fumbling hand,
A heart that leaps to a fife band:
Set these against your water-shafted air
Of amethyst and moonstone, the horses' feet like bells of
    hair
Shambling beneath the orange cart, the beer-brown spring
Guzzling between the heather, the green gush of Irish
    spring.
Cursèd be he that curses his mother. I cannot be
Anyone else than what this land engendered me:
In the back of my mind are snips of white, the sails
Of the Lough's fishing-boats, the bellropes lash their tails
When I would peal my thoughts, the bells pull free –
Memory in apostasy.
I would tot up my factors
But who can stand in the way of his soul's steam-tractors?
I can say Ireland is hooey, Ireland is
A gallery of fake tapestries,
But I cannot deny my past to which my self is wed,
The woven figure cannot undo its thread.
On a cardboard lid I saw when I was four
Was the trade-mark of a hound and a round tower,
And that was Irish glamour, and in the cemetery
Sham Celtic crosses claimed our individuality,
And my father talked about the West where years back
He played hurley on the sands with a stick of wrack.
Park your car in Killarney, buy a souvenir
Of green marble or black bog-oak, run up to Clare,
Climb the cliff in the postcard, visit Galway city,
Romanticise on our Spanish blood, leave ten per cent of pity
Under your plate for the emigrant,
Take credit for our sanctity, our heroism and our sterile want
Columba Kevin and briny Brandan the accepted names,
Wolfe Tone and Grattan and Michael Collins the accepted
    names,
Admire the suavity with which the architect
Is rebuilding the burnt mansion, recollect
The palmy days of the Horse Show, swank your fill,
But take the Holyhead boat before you pay the bill;

Before you face the consequence
Of inbred soul and climatic maleficence
And pay for the trick beauty of a prism
In drug-dull fatalism.
I will exorcise my blood
And not to have my baby-clothes my shroud
I will acquire an attitude not yours
And become as one of your holiday visitors,
And however often I may come
Farewell, my country, and in perpetuum;
Whatever desire I catch when your wind scours my face
I will take home and put in a glass case
And merely look on
At each new fantasy of badge and gun.
Frost will not touch the hedge of fuchsias,
The land will remain as it was,
But no abiding content can grow out of these minds
Fuddled with blood, always caught by blinds;
The eels go up the Shannon over the great dam;
You cannot change a response by giving it a new name.
Fountain of green and blue curling in the wind
I must go east and stay, not looking behind,
Not knowing on which day the mist is blanket-thick
Nor when sun quilts the valley and quick
Winging shadows of white clouds pass
Over the long hills like a fiddle's phrase.
If I were a dog of sunlight I would bound
From Phoenix Park to Achill Sound,
Picking up the scent of a hundred fugitives
That have broken the mesh of ordinary lives,
But being ordinary too I must in course discuss
What we mean to Ireland or Ireland to us;
I have to observe milestone and curio
The beaten buried gold of an old king's bravado,
Falsetto antiquities, I have to gesture,
Take part in, or renounce, each imposture;
Therefore I resign, good-bye the chequered and the quiet
    hills,
The gaudily-striped Atlantic, the linen-mills

That swallow the shawled file, the black moor where half
A turf-stack stands like a ruined cenotaph;
Good-bye your hens running in and out of the white house
Your absent-minded goats along the road, your black cows
Your greyhounds and your hunters beautifully bred
Your drums and your dolled-up Virgins and your ignorant
   dead.

198   Prognosis

Good-bye, Winter,
The days are getting longer,
The tea-leaf in the teacup
Is herald of a stranger.

Will he bring me business
Or will he bring me gladness
Or will he come for cure
Of his own sickness?

With a pedlar's burden
Walking up the garden
Will he come to beg
Or will he come to bargain?

Will he come to pester,
To cringe or to bluster,
A promise in his palm
Or a gun in his holster?

Will his name be John
Or will his name be Jonah
Crying to repent
On the Island of Iona?

Will his name be Jason
Looking for a seaman
Or a mad crusader
Without rhyme or reason?

What will be his message –
War or work or marriage?
News as new as dawn
Or an old adage?

Will he give a champion
Answer to my question
Or will his words be dark
And his ways evasion?

Will his name be Love
And all his talk be crazy?
Or will his name be Death
And his message easy?

199   Who stands, the crux left of the watershed

Who stands, the crux left of the watershed,
On the wet road between the chafing grass
Below him sees dismantled washing-floors,
Snatches of tramline running to the wood,
An industry already comatose,
Yet sparsely living. A ramshackle engine
At Cashwell raises water; for ten years
It lay in flooded workings until this,
Its latter office, grudgingly performed,
And further here and there, though many dead
Lie under the poor soil, some acts are chosen
Taken from recent winters; two there were
Cleaned out a damaged shaft by hand, clutching
The winch the gale would tear them from; one died
During a storm, the fells impassable,
Not at his village, but in wooden shape
Through long abandoned levels nosed his way
And in his final valley went to ground.

Go home, now, stranger, proud of your young stock,
Stranger, turn back again, frustrate and vexed:
This land, cut off, will not communicate,
Be no accessory content to one
Aimless for faces rather there than here.
Beams from your car may cross a bedroom wall,
They wake no sleeper; you may hear the wind
Arriving driven from the ignorant sea
To hurt itself on pane, on bark of elm
Where sap unbaffled rises, being Spring;
But seldom this. Near you, taller than grass,
Ears poise before decision, scenting danger.

200   'Taller to-day'

Taller to-day, we remember similar evenings,
Walking together in the windless orchard
Where the brook runs over the gravel, far from the glacier.

Again in the room with the sofa hiding the grate,
Look down to the river when the rain is over,
See him turn to the window, hearing our last
Of Captain Ferguson.

It is seen how excellent hands have turned to commonness.
One staring too long, went blind in a tower,
One sold all his manors to fight, broke through, and
    faltered.

Nights come bringing the snow, and the dead howl
Under the headlands in their windy dwelling
Because the Adversary put too easy questions
On lonely roads.

But happy now, though no nearer each other,
We see the farms lighted all along the valley;
Down at the mill-shed the hammering stops
And men go home.

Noises at dawn will bring
Freedom for some, but not this peace
No bird can contradict: passing, but is sufficient now
For something fulfilled this hour, loved or endured.

201   From scars where kestrels hover

From scars where kestrels hover,
The leader looking over
Into the happy valley,

Orchard and curving river,
May turn away to see
The slow fastidious line
That disciplines the fell,
Hear curlew's creaking call
From angles unforeseen,
The drumming of a snipe
Surprise where driven sleet
Had scalded to the bone
And streams are acrid yet
To an unaccustomed lip.
The tall unwounded leader
Of doomed companions, all
Whose voices in the rock
Are now perpetual,
Fighters for no one's sake,
Who died beyond the border.

Heroes are buried who
Did not believe in death
And bravery is now
Not in the dying breath
But resisting the temptations
To skyline operations.
Yet glory is not new;
The summer visitors
Still come from far and wide,
Choosing their spots to view
The prize competitors,
Each thinking that he will
Find heroes in the wood,
Far from the capital
Where lights and wine are set
For supper by the lake,
But leaders must migrate:
'Leave for Cape Wrath to-night',
And the host after waiting
Must quench the lamps and pass
Alive into the house.

Get there if you can and see the land you once were proud to
     own
Though the roads have almost vanished and the expresses
     never run:

Smokeless chimneys, damaged bridges, rotting wharves and
     choked canals,
Tramlines buckled, smashed trucks lying on their side across
     the rails;

Power-stations locked, deserted, since they drew the boiler
     fires;
Pylons fallen or subsiding, trailing dead high-tension wires;

Head-gears gaunt on grass-grown pit-banks, seams
     abandoned years ago;
Drop a stone and listen for its splash in flooded dark below.

Squeeze into the works through broken windows or through
     damp-sprung doors;
See the rotted shafting, see holes gaping in the upper floors;

Where the Sunday lads come talking motor-bicycle and girl,
Smoking cigarettes in chains until their heads are in a whirl.

Far from there we spent the money, thinking we could well
     afford,
While they quietly undersold us with their cheaper trade
     abroad;

At the theatre, playing tennis, driving motor-cars we had,
In our continental villas, mixing cocktails for a cad.

These were boon companions who devised the legends for
     our tombs,
These who have betrayed us nicely while we took them to
     our rooms.

Newman, Ciddy, Plato, Fronny, Pascal, Bowdler,
   Baudelaire,
Doctor Frommer, Mrs Allom, Freud, the Baron, and
   Flaubert.

Lured with their compelling logic, charmed with beauty of
   their verse,
With their loaded sideboards whispered 'Better join us, life
   is worse.'

Taught us at the annual camps arranged by the big business
   men
'Sunbathe, pretty till you're twenty. You shall be our
   servants then.'

Perfect pater. Marvellous mater. Knock the critic down who
   dares –
Very well, believe it, copy, till your hair is white as theirs.

Yours you say were parents to avoid, avoid then if you
   please
Do the reverse on all occasions till you catch the same
   disease.

When we asked the way to Heaven, these directed us ahead
To the padded room, the clinic and the hangman's little
   shed.

Intimate as war-time prisoners in an isolation camp,
Living month by month together, nervy, famished, lousy,
   damp.

On the sopping esplanade or from our dingy lodgings we
Stare out dully at the rain which falls for miles into the sea.

Lawrence, Blake and Homer Lane, once healers in our
   English land;
These are dead as iron for ever; these can never hold our
   hand.

Lawrence was brought down by smut-hounds, Blake went
  dotty as he sang,
Homer Lane was killed in action by the Twickenham Baptist
  gang.

Have things gone too far already? Are we done for? Must we
  wait
Hearing doom's approaching footsteps regular down miles
  of straight;

Run the whole night through in gumboots, stumble on and
  gasp for breath,
Terrors drawing close and closer, winter landscape, fox's
  death;

Or, in friendly fireside circle, sit and listen for the crash
Meaning that the mob has realised something's up, and start
  to smash;

Engine-drivers with their oil-cans, factory girls in overalls
Blowing sky-high monster stores, destroying intellectuals?

Hope and fear are neck and neck: which is it near the
  course's end
Crashes, having lost his nerve; is overtaken on the bend?

Shut up talking, charming in the best suits to be had in
  town,
Lecturing on navigation while the ship is going down.

Drop those priggish ways for ever, stop behaving like a
  stone:
Throw the bath-chairs right away, and learn to leave
  ourselves alone.

If we really want to live, we'd better start at once to try;
If we don't it doesn't matter, but we'd better start to die.

203   Who will endure

Who will endure
Heat of day and winter danger,
Journey from one place to another,
Nor be content to lie
Till evening upon headland over bay,
Between the land and sea;
Or smoking wait till hour of food,
Leaning on chained-up gate
At edge of wood?

Metals run
Burnished or rusty in the sun
From town to town,
And signals all along are down;
Yet nothing passes
But envelopes between these places,
Snatched at the gate and panting read indoors,
And first spring flowers arriving smashed,
Disaster stammered over wires,
And pity flashed.
For should professional traveller come,
Asked at the fireside he is dumb,
Declining with a small mad smile,
And all the while
Conjectures on the maps that lie
About in ships long high and dry
Grow stranger and stranger.

There is no change of place
But shifting of the head
To keep off glare of lamp from face,
Or climbing over to wall-side of bed;
No one will ever know
For what conversion brilliant capital is waiting,
What ugly feast may village band be celebrating;
For no one goes
Further than railhead or the ends of piers,

Will neither go nor send his son
Further through foothills than the rotting stack
Where gaitered gamekeeper with dog and gun
Will shout 'Turn back'.

204   What siren zooming is sounding our coming

To Edward Upward, schoolmaster

What siren zooming is sounding our coming
Up frozen fjord forging from freedom
     What shepherd's call
     When stranded on hill,
     With broken axle
     On track to exile?

With labelled luggage we alight at last
Joining joking at the junction on the moor
     With practised smile
     And harmless tale
     Advance to meet
     Each new recruit.

Expert from uplands, always in oilskins,
Recliner from library, laying down law,
     Owner from shire,
     All meet on this shore
     Facing each prick
     With ginger pluck.

Our rooms are ready, the register signed,
There is time to take a turn before dark,
     See the blistered paint
     On the scorching front,
     Or icicles sombre
     On pierhead timber.

To climb the cliff path to the coastguard's point
Past the derelict dock deserted by rats,
          Look from concrete sill
          Of fort for sale
          To the bathers' rocks
          The lovers' ricks.

Our boots will be brushed, our bolsters pummelled,
Cupboards are cleared for keeping our clothes.
          Here we shall live
          And somehow love
          Though we only master
          The sad posture.

Picnics are promised and planned for July
To the wood with the waterfall, walks to find,
          Traces of birds,
          A mole, a rivet,
          In factory yards
          Marked strictly private.

There will be skating and curling at Christmas – indoors
Charades and ragging; then riders pass
          Some afternoons
          In snowy lanes
          Shut in by wires
          Surplus from wars.

In Spring we shall spade the soil on the border
For blooming of bulbs; we shall bow in Autumn
          When trees make passes,
          As high gale pushes,
          And bewildered leaves
          Fall on our lives.

We are here for our health, we have not to fear
The fiend in the furze or the face at the manse;
        Proofed against shock
        Our hands can shake;
        The flag at the golf-house flutters
        And nothing matters.

We shall never need another new outfit;
These grounds are for good, we shall grow no more,
        But lose our colour
        With scurf on collar
        Peering through glasses
        At our own glosses.

This life is to last, when we leave we leave all,
Though vows have no virtue, though voice is in vain,
        We live like ghouls
        On posts from girls
        What the spirit utters
        In formal letters.

Watching through windows the wastes of evening,
The flare of foundries at fall of the year.
        The slight despair
        At what we are,
        The marginal grief
        Is source of life.

In groups forgetting the gun in the drawer
Need pray for no pardon, are proud till recalled
        By music on water
        To lack of stature
        Saying Alas
        To less and less.

Till holding our hats in our hands for talking
Or striding down streets for something to see
       Gas-light in shops
       The fate of ships
       And the tide-wind
       Touch the old wound.

Till the town is ten and the time is London
And nerves grow numb between north and south
       Hear last in corner
       The pffwungg of burner
       Accepting dearth
       The shadow of death.

205   'O who can ever gaze his fill'

'O who can ever gaze his fill',
    Farmer and fisherman say,
'On native shore and local hill,
Grudge aching limb or callus on the hand?
Fathers, grandfathers stood upon this land,
And here the pilgrims from our loins shall stand.'
    So farmer and fisherman say
    In their fortunate heyday:
    But Death's soft answer drifts across
    Empty catch or harvest loss
    Or an unlucky May:
The earth is an oyster with nothing inside it
    Not to be born is the best for man
The end of toil is a bailiff's order
    Throw down the mattock and dance while you can.

'O life's too short for friends who share',
    Travellers think in their hearts,
'The city's common bed, the air,
The mountain bivouac and the bathing beach,
Where incidents draw every day from each
Memorable gesture and witty speech.'

So travellers think in their hearts,
Till malice or circumstance parts
Them from their constant humour:
And slyly Death's coercive rumour
    In the silence starts:
A friend is the old old tale of Narcissus
    Not to be born is the best for man
An active partner is something disgraceful
    Change your partner, dance while you can.

'O stretch your hands across the sea',
    The impassioned lover cries,
'Stretch them towards your harm and me.
Our grass is green, and sensual our brief bed,
The stream sings at its foot, and at its head
The mild and vegetarian beasts are fed.'
    So the impassioned lover cries
    Till his storm of pleasure dies:
    From the bedpost and the rocks
    Death's enticing echo mocks,
        And his voice replies:
The greater the love, the more false to its object
    Not to be born is the best for man
After the kiss comes the impulse to throttle
    Break the embraces, dance while you can.

'I see the guilty world forgiven',
    Dreamer and drunkard sing,
'The ladders let down out of heaven;
The laurel springing from the martyr's blood;
The children skipping where the weepers stood;
The lovers natural, and the beasts all good.'
    So dreamer and drunkard sing
    Till day their sobriety bring:
    Parrotwise with death's reply
    From whelping fear and nesting lie,
        Woods and their echoes ring:

The desires of the heart are as crooked as corkscrews
*   Not to be born is the best for man*
The second best is a formal order
*   The dance's pattern, dance while you can.*
Dance, dance, for the figure is easy
*   The tune is catching and will not stop*
Dance till the stars come down with the rafters
*   Dance, dance, dance till you drop.*

206   Johnny

O the valley in the summer where I and my John
Beside the deep river would walk on and on
While the flowers at our feet and the birds up above
Argued so sweetly on reciprocal love,
And I leaned on his shoulder; 'O Johnny, let's play':
But he frowned like thunder and he went away.

O that Friday near Christmas as I well recall
When we went to the Charity Matinee Ball,
The floor was so smooth and the band was so loud
And Johnny so handsome I felt so proud;
'Squeeze me tighter, dear Johnny, let's dance till it's day':
But he frowned like thunder and he went away.

Shall I ever forget at the Grand Opera
When music poured out of each wonderful star?
Diamonds and pearls they hung dazzling down
Over each silver or golden silk gown;
'O John I'm in heaven', I whispered to say:
But he frowned like thunder and he went away.

O but he was as fair as a garden in flower,
As slender and tall as the great Eiffel Tower,
When the waltz throbbed out on the long promenade
O his eyes and his smile they went straight to my heart;
'O marry me, Johnny, I'll love and obey':
But he frowned like thunder and he went away.

O last night I dreamed of you, Johnny, my lover,
You'd the sun on one arm and the moon on the other,
The sea it was blue and the grass it was green,
Every star rattled a round tambourine;
Ten thousand miles deep in a pit there I lay:
But you frowned like thunder and you went away.

207   As I walked out one evening

As I walked out one evening,
    Walking down Bristol Street,
The crowds upon the pavement
    Were fields of harvest wheat.

And down by the brimming river
    I heard a lover sing
Under an arch of the railway:
    'Love has no ending.

'I'll love you, dear, I'll love you
    Till China and Africa meet
And the river jumps over the mountain
    And the salmon sing in the street.

'I'll love you till the ocean
    Is folded and hung up to dry
And the seven stars go squawking
    Like geese about the sky.

'The years shall run like rabbits
        For in my arms I hold
The Flower of the Ages
        And the first love of the world.'

But all the clocks in the city
        Began to whirr and chime:
'O let not Time deceive you,
        You cannot conquer Time.

'In the burrows of the Nightmare
        Where Justice naked is,
Time watches from the shadow
        And coughs when you would kiss.

'In headaches and in worry
        Vaguely life leaks away,
And Time will have his fancy
        To-morrow or to-day.

'Into many a green valley
        Drifts the appalling snow;
Time breaks the threaded dances
        And the diver's brilliant bow.

'O plunge your hands in water,
        Plunge them in up to the wrist;
Stare, stare in the basin
        And wonder what you've missed.

'The glacier knocks in the cupboard,
        The desert sighs in the bed,
And the crack in the tea-cup opens
        A lane to the land of the dead.

'Where the beggars raffle the banknotes
        And the Giant is enchanting to Jack,
And the Lily-white Boy is a Roarer
        And Jill goes down on her back.

274

'O look, look in the mirror,
    O look in your distress;
Life remains a blessing
    Although you cannot bless.

'O stand, stand at the window
    As the tears scald and start;
You shall love your crooked neighbour
    With your crooked heart.'

It was late, late in the evening,
    The lovers they were gone;
The clocks had ceased their chiming
    And the deep river ran on.

208   Fable

O the vines were golden, the birds were loud,
The orchard showered, the honey flowed,
The Venice glasses were full of wine,
The women were geese and the men were swine,

And the lamp then flickered over the door,
And the gulls went screaming along the shore,
And the wolf crept down from the milkwhite hill
And the stars lay bright in the frozen well:

O my world, O what have you done to me?
For my love has turned to a laurel tree,
The axe hangs trembling over the Isles,
The Lyre has loosened her flaming miles,

And the door is locked and the key is lost
And the gulls lie stiffening in the frost
And the rippled snow is tracked with blood
And my love lies cold in the burning wood.

KENNETH ALLOTT

209   Lament for a Cricket Eleven

For S. T.

Beyond the edge of the sepia
Rises the weak photographer
With the moist moustaches and the made-up tie.
He looked with his mechanical eye,
And the upshot was that they had to die.

Portrait of the Eleven nineteen-o-five
To show when these missing persons were last alive.
Two sit in Threadneedle Street like gnomes.
One is a careless schoolmaster
Busy with carved desks, honour and lines.
He is eaten by a wicked cancer.
They have detectives to watch their homes.

From the camera hood he looks at the faces
Like the spectral pose of the praying mantis.
Watch for the dicky-bird. But, O my dear,
That bird will not migrate this year.
Oh for a parasol, oh for a fan
To hid my weak chin from the little man.

One climbs mountains in a storm of fear,
Begs to be unroped and left alone.
One went mad by a tape-machine.
One laughed for a fortnight and went to sea.
Like a sun one follows the jeunesse dorée.

With his hand on the bulb he looks at them.
The smiles on their faces are upside down.
'I'll turn my head and spoil the plate.'
'Thank you, gentlemen.' Too late. Too late.

One greyhead was beaten in a prison riot.
He needs injections to keep him quiet.
Another was a handsome clergyman,
But mortification has long set in.
One keeps six dogs in a unlit cellar.
The last is a randy bachelor.

The photographer in the norfolk jacket
Sits upstairs in his darkroom attic.
His hand is expert at scissors and pin.
The shadows lengthen, the days draw in,
And the mice come out round the iron stove.
'What I am doing, I am doing for love.
When shall I burn this negative
And hang the receiver up on grief?'

210   Patch

Caught into a brown study with the stars
Tonight the foreign bodies of the hills,
As innocent of every care
As the old lovers in the garden were,
Shrug at our vehement blood:
The wind clamps the ice on the random fells.

Tomorrow we may rub our eyes and cry,
The livestock perish in the floods,
The timepiece cease to item in the weeds,
And one of us be sent incognito
Beyond the last peak and the flurried snow,
And no philosopher discover why.

Meanwhile the timbers creak and the lake blows white
Against the lost circumference of the shore,
Yet like the comfort of the Israelite
Even the wolvish pines tonight
Queerly affirm as more than rumour
The meticulous sweetness of the indifferent year.

LAWRENCE DURRELL

211   In a Time of Crisis

For Nancy

My love on Wednesday letting fall her body
From upright walking won by weariness,
As on a bed of flesh by ounces counted out,
Softer than snuff or snow came where my body was.

So in the aboriginal waterways of the mind,
No words being spoken by a familiar girl,
One may have a clear apprehension of ghostly matters,
Audible, as perhaps in a sea-shell's helix.

The Gulf Stream can rub soft music from a pebble,
Like quiet rehearsal of the words 'Kneel down';
And cool on the inner corridors of the ear
Can blow on memory and conscience like a sin.

The inner man is surely the native of God,
And his wife a brilliant novice of nature.
The woman walks in the dark like a swinging lantern,
A white spark blown between points of pain.

We do not speak, embracing with the blood,
The tolling heart marking its measures in darkness
Like the scratch of a match, or the fire-stone
Struck to a spark in the dark by a colder one.

So lying close, an enchanted boy may hear
Soon from Tokyo the crass drum sounding:
From the hero's hearth the merry crotchet of war.
Flame shall swallow the lady.

Tall men shall come to cool the royal bush,
Over the grey waters the bugler's octaves
Publish aloud a new resurrection of terror.
Many shall give suck at the bomb's cold nipple.

We are the tiny lords and ladies in waiting,
Kneel on a sharp equator between possible climates;
They reserve for us the monarch's humiliations,
To be pricked in the heart by a queen's golden pin.

Empty your heart or fill from a purer source,
That what is in a man can weep, having eyes,
That what is Truth can speak from the responsible dust,
And O the rose be in the middle of the great world.

212 Epidaurus

The islands which whisper to the ambitious,
Washed all winter by the surviving stars
Are here hardly remembered: or only as
Stone choirs for the sea-bird,
Stone chairs for the statues of fishermen.
This civilised valley was dedicated
To the culture of circles, the contemplation
And corruption of human maladies
Which the repeating flesh has bred in us
By continuous childhood like the worm in meat.

Here we can carry our own small deaths
With the resignation of place and identity:
The temple set severely like a dice
At the vale's end; and apparently once
Ruled from the whitest light of the summer:

A formula for marble when the clouds
Troubled the architect, and the hill spoke
Volumes of thunder, the sibyllic god wept.
Here we are safe from everything but ourselves,
The dying leaves and the reports of love.

The only disorder is in what we bring.
Cars falling like leaves into the valleys,
The penetration of clocks striking in Geneva,
The composure of the doll and the fanatic;
Financed migrations to the oldest sources,
Theatres where repentance was enacted,
Complicated by fear, the stones heavy with dew.
The olive signs the hill signifying revival:
The swallow's cot built in the ruins seems now
So small yet defiant an exaggeration of love.

Northward the gunners have buckled their belts.
The lion is out on his walks. The spring
Threatens a rain of brides by the Latin sea.
We have no right, surely, walking upon
Grass dedicated to myth, to renounce our own:
The somnambulists with the long black rifles.
Sex and hunger, the old partners, on the march,
Together again, paced by the stylistic drums.
The detonations of clocks in the memory,
The detonation of each grain in the hour-glass.

We, like the winter, are only visitors,
To prosper here from the breathing grass,
Encouraging petals on a terrace, disturbing
Nothing, enduring the sun like girls
In a town window. The earth's fine flower
Blows here original with every spring,
Grows with the shining of man's age
Into grave texts and precedents for time,
Everything here feels the ancestral order,
The old captains smiling in their tombs.

Then smile, my dear, above the holy wands,
Make a last poignant and inadequate
Gesture of the hands unlocking here
A world that is not our world.
The rest is metaphor: who shall persuade
The awkward swan to death before her time?
Her will to sleep moves in a naked singing
Across the unsleeping house of history.
So small is all we have to give: a gift of breath,
All causes ending in the great Because.

213   Winter Night

An owl is hooting in the grove,
The moonlight makes the night air mauve,
The trees are regular as crystals,
The thawing road shines black as pistols,
And muffled by the quiet snow
The wind is only felt to blow.
Dread bird that punctually calls!
Its sound inhuman strangely falls
Within the human scale; and I
Am forced to place, besides the cry,
The moon, the trees, the swollen snow,
Reluctantly with what I know.
Even the road conveys the sense
Of being outside experience;
As though, this winter night of war,
The world men made were man's no more.

R. S. THOMAS

214   The Welsh Hill Country

Too far for you to see
The fluke and the foot-rot and the fat maggot
Gnawing the skin from the small bones,
The sheep are grazing at Bwlch-y-Fedwen,
Arranged romantically in the usual manner
On a bleak background of bald stone.

Too far for you to see
The moss and the mould on the cold chimneys,
The nettles growing through the cracked doors,
The houses stand empty at Nant-yr-Eira,
There are holes in the roofs that are thatched with sunlight,
And the fields are reverting to the bare moor.

Too far, too far to see
The set of his eyes and the slow phthisis
Wasting his frame under the ripped coat,
There's a man still farming at Ty'n-y-Fawnog,
Contributing grimly to the accepted pattern,
The embryo music dead in his throat.

215   Depopulation of the Hills

Leave it, leave it – the hole under the door
Was a mouth through which the rough wind spoke
Ever more sharply; the dank hand
Of age was busy on the walls
Scrawling in blurred characters
Messages of hate and fear.

Leave it, leave it – the cold rain began
At summer end – there is no road
Over the bog, and winter comes
With mud above the axletree.

Leave it, leave it – the rain dripped
Day and night from the patched roof
Sagging beneath its load of sky.

Did the earth help them, time befriend
These last survivors? Did the spring grass
Heal winter's ravages? The grass
Wrecked them in its draughty tides,
Grew from the chimney-stack like smoke,
Burned its way through the weak timbers.
That was nature's jest, the sides
Of the old hulk cracked, but not with mirth.

216   The Hill Farmer Speaks

I am the farmer, stripped of love
And thought and grace by the land's hardness;
But what I am saying over the fields'
Desolate acres, rough with dew,
Is, Listen, listen, I am a man like you.

The wind goes over the hill pastures
Year after year, and the ewes starve,
Milkless, for want of the new grass.
And I starve, too, for something the spring
Can never foster in veins run dry.

The pig is a friend, the cattle's breath
Mingles with mine in the still lanes;
I wear it willingly like a cloak
To shelter me from your curious gaze.

The hens go in and out at the door
From sun to shadow, as stray thoughts pass
Over the floor of my wide skull.
The dirt is under my cracked nails;
The tale of my life is smirched with dung;
The phlegm rattles. But what I am saying
Over the grasses rough with dew
Is, Listen, listen, I am a man like you.

217 Song

Wandering, wandering, hoping to find
The ring of mushrooms with the wet rind,
Cold to the touch, but bright with dew,
A green asylum from time's range.

And finding instead the harsh ways
Of the ruinous wind and the clawed rain;
The storm's hysteria in the bush;
The wild creatures and their pain.

218 Welsh Landscape

To live in Wales is to be conscious
At dusk of the spilled blood
That went to the making of the wild sky,
Dyeing the immaculate rivers
In all their courses.
It is to be aware,
Above the noisy tractor
And hum of the machine
Of strife in the strung woods,
Vibrant with sped arrows.
You cannot live in the present,
At least not in Wales.
There is the language for instance,
The soft consonants
Strange to the ear.
There are cries in the dark at night
As owls answer the moon,
And thick ambush of shadows,
Hushed at the fields' corners
There is no present in Wales,
And no future;
There is only the past,
Brittle with relics,
Wind-bitten towers and castles
With sham ghosts;

Mouldering quarries and mines;
And an impotent people,
Sick with inbreeding,
Worrying the carcase of an old song.

219   The Lonely Farmer

Poor hill farmer astray in the grass:
There came a movement and he looked up, but
All that he saw was the wind pass.
There was a sound of voices on the air,
But where, where? It was only the glib stream talking
Softly to itself. And once when he was walking
Along a lane in spring he was deceived
By a shrill whistle coming through the leaves:
Wait a minute, wait a minute – four swift notes;
He turned, and it was nothing, only a thrush
In the thorn bushes easing its throat.
He swore at himself for paying heed,
The poor hill farmer, so often again
Stopping, staring, listening, in vain,
His ear betrayed by the heart's need.

220   A Welshman to Any Tourist

We've nothing vast to offer you, no deserts
Except the waste of thought
Forming from mind erosion;
No canyons where the pterodactyl's wing
Falls like a shadow.
The hills are fine, of course,
Bearded with water to suggest age
And pocked with caverns,
One being Arthur's dormitory;
He and his knights are the bright ore
That seams our history,
But shame has kept them late in bed.

221 Children's Song

We live in our own world,
A world that is too small
For you to stoop and enter
Even on hands and knees,
The adult subterfuge.
And though you probe and pry
With analytic eye,
And eavesdrop all our talk
With an amused look,
You cannot find the centre
Where we dance, where we play,
Where life is still asleep
Under the closed flower,
Under the smooth shell
Of eggs in the cupped nest
That mock the faded blue
Of your remoter heaven.

DYLAN THOMAS

222   The Hunchback in the Park

The hunchback in the park
A solitary mister
Propped between trees and water
From the opening of the garden lock
That lets the trees and water enter
Until the Sunday sombre bell at dark

Eating bread from a newspaper
Drinking water from the chained cup
That the children filled with gravel
In the fountain basin where I sailed my ship
Slept at night in a dog kennel
But nobody chained him up.

Like the park birds he came early
Like the water he sat down
And Mister they called Hey mister
The truant boys from the town
Running when he had heard them clearly
On out of sound

Past lake and rockery
Laughing when he shook his paper
Hunchbacked in mockery
Through the loud zoo of the willow groves
Dodging the park keeper
With his stick that picked up leaves.

And the old dog sleeper
Alone between nurses and swans
While the boys among willows
Made the tigers jump out of their eyes
To roar on the rockery stones
And the groves were blue with sailors

Made all day until bell time
A woman figure without fault
Straight as a young elm
Straight and tall from his crooked bones
That she might stand in the night
After the locks and chains

All night in the unmade park
After the railings and shrubberies
The birds the grass the trees the lake
And the wild boys innocent as strawberries
Had followed the hunchback
To his kennel in the dark.

ROBERT CONQUEST

223   Watering Place

Through flowers fat after so much flattery
And pompous roses cured by tricky surgery
A rash on the garden's shoddy upholstery,

At the end of their six-hour parabola, the masters,
Careful as porcelain with consoling gestures
Return to nibble at their ancestors:

Fumbling with flesh beside the undrinkable ocean,
Drawing nourishment for the will's exhaustion,
The twin manna seeking under clouds of desolation,

Now (as they say that some whose breath is needed,
Spinning downwater, from black ships unthreaded,
Fear more than drowning the cold slime of the seabed)

Worse than war's open furnace of the null,
More frightful than all bombings, they must feel
The sulphurous fires of an inner hell,

And caught at last by the nude accusing ache
Freeze in that moonlight where, a measured snake,
The tongue bleeds out its metaphors of heartbreak.

ROGER WODDIS

224   The Hero

On the Birmingham pub bombings of 21 November 1974

I went out to the city streets,
Because a fire was in my head,
And saw the people passing by,
And wished the youngest of them dead,
And twisted by a bitter past,
And poisoned by a cold despair,
I found at last a resting-place
And left my hatred ticking there.

When I was fleeing from the night
And sweating in my room again,
I heard the old futilities
Exploding like a cry of pain;
But horror, should it touch the heart,
Would freeze my hand upon the fuse,
And I must shed no tears for those
Who merely have a life to lose.

Though I am sick with murdering,
Though killing is my native land,
I will find out where death has gone,
And kiss his lips and take his hand;
And hide among the withered grass,
And pluck, till love and life are done,
The shrivelled apples of the moon,
The cankered apples of the sun.

The Song of Wandering Aengus

I went out to the hazel wood,
Because a fire was in my head,
And cut and peeled a hazel wand,
And hooked a berry to a thread;
And when white moths were on the wing,
And moth-like stars were flickering out,
I dropped the berry in a stream
And caught a little silver trout.

When I had laid it on the floor
I went to blow the fire aflame,
But something rustled on the floor,
And someone called me by my name:
It had become a glimmering girl
With apple blossom in her hair
Who called me by my name and ran
And faded through the brightening air.

Though I am old with wandering
Through hollow lands and hilly lands.
I will find out where she has gone,
And kiss her lips and take her hands;
And walk among long dappled grass,
And pluck till time and times are done
The silver apples of the moon,
The golden apples of the sun.

DONALD DAVIE

225   The Garden Party

Above a stretch of still unravaged weald
In our Black Country, in a cedar-shade,
I found, shared out in tennis courts, a field
Where children of the local magnates played.

And I grew envious of their moneyed ease
In Scott Fitzgerald's unembarrassed vein.
Let prigs, I thought, fool others as they please,
I only wish I had my time again.

To crown a situation as contrived
As any in 'The Beautiful and Damned',
The phantom of my earliest love arrived;
I shook absurdly as I shook her hand.

As dusk drew in on cultivated cries,
Faces hung pearls upon a cedar-bough;
And gin could blur the glitter of her eyes,
But it's too late to learn to tango now.

My father, of a more submissive school,
Remarks the rich themselves are always sad.
There is that sort of equalizing rule;
But theirs is all the youth we might have had.

226 'Climbing the hill'

Climbing the hill within the deafening wind
The blood unfurled itself, was proudly borne
High over meadows where white horses stood;
Up the steep woods it echoed like a horn
Till at the summit under shining trees
It cried: Submission is the only good;
Let me become an instrument sharply stringed
For all things to strike music as they please.

How to recall such music, when the street
Darkens? Among the rain and stone places
I find only an ancient sadness falling,
Only hurrying and troubled faces,
The walking of girls' vulnerable feet,
The heart in its own endless silence kneeling.

227 Coming

On longer evenings,
Light, chill and yellow,
Bathes the serene
Foreheads of houses.
A thrush sings,
Laurel-surrounded
In the deep bare garden,
Its fresh-peeled voice
Astonishing the brickwork.
It will be spring soon,
It will be spring soon –
And I, whose childhood
Is a forgotten boredom,

Feel like a child
Who comes on a scene
Of adult reconciling,
And can understand nothing
But the unusual laughter,
And starts to be happy.

228 Born Yesterday

For Sally Amis

Tightly-folded bud,
I have wished you something
None of the others would:
Not the usual stuff
About being beautiful,
Or running off a spring
Of innocence and love –
They will all wish you that,
And should it prove possible,
Well, you're a lucky girl.

But if it shouldn't, then
May you be ordinary;
Have, like other women,
An average of talents:
Not ugly, not good-looking,
Nothing uncustomary
To pull you off your balance,
That, unworkable itself,
Stops all the rest from working.
In fact, may you be dull –
If that is what a skilled,
Vigilant, flexible,
Unemphasised, enthralled
Catching of happiness is called.

229   Mr Bleaney

'This was Mr Bleaney's room. He stayed
The whole time he was at the Bodies, till
They moved him.' Flowered curtains, thin and frayed,
Fall to within five inches of the sill,

Whose window shows a strip of building land,
Tussocky, littered. 'Mr Bleaney took
My bit of garden properly in hand.'
Bed, upright chair, sixty-watt bulb, no hook

Behind the door, no room for books or bags –
'I'll take it.' So it happens that I lie
Where Mr Bleaney lay, and stub my fags
On the same saucer-souvenir, and try

Stuffing my ears with cotton-wool, to drown
The jabbering set he egged her on to buy.
I know his habits – what time he came down,
His preference for sauce to gravy, why

He kept on plugging at the four aways –
Likewise their yearly frame: the Frinton folk
Who put him up for summer holidays,
And Christmas at his sister's house in Stoke.

But if he stood and watched the frigid wind
Tousling the clouds, lay on the fusty bed
Telling himself that this was home, and grinned,
And shivered, without shaking off the dread

That how we live measures our own nature,
And at his age having no more to show
Than one hired box should make him pretty sure
He warranted no better, I don't know.

230 Nothing To Be Said

For nations vague as weed,
For nomads among stones,
Small-statured cross-faced tribes
And cobble-close families
In mill-towns on dark mornings
Life is slow dying.

So are their separate ways
Of building, benediction,
Measuring love and money
Ways of slow dying.
The day spent hunting pig
Or holding a garden-party,

Hours giving evidence
Or birth, advance
On death equally slowly.
And saying so to some
Means nothing; others it leaves
Nothing to be said.

231 For Sidney Bechet

That note you hold, narrowing and rising, shakes
Like New Orleans reflected on the water,
And in all ears appropriate falsehood wakes,

Building for some a legendary Quarter
Of balconies, flower-baskets and quadrilles,
Everyone making love and going shares –

Oh, play that thing! Mute glorious Storyvilles
Others may license, grouping round their chairs
Sporting-house girls like circus tigers (priced

Far above rubies) to pretend their fads,
While scholars *manqués* nod around unnoticed
Wrapped up in personnels like old plaids.

On me your voice falls as they say love should,
Like an enormous yes. My Crescent City
Is where your speech alone is understood,

And greeted as the natural noise of good,
Scattering long-haired grief and scored pity.

232 First Sight

Lambs that learn to walk in snow
When their bleating clouds the air
Meet a vast unwelcome, know
Nothing but a sunless glare.
Newly stumbling to and fro
All they find, outside the fold,
Is a wretched width of cold.

As they wait beside the ewe,
Her fleeces wetly caked, there lies
Hidden round them, waiting too,
Earth's immeasurable surprise.
They could not grasp it if they knew,
What so soon will wake and grow
Utterly unlike the snow.

'Dockery was junior to you,
Wasn't he?' said the Dean. 'His son's here now.'
Death-suited, visitant, I nod. 'And do
You keep in touch with —' Or remember how
Black-gowned, unbreakfasted, and still half-tight
We used to stand before that desk, to give
'Our version' of 'these incidents last night'?
I try the door of where I used to live:

Locked. The lawn spreads dazzlingly wide.
A known bell chimes. I catch my train, ignored.
Canal and clouds and colleges subside
Slowly from view. But Dockery, good Lord,
Anyone up today must have been born
In '43, when I was twenty-one.
If he was younger, did he get this son
At nineteen, twenty? Was he that withdrawn

High-collared public-schoolboy, sharing rooms
With Cartwright who was killed? Well, it just shows
How much . . . How little . . . Yawning, I suppose
I fell asleep, waking at the fumes
And furnace-glares of Sheffield, where I changed,
And ate an awful pie, and walked along
The platform to its end to see the ranged
Joining and parting lines reflect a strong

Unhindered moon. To have no son, no wife,
No house or land still seemed quite natural.
Only a numbness registered the shock
Of finding out how much had gone of life,
How widely from the others. Dockery, now:
Only nineteen, he must have taken stock
Of what he wanted, and been capable
Of . . . No, that's not the difference: rather, how

Convinced he was he should be added to!
Why did he think adding meant increase?
To me it was dilution. Where do these
Innate assumptions come from? Not from what
We think truest, or most want to do:
Those warp tight-shut, like doors. They're more a style
Our lives bring with them: habit for a while,
Suddenly they harden into all we've got

And how we got it; looked back on, they rear
Like sand-clouds, thick and close, embodying
For Dockery a son, for me nothing,
Nothing with all a son's harsh patronage.
Life is first boredom, then fear.
Whether or not we use it, it goes,
And leaves what something hidden from us chose,
And age, and then the only end of age.

234   Reference Back

That was a pretty one, I heard you call
From the unsatisfactory hall
To the unsatisfactory room where I
Played record after record, idly,
Wasting my time at home, that you
Looked so much forward to.

Oliver's *Riverside Blues*, it was. And now
I shall, I suppose, always remember how
The flock of notes those antique negroes blew
Out of Chicago air into
A huge remembering pre-electric horn
The year after I was born
Three decades later made this sudden bridge
From your unsatisfactory age
To my unsatisfactory prime.

Truly, though our element is time,
We are not suited to the long perspectives
Open at each instant of our lives.
They link us to our losses: worse,
They show us what we have as it once was,
Blindingly undiminished, just as though
By acting differently we could have kept it so.

235   Going, Going

I thought it would last my time –
The sense that, beyond the town,
There would always be fields and farms,
Where the village louts could climb
Such trees as were not cut down;
I knew there'd be false alarms

In the papers about old streets
And split-level shopping, but some
Have always been left so far;
And when the old parts retreat
As the bleak high-risers come
We can always escape in the car.

Things are tougher than we are, just
As earth will always respond
However we mess it about;
Chuck filth in the sea, if you must:
The tides will be clean beyond.
– But what do I feel now? Doubt?

Or age, simply? The crowd
Is young in the M1 café;
Their kids are screaming for more –
More houses, more parking allowed,
More caravan sites, more pay.
On the Business Page, a score

Of spectacled grins approve
Some takeover bid that entails
Five per cent profit (and ten
Per cent more in the estuaries): move
Your works to the unspoilt dales
(Grey area grants)! And when

You try to get near the sea
In summer . . .
                    It seems, just now,
To be happening so very fast;
Despite all the land left free
For the first time I feel somehow
That it isn't going to last,

That before I snuff it, the whole
Boiling will be bricked in
Except for the tourist parts –
First slum of Europe: a role
It won't be so hard to win,
With a cast of crooks and tarts.

And that will be England gone,
The shadows, the meadows, the lanes,
The guildhalls, the carved choirs.
There'll be books; it will linger on
In galleries; but all that remains
For us will be concrete and tyres.

Most things are never meant.
This won't be, most likely: but greeds
And garbage are too thick-strewn
To be swept up now, or invent
Excuses that make them all needs.
I just think it will happen, soon.

236 Dublinesque

Down stucco sidestreets,
Where light is pewter
And afternoon mist
Brings lights on in shops
Above race-guides and rosaries,
A funeral passes.

The hearse is ahead,
But after there follows
A troop of streetwalkers
In wide flowered hats,
Leg-of-mutton sleeves,
And ankle-length dresses.

There is an air of great friendliness,
As if they were honouring
One they were fond of;
Some caper a few steps,
Skirts held skilfully
(Someone claps time),

And of great sadness also.
As they wend away
A voice is heard singing
Of Kitty, or Katy,
As if the name meant once
All love, all beauty.

237 Cut Grass

Cut grass lies frail:
Brief is the breath
Mown stalks exhale.
Long, long the death

It dies in the white hours
Of young-leafed June
With chestnut flowers,
With hedges snowlike strewn,

White lilac bowed,
Lost lanes of Queen Anne's lace,
And that high-builded cloud
Moving at summer's pace.

238   Salamnbo

Alive again, sometimes she went to stand
Beside the window when the afternoon
Subtracted clearness from the hateful land.
Light waved no longer like a dandelion;
Rouen lay white as Carthage in the moon.

Calm, chiselled ghost, indifferent, clad in iron
Temptations of the desert, she had moved
To slumber and desire the amorous man
Whom fame had tortured from the embrace he loved
And laid once more beside his Bovary.

Salamnbo watched. Though he implored her bright
And copious eyes, as ignorant as history,
She never knew it was her African
Body he cried for in the Norman night.

ELIZABETH JENNINGS

239 Time

Why should we think of ends, beginnings,
Who for a moment draw our pace
Through moons and sunsets, rising, wanings,
Who brush the moment, seek a place
More than a minute's hopes and winnings?

Why cannot we accept the hour,
The present, be observers and
Hold a full knowledge in our power,
Arrest the falling of the sand?
And keep the watchful moment, pour
Its meaning in the hurried hand?

240 The Rabbit's Advice

I have been away too long.
Some of you think I am only a nursery tale,
One which you've grown out of.
Or perhaps you saw a movie and laughed at my ears
But rather envied my carrot.
I must tell you that I exist.

I'm a puff of wool leaping across a field,
Quick to all noises,
Smelling my burrow of safety.
I am easily frightened. A bird
Is tame compared to me.
Perhaps you have seen my fat white cousin who sits,
Constantly twitching his nose,
Behind bars in a hutch at the end of a garden.

If not, imagine those nights when you lie awake
Afraid to turn over, afraid
Of night and dawn and sleep.
Terror is what I am made
Of partly, partly of speed.

But I am a figure of fun.
I have no dignity
Which means I am never free.
So, when you are frightened or being teased, think of
My twitching whiskers, my absurd white puff of a tail,
Of all that I mean by 'me'
And my ludicrous craving for love.

241   At Birth

Come from a distant country,
Bundle of flesh, of blood,
Demanding painful entry,
Expecting little good:
There is no going back
Among those thickets where
Both night and day are black
And blood's the same as air.

Strangely you come to meet us,
Stained, mottled, as if dead:
You bridge the dark hiatus
Through which your body slid
Across a span of muscle,
A breadth my hand can span.
The gorged and brimming vessel
Flows over, and is man.

Dear daughter, as I watched you
Come crumpled from the womb,
And sweating hands had fetched you
Into this world, the room
Opened before your coming
Like water struck from rocks
And echoed with your crying
Your living paradox.

242   Annunciation, Visitation

Elizabeth and Zechariah
Walk into the house of fire
Where the angels wreathe the spire
And one old man alone
In the temple finds desire
Like a dog his bone.

Gabriel, Elizabeth
Is shaken with your burning breath,
Meanwhile in humble Nazareth
The virgin in the house
Attends upon a birth and death
And trembles like a mouse.

Look at her, unwind your scroll,
Let the heavenly message roll
Like thunder through her pale white soul
As ghostly as her room,
Trample like an angry bull
About her seedless womb.

Hail Elizabeth! Our meeting
Sees our children leap in greeting,
Hear their fists and foreheads beating
Hard against the wall,
While the lambs in flocks are bleating,
Come one, come two, come all.

Come one, come two, come all to feast,
Come the lesser and the least,
Come to us out of the East,
While one old man alone
Becomes as dumb as any beast
And still as any stone.

NOTES

NOTE ON THE NOTES

Some of these notes provide information. They are meant to explain difficult words and what may be obscure references, in the belief that the better a poem is understood, the more interesting and enjoyable it becomes, and ordinary gumption will stretch only so far. To take an extreme case, almost no unassisted reader could hope to get more than a kind of shimmer out of poem **39**, whereas to lay it aside would be a loss. To take a more typical case, the word *ball* in **27** is only one word, but not knowing what sort of ball is meant muddies the close of that lucid poem.

My annotations ignore merely uncommon or obsolete words and expressions that readers can look up for themselves in a good standard dictionary like *The Concise Oxford Dictionary*, a policy which might encourage that healthy habit and certainly saves space. But I try to explain very rare words, and also uncommon or obsolete usages of familiar words that might mislead the unwary, like *gentle* in **3**. In the same spirit of economy I pass over references that can be traced in standard encyclopedias and the like. Thus, again in **3**, I indicate that *Isaphill* is an old form of Hypsipyle and nothing more. I will just say here that she was a mythical princess of Lemnos who became the subject of a play by Euripides known to us only from fragments. I suspect that she herself was known to Skelton only by name, a name which rhymes handily. *Cassander* I thought it safe to leave unglossed.

Other notes, not all of them easy to separate from the first kind, raise historical, biographical and even critical points, and others again bring in matters of personal reminiscence and reaction that may not be out of place in an anthology such as this. Anyway, it seemed a good chance to get them into print.

Two cautions. It should not be thought that the more I (or anyone else) may find to say about a poem or a poet, the better or more interesting the poem or poems will be. And read the poem before looking at the notes on it, not the other way round.

313

The word or short phrase between the number and the author's name, as in **7**. Son (Ralegh) and **9**. Lacking my love (Spenser), is intended not to be clever or anything but just to remind readers what poem it is and save them from having to turn back to the text.

NOTES

1. Lyarde (Lydgate). *more*: any more, any longer.

2. Adam (Anon). *four thousand winter*: God was traditionally supposed to have created the world (and Adam with it) about the year 4000 BC.

3. Margaret (Skelton). *gentle*: of excellent breed or spirit. A falcon-gentle was also the female of the peregrine falcon, a species highly thought of for hawking. *of the tower*: capable of lofty flight. *Isaphill*: Hypsipyle.

4. Women (Heath). Nobody has been able to find Heath's Christian name. A look at the poem suggests that he might have preferred not to have it known.

5. Islington (Anon). Today we would use the less formally correct expression, 'the bailiff of Islington's daughter'.

bailiff: then the representative of the Crown in a village or district. *puggish*: a pug was many things, including a prostitute and a bargeman. A puggard was a thief. Whatever the exact kind of attire this respectable girl put on, it was clearly below her station.

7. Son (Ralegh). Probably his elder son, also Walter, born 1593, killed 1618 by Spaniards in a skirmish in South America, where he had gone on an expedition led by his father. The latter was himself executed later in the same year, not by the hangman but by the headsman.

8. Walsingham (Ralegh). The second speaker had been on a pilgrimage to Walsingham Abbey in Norfolk, once visited by pilgrims from all over Europe.

9. Lacking my love (Spenser). *herself*: the unmodernised text reads 'her self' in both cases. As was customary at his time, Spenser made two words of what we now customarily write as one. We are the losers in this case, for by writing 'her self' he was able to suggest both our word 'herself' and the quite different expression 'her self'. Both times in this poem, especially the first time, he clearly very much means 'her self' as well as 'herself'.

10. Myra (Brooke). This is the only poem in this book written by a Chancellor of the Exchequer (appointed 1614). The site of the poet's house is commemorated by Greville Street and Brooke Street in Holborn. He appears to have invented the name Myra.

chimneys: glossed by Sir Arthur Quiller-Couch as '*cheminées*, chimney-screens of tapestry-work', which makes excellent sense but I cannot find supported anywhere else in French or English. *washing the water with her beauty's white*, i.e. whiteness. I have preferred Quiller-Couch's reading to other possibilities, such as

Washing the water with her beauties white,

i.e. her white beauties,

and

Washing the water, with her beauties, white,

i.e. perfectly transparent. Brooke must have written this stunning hyperbole as

Washing the water with her beautys white

and got all three meanings in one.

11. Elegy (Tichborne). The poet wrote this three days before his execution by the hangman in 1586 as a Catholic conspirator against Queen Elizabeth I. It was first published in the same year in an anthology called, without conscious irony, *Verses of Praise and Joy*. Tichborne is not known to have written anything else.

12. Chopcherry (Peele). This song from the play *The Old Wives' Tale* surprised the young Amis by showing that proper poetry could be about *that* too.

14. Phillida (Anon). The central figure's touches of the homespun and the self-mocking separate him from untold thousands of flouted lovers.

whig: a drink made of whey, sometimes fermented and flavoured with herbs.

15. Agincourt (Drayton). This historical poem commemorates an event that took place a century and a half before Drayton was born.

16. Laura (Campion). First came out in a pamphlet that was part of a long-forgotten controversy. Campion was trying to prove that rhyme was unnecessary, indeed vulgar, in English poetry. All he did prove was that one first-rate unrhymed lyric could be written in the language, but that was much more than any of the other disputants achieved.

concent: harmony. *still*: constantly, always, the usual sense of the word at this period, as again in **24**.

17. Sweet and kind (Ford). There was once a popular drawing-room ballad using the first, second and last verses of this poem. I think the unbowdlerised version is better.

free: free and easy, unselfconscious. *sphere*: station in the heavens.

18. Kind and true (Townshend). *free*: see note on **17**. *confide*: feel safe.

19. Life (King). *to night*: also meaning 'tonight'. See note on *herself* in **9**.

23. Love (Herbert). We are to imagine Love (= Christ, God) as an innkeeper greeting and receiving the poet (= the Christian soul) as a weary traveller. 'Welcome!' was at this time the customary first word of a real innkeeper to a guest and 'What do you lack?' is not far off the modern 'What can I get you?' The final lines allude to Holy Communion.

ʃʃ Suckling is usually remembered as an elegantly lyrical Cavalier poet (and the inventor of the game of cribbage). Some of his work, however, cuts a little deeper, like these two rather cryptic poems, which show us a womaniser sadly aware of the cruel transience of sexual attraction.

24. Prithee (Suckling). *gentle boy*: Cupid. *say grace*: i.e. after the meal.

25. Fruition (Suckling). *chameleon*: it was generally believed that chameleons fed on air. Hamlet thought so, or so he said.

26. Resolved soul (Marvell). *resolved*: determined, resolute (in the pursuit of virtue). *created*: i.e. non-spiritual. *bait*: halt for refreshment. *crystal*: mirror. *chordage*: a famous Metaphysical pun. It is worth remembering that in fact cords are easier to break than chains; and noticing that music is the only temptation that the Soul needs four lines to demolish.

centre: i.e. the Earth, as the supposed centre of the universe.

27. Mistress (Marvell). *coy*: not just shy or modest in manner, but not responding to amorous advances. *mistress*: woman being courted, not a mistress in the modern sense. (This one was probably an imaginary figure rather than a real girl in

Marvell's life.) *Humber*: Marvell grew up in Hull and was elected its MP in 1659. *slow-chapped*: slowly moving his chaps or chops, slowly chewing. *ball*: Marvell must have been thinking of a cannon-ball. See F. W. Bateson, *English Poetry: a critical introduction* (1950, p. 9). (But treat his general arguments with reserve.)

28. Garden (Marvell). I love the constant play of classical-mythological-philosophical-religious reference here (as much as I understand of it, that is), though things do get a little fine-spun now and again. For instance, the poet alludes to the story in which Apollo amorously pursued Daphne, a river-god's daughter, who eluded him by being changed into a laurel or bay-tree. He made the best of the situation by adopting the laurel as his emblem and awarding crowns of it (the 'bays' of line 2) to distinguished poets. Marvell pretends that Apollo was only ever interested in Daphne as a potential source of laurel and that Pan similarly set things up with Syrinx in order to come by his pipes. This kind of donnish waggery goes poorly with most of the other parts of the poem and is pretty thin stuff anyway.

29. Ancient lover (Rochester). I know of no other piece of literature which unites tenderness with obscenity (or whatever it is to be called) as Rochester does here.

30. Mankind (Rochester). This is one of the first and greatest of all Leftie poems. It exists in two versions, of which this is the shorter; the longer includes a further passage which is evidently a 'Postscript' as it is sometimes headed, an answer to possible criticisms of the original. The postscript is not nearly as angry or as good as the original, but I give its last ten lines here for interest's sake:

> But a meek humble man of modest sense,
> Who, preaching peace, does practise continence,
> Whose pious life's a proof he does believe
> Mysterious truths which no man can conceive;
> If upon earth there dwell such godlike men
> I'll here recant my paradox to them,
> Adore those shrines of virtue, homage pay,
> And, with the rabble world, their laws obey.

If such there are, yet grant me this at least,
Man differs more from man than man from beast.

fenny bogs: Rochester was an Oxford man, or boy; he went up to Wadham at the then not ridiculously early age of twelve. This reference must be a sneer at contemporary Cambridge philosophy. *makes him try*: it seems it must be reason that makes him try, but the sentence is getting out of hand. *wretch*: in those days a shameful as well as an abject thing to be.

32. Hye nonny (Anon). The source of this is John Aubrey's *Brief Lives*, and the life in question is that of one John Overall, Dean of St Paul's, later Bishop of Norwich, on whose wife's amatory career the poem is evidently founded. Auden printed three verses in *The Oxford Book of Light Verse* of 1938 without understanding the harmless obscenity of the refrain.

for why: because.

33. Daphne (Swift). *squares*: conventions, rules.

34. Unfortunate lady (Pope). Pope ingeniously gives the impression that the background to this poem, the story of a lady who killed herself for love, was a well-known real case with which he had had something to do. But he made it all up, creating what is in effect a highly compressed and emotional short story in verse.

a Roman's part: by committing suicide. *the ball*: the globe, the Earth. Pope has taken stick for dragging in the Earth's shape to get a rhyme, but he must have been alluding to the emblematic ball carried by figures personifying Justice.

35. Molly (Farewell). I came across this poem and this poet for the first time in 1984, in Roger Lonsdale's splendid selection, *The New Oxford Book of Eighteenth-Century Verse*. The name Farewell is almost certainly a pseudonym, that of an Englishman domiciled, for whatever reason, in France.

36. Prologue (Johnson). I cannot discover who wrote *A Word to the Wise*, but the poem says everything necessary about him and it.

37. Spring (Gray). Until its last verse, this seems like a well-written variation on a quite sufficiently familiar theme of eighteenth-century and earlier poetry, the trivial and transitory nature of worldly concerns like power and pleasure. But then, instead of the expected walkover for the contemplative life, the conclusion is that the gadabouts have the best of the game and the sober moralist is a miserable fuddy-duddy. From this exhilarating vantage-point the passage where the Muse and the poet sit companionably down to pass judgement (at ease reclined in rustic state, and in brackets too) reads like an unkind parody, and even the graceful opening lines seem to carry an anticipatory snigger. Altogether, this is exactly the poem that might have been written by a clever fellow who had heard the 'Elegy Written in a Country Churchyard' praised just once too often, instead of by the young man of twenty-five who soon enough was going to be the author of that very 'Elegy'. There can be few other cases of a poet sawing off with such dedication the branch he was yet to occupy.

38. Elegy (Gray). Whatever doubts it may stir up (and see note to **37**) the 'Elegy' remains a great poem, and incidentally a great Rightie poem; no work of literature ever argued more persuasively that the poor and ignorant are better off as they are. It is also a good poem, good enough to produce in me the illusion that it was written specially for me. And, into the bargain, a favourite-poem anthology in 1985 showed it to be the favourite poem of Margaret Thatcher, James Callaghan and Philip Larkin.

Country Churchyard: but which one? Peter Watson-Smyth writes:

'The myth of Stoke Poges churchyard as the scene of the Elegy arose mainly because Gray, for personal reasons not understood by his contemporaries, chose never to reveal when, where or why he had written his masterpiece.

'Because, on several superficial counts, Stoke Poges seemed the likeliest spot, the myth took hold and flourished until comparatively recent scholars pointed out, inter alia, that its churchyard

    a) is not on high ground as implied in the opening stanzas,

    b) had no elm trees, and

    c) had a church tower which could never have been *yonder* to the meticulously observant and precise Gray.

'It is largely due to that faculty, dinned into him by his uncle/tutor at Eton, that we can now not only positively identify the churchyard of nearby St Peter's, Burnham as the true birthplace of the poem, but even pinpoint the time of birth as just after 8.0 p.m. on Sunday, 18 August 1737, a few months before the poet's twenty-first birthday. It was then that the first four descriptive stanzas were almost certainly written.

'Gray's inspiration was twofold. First, his openly confessed (22 August) envy of the elegy *in English* which his friend Richard West had just composed, Gray having until then only produced completed poems in Latin. Second, the contrast between the Westminster Abbey funeral service of his best friend's mother, Lady Walpole (24 August), and that of his uncle/tutor seven years earlier at humble St Peter's, where he had just attended Evensong.'

Some scholars have rejected Watson-Smyth's conclusions without overthrowing his arguments. He gives a much fuller account of the matter in the *Spectator* of 31 July 1971, to mark the bicentenary of Gray's death.

For thee, who mindful of the unhonoured dead etc.: hereabouts there is a difficulty. In *thee* the poet must be addressing himself, and the general sense must run, 'If a sympathetic visitor to the village should ask what happened to the man who wrote the foregoing lines, some hoary-headed swain might describe how the villagers used to see him walking or mooning about the place, always alone, until the day he died and was duly buried in the churchyard.' But nothing like that ever happened to Gray, who went to Eton and Peterhouse and became a famous poet. What then is intended?

There is other evidence that at some point between the line *With incense kindled at the Muse's flame* and the appearance of the hoary-headed swain Gray was visited by a new idea, or decided to join something on, rather than continuing with the poem he had all along set out to write. The new idea or the something-else, it seems, was a picture of himself or a version of himself as he would have been if he had been a villager, of *humble birth* and *to fortune unknown*, instead of the child of a prosperous middle-class London household. The important

321

difference between villager-Gray and historical-Gray, as shown here, is that villager-Gray would have been illiterate. As such he could never have become a poet of any recognisable sort; instead, a poor half-crazed fellow plagued by impulses he could make nothing of, *muttering his wayward fancies* to nobody but himself, *drooping, woeful, wan* and perishing out of hopelessness while still a youth, a Gray mute and inglorious for a very practical reason.

It would no doubt have been difficult for the poet to have explained the transition from his comparatively straightforward account of the significance of humble village life to his rather fanciful vision of himself as he might have been. He correctly calculated that the tremendous momentum and authority of his four-line stanza would overpower any uncertainties or questionings on the part of the reader.

This reading affects the rhythm of the line *Approach and read (for thou canst read) the lay*. When, at a tender age, I first encountered it, I thought that *for thou canst read* was just a conventional rustic compliment o a gentlemanly stranger, and as such would carry a roughly equal stress on *thou* and *canst*, unsatisfactorily counter to the very strongly regular iambic run of the verse. (No doubt I would not then have put the matter to myself quite like that.) The notion of the illiterate villager-Gray restores the flow. '*Approach and read*,' says the hoary-headed swain, '*for* thou *canst read*' – which is more than *he*, the subject of the epitaph, could do.

I can find no indication in the poem (or anywhere else) that Gray ever came near applying his hierarchical view of society to himself and wondering whether he might not have been better off, or at least a worthier citizen, as an illiterate solitary among all the village-Hampdens and guiltless Cromwells.

Reprinting here such a well-known poem may seem more justified if I also reprint what is less well known: the extra verses Gray sketched during composition and eventually either cut out altogether or adapted into a shorter form in the poem as he published it, as follows:

After *With incense kindled at the Muse's flame*:

> The thoughtless world to majesty may bow,
> Exalt the brave, and idolise success,
> But more to innocence their safety owe
> Than power and genius e'er conspired to bless.
>
> And thou, who mindful of the unhonoured dead,
> Dost in these notes their artless tale relate,
> By Night and lonely Contemplation led
> To linger in the gloomy walks of fate –
>
> Hark how the sacred Calm that broods around
> Bids every fierce tumultuous passion cease,
> In still small accents whispering from the ground
> A grateful earnest of eternal peace.
>
> No more with Reason and thyself at strife
> Give anxious cares and endless wishes room,
> But through the cool sequestered vale of life
> Pursue the silent tenor of thy doom.

After *Some kindred spirit shall inquire thy fate*:

> If chance that e'er some pensive spirit more,
> By sympathetic musings here delayed,
> With vain though kind inquiry shall explore
> Thy once-loved haunt, this long-deserted shade.

After *To meet the sun upon the upland lawn*:

> Him have we seen the greenwood side along,
> While o'er the heath we hied, our labours done,
> Oft as the woodlark piped her farewell song,
> With wistful eyes pursue the setting sun.

After *Graved on the stone beneath yon aged thorn*:

> There scattered oft, the earliest of the year,
> By hands unseen, are showers of violets found;
> The redbreast loves to build and warble there,
> And little footsteps lightly print the ground.

39. Lament for Flodden (Elliot). This very different kind of elegy must have great power to reach someone like myself who has not a drop of Scottish blood and has never lived in Scotland. Jean Elliot's poem, written about 1763, is the most popular version of an older lament for the Scottish dead at the battle of Flodden in 1513. (Flodden is on the English side of the border, and the Scots were invading England at the time, a fact their descendants often forget.)

Some readers may find the various Scottish words a nuisance or even quaintly pretty, others neither.

ilka: every. *loaning*: milking-ground. *flowers of the forest*: in the first place bluebells, though not, as it happens, what most of the world means by bluebells: a bluebell to a Scotsman is a harebell to others. Anyway, in the second place the phrase is a synonym, once universal among Scots, for Scottish warriors, and there is an elegiac pipe tune named for them. They were often known as 'blue bonnets' from their traditional headgear, blue being the national colour, as on the flag, and a bonnet in this context being not a floppy affair tied under the chin but a round flat brimless cap. (I am afraid this has turned into the sort of note that gets notes a bad name.) *wede*: weeded, uprooted. *boughts*: milking-pens. *scorning*: boasting. *dowie*: dismal. *daffing*: frolicking. *leglen*: milk-pail. *har'st*: harvest. *bandsters*: binders of sheaves. *lyart*: silver-haired. *fleeching*: coaxing. *bogle*: a bogle is a 'bogey' or scarecrow, so presumably this was some elementary jumping-out-and-shouting-bo! game.

41. Auguries (Blake). As mentioned in the Introduction I have retained Blake's individual capitalisation and other details.

43. Anderson (Burns). *jo*: beloved. *brent*: smooth, unwrinkled. *pow*: head. *canty*: jolly.

45. Blenheim (Southey). At Blenheim in Bavaria in 1704, English forces under the Duke of Marlborough and Austrians under Prince Eugene defeated French and Bavarians in a decisive battle of the War of the Spanish Succession. The battle gave its name to the mansion and estate in Oxfordshire awarded to Marlborough for his services in the war. 'What good came of it at last' was the curbing of French aggression for a generation or so, though that might not have seemed good enough to an Englishman of Southey's time, with Napoleon on the rampage. But it was certainly a famous enough victory to suit his forceful anti-war poem.

46. Ullin (Campbell). *water-wraith*: spirit of the waters.

47. Baltic (Campbell). Here Campbell celebrates Nelson's victory at Copenhagen in 1801. It was the battle at which he put his telescope to his blind eye in order to disregard a signal to withdraw.

Riou: a British captain mentioned in Nelson's dispatches.

48. Hohenlinden (Campbell). At Hohenlinden in (West) Germany in 1800 a French army heavily defeated the Austrians. No British were present. Campbell had some idea of what battles were like, not as a participant, true, but as an eye-witness.

50. Greenland (Heber). Heber was the Anglican bishop of Calcutta until his early death. (His entry in *The Oxford Companion to English Literature* gives him the dates of his half-brother Richard Heber.) The sentiments expressed in this hymn may read strangely today, but nobody could have expressed them better.

52. Newark (Peacock). The ruins of Newark Priory, as it is more usually known, still stand near Woking in Surrey.

53. Corunna (Wolfe). At the battle of Corunna (La Coruña) in northern Spain in 1808, Sir John Moore's command successfully withdrew by sea in the face of a numerically superior French force. Wolfe read a magazine account of it and years later wrote his poem at a sitting in the rooms of a friend at Trinity College, Dublin.

sullenly: when I first read it as a schoolboy I thought this word was used differently from all the other words in the poem.

54. Household graves (Hemans). While there were still such things as famous lines of English poetry Mrs Hemans was remembered for 'The boy stood on the burning deck,' though a million knew the line for every one who knew her name (or the next three lines). The child of a Liverpool merchant, she married an army officer and became a very widely-read poetess, especially in America. With my classmates I once had to turn this poem into Latin verses, and some of us were surprised to find how readily it took to being translated into those strict measures.

55. Abide (Lyte). Hymns are obviously public poems but, from 'All people that on Earth do dwell' onwards, even the most public usually have in them some communication from the writer to God. There is so much of the latter throughout 'Abide with Me' that it is hard to believe it ever became material for congregations to sing, even in the usual cut version (I give all of it here). It is sometimes thought of as characteristically Victorian, but its author's dates show it is a little early for that.

   condescending: behaving as far as possible like an equal.

56. Melancholy (Keats). *Psyche*: Psyche, the soul, was once represented as a butterfly.

59. Ruth (Hood). *she stood breast high amid the corn*: Hood is thinking of the Ruth in Keats, who 'stood in tears amid the alien corn', rather than the Ruth in the Old Testament, who as a mere gleaner of the corn had no chance of standing breast-high amid it.

60. Winter's Night (Barnes). Barnes was a schoolmaster, grammarian and parson who wrote most of his poems in an attempted representation of Dorset dialect. Those who can read them often prefer them to his English poems.

61. Hiawatha (Longfellow). *The Song of Hiawatha* was immensely popular in its own day in all English-speaking countries. Though often ridiculed, it is a decent and respectful attempt, more successful than is nowadays conceded, at an American epic, concerned with the doings of legendary North American Indians. This excerpt – admitted under my rules because it is largely complete in itself – is a song addressed to the maiden Onaway at Prince Hiawatha's wedding-feast.

62. Slave (Longfellow). *Caffre*: Kaffir, here = native African.

63. Mariana (Tennyson). Tennyson said, 'The *moated grange* was no particular grange, but one that rose to the music of Shakespeare's words.'

65. O maid (Tennyson). *silver horns*: snowy peaks. *azure pillars*: smoke from cottage fires.

66. Tithonus (Tennyson). Tithonus, a prince of Troy, was loved by Eos, or Aurora, the dawn-goddess, who was empowered to grant him one wish. He thoughtlessly chose eternal life, not eternal youth, with the results Tennyson alludes to. The setting of the poem is some undefined region of the skies.

goal of ordinance: Tennyson supplied the meaning 'appointed limit'. *that strange song*: Apollo created the city of Ilion (Troy) by the power of his song.

67. Milton (Tennyson). *Alcaics*: as his contemporary readers were qualified to notice, this poem of Tennyson's keeps all the strict rules of the Greek/Latin metre as well as making prosodic sense in English.

68. Confessional (Browning). I first came across this poem in 1941 when the Oxford University Ballet Club staged a ballet called *Confessional*, presented by Cyril Frankel, danced by Sally Gilmour and Walter Gore, choreography W. Gore. The music, played on gramophone records, was taken from Sibelius's incidental music to *Pelléas et Mélisande* and Browning's poem was read off-stage by Meric Dobson. The combination bowled me over and I still think it was a brilliant use of small resources.

stapled: the block had an iron collar driven into it. Beltran was not hanged but garrotted, i.e. ceremonially strangled, the usual Spanish method of capital punishment.

69. Galuppi (Browning). Baldassare (*sic*) Galuppi was an eighteenth-century comic-opera composer and keyboard-player in Venice (though he made an extended visit to England). A toccata or 'touch-piece' shows off the performer's technique, but as we see here it can perhaps do more than that. Some will think the musical technicalities a little hastily applied. One critic wrote that 'mentioning diminished sixths in this offhand way is rather like casually speaking of breakfasting off roc's egg as a matter of everyday occurrence.' This has been contested.

when the kissing had to stop: this group of words was taken as the title of a novel by Constantine FitzGibbon in 1960 and has since become a catchphrase. I mention this because ignorant modern readers are perpetually coming across something an author invented and thinking he has fallen back on a cliché, as when a dunce recently accused Graham Greene of having resorted to a banality by calling a film/book *The Third Man*. Greene *originated* the expression. Compare *the many-splendoured thing* in **90**.

70. Gustibus (Browning). These days one must just say flatly that the title is half a Latin tag of which the whole means 'There is no arguing about tastes.' For Browning it was extravagantly generous to devote thirteen whole lines to the other fellow's taste as against a mere thirty-three to his own.

the liver-wing: a nineteenth-century colloquialism for the right arm. 'The right wing of a fowl, etc.,' says the *OED*, '. . . when dressed for cooking, has the liver tucked under it.' *his Bourbon arm*: same arm. The king in question, Ferdinand II of the Two Sicilies, was a member of the royal house of Bourbon. This and the next line are not among Browning's most rewarding. *Calais*: still pronounced 'Callis' then.

71. Kingdom (Anon). This poem, if that is what it is, exists in several versions. My text, first printed 1844 in a collection of nursery rhymes, is taken from Auden's *Oxford Book of Light Verse*.

72. Greenhorn (Kingsley). *Dan Horace*: this is Kingsley's reproduction-medieval way of referring to the Roman poet, who no doubt does say something of the sort somewhere. *saint*: must be wrong, the result of the printer's eye having fallen on the word five lines later. What should it be? Throne? Club? Cross?

73. North-easter (Kingsley). *zephyr*: soft, mild, gentle wind or breeze, like the ones disparaged later in the poem. *Chime*: refers to the concerted barking of hounds when they are all sure of the scent or sight of a fox. Surtees uses the word in this sense.

74. Fishers (Kingsley). *the harbour bar be moaning*: a phrase nobody I know of has even tried to explain in print. The late Philip Hope-Wallace told me that, in the common estuary of the rivers Taw and Torridge in Barnstaple (or Bideford) Bay, the joining of their waters and the incoming sea can between them, if conditions are just right, produce a loud moaning sound above the sand-bar at the mouth of the inlet. Kingsley had lived in that part of north Devon and was no doubt referring to a local superstition. 'And may there be no moaning at the bar' in Tennyson's 'Crossing the Bar' seems to be merely an uncomprehending echo of Kingsley's line.

75. Merman (Arnold). Arnold wrote this in his twenties after (not necessarily straight after) reading an English summary of a Danish ballad, 'Agnes and the Merman', in a London paper. If you like Arnold's poem you might think it does some damage to the widely held view that proper poetry can only come out of personal experience, emotional involvement, etc. Of course it can always be argued that Arnold must have had that sort of experience already without realising it until reading the summary brought it to his mind, but that would be rather shifty, I think. 53 raises the same point on a different level.

76. Rugby (Arnold). When Arnold's father, Dr Thomas Arnold, Headmaster of Rugby School 1828–1842, died in the latter year at the age of forty-seven, Matthew was nineteen. He began the poem, as he says in it, fifteen years later. It is hard for us today not to feel from time to time, when words like *arosest* or *beckonedst* come along, that the forms of the second person plural would have been more natural. But to Arnold's readers in the 1850s, in that context, they might very well have seemed intolerably familiar and indecorous. If faced with the counter-argument that a poet should make a point of not catering to his readers' expectations, one could answer in turn that he should not bother with such trivial concerns when writing about something as important as his father's life and death.

77. Heraclitus (Cory). Cory is remembered today only as the author of the Eton Boating Song and this poem. The latter is a translation of an epigram of Callimachus, a Greek poet of the third century BC. The translation uses more than twice as many words as the original, not only because of the structures of the respective languages but also because Cory tends to say twice (*they told me . . . they told me*, etc.) what Callimachus says once. This is not to say that Cory's version is somehow enervated or puffed up. What is remarkable is how different it is from the Callimachus while remaining a very close translation, in the sense that the one introduces no ideas that are not in the other.

thy nightingales: said to be the title of the poems left by Heraclitus.

78. Summer (Rossetti). Written in mid-January in London.

82. Elwy (Hopkins). The first bad poet in our language, as opposed to many who are merely no good, is needless to say an American, E. A. Poe (1809–1849). His first cisatlantic counterpart, or perhaps the poet who, while very talented, fully epitomises a particular poetic fallacy, is Hopkins. For me, he most nearly escaped from it in this poem, though the eighth line and the last two are touched with his obsessive affectation of singularity.

83. Parted (Meynell). Like many Victorian poets, Alice Meynell was constantly being very nearly very good without quite getting there. Here I think she pulls it off, even if there may be a slight stumble at the end.

84. Margaritae Sorori (Henley). Title: To (my) sister Margaret, In Memoriam. Henley's sister of that name died in 1886.

my task accomplished and the long day done: Henley, who was ill from childhood on, is hoping or praying for a full life-span in which to complete his work. He wrote this poem when he was twenty-seven and died at the age of fifty-four.

87. Requiem (Stevenson). I give here, rather than in the text, Housman's poem 'R.L.S.':

> Home is the sailor, home from sea:
>   Her far-borne canvas furled
> The ship pours shining on the quay
>   The plunder of the world.
>
> Home is the hunter from the hill:
>   Fast in the boundless snare
> All flesh lies taken at his will
>   And every fowl of air.
>
> 'Tis evening on the moorland free,
>   The starlit wave is still:
> Home is the sailor from the sea,
>   The hunter from the hill.

A comparison with Stevenson's poem suggests that small differences sometimes make a lot of difference, and that it is possible to say more in an indirect way than directly.

88. Harlot (Wilde). I stir uncomfortably at those 'Treues Liebes Herz', but the final image never fades.

89. Stag (Davidson). For years I read this as a passionate attack on one particular form of selfish behaviour, made the more effective by fully celebrating the attraction of that behaviour. Then I thought of it as an attack on all selfishness and irresponsibility, one that said, This is the kind of terrible, pitiful thing you do when you enjoy yourself regardless of others, and it serves you right when, as often happens, you don't even get what you were after. Now I see in it not so much indignation as sorrowful acceptance of human blundering. A less 'Victorian' poem it would be hard to imagine.

It is remarkable that Davidson himself died by drowning in circumstances that pointed to suicide.

harboured: traced to his lair. *feathered*: set the hounds on (the trail). *Brow, bay and tray*: the three antlers or branches of a stag's horn (reading upwards). *brocket*: immature stag. *beamed*: having an antler of the fourth year. *tined*: with a full set of antlers. *tufted*: beat, dislodged by beating. The presence and the accuracy of these technical terms are important, much more so than they would be in a straightforward poem on the subject, in establishing the narrator's credentials as a proper stag-hunting man.

90. Kingdom (Thompson). *the many-splendoured thing*: Thompson's own phrase. Compare *when the kissing had to stop* in **69**.

∫∫The man who taught me most about English literature, the Rev. C. J. Ellingham of the City of London School, surprised me exceedingly at one stage by announcing that Housman was his favourite poet – this from a very unequivocal Christian. That was when I finally learnt that you need not agree with a poem to value it or be moved by it. Later I came to share Mr Ellingham's preference, which makes selection difficult.

Of course I think it ungrateful and wrong that Housman should never have been conventionally admitted as a great

English poet, one of the greatest since Arnold, but not so surprising when you consider some of the people who have been so admitted. What are the objections to him? His homosexuality cannot possibly be one. He lacks bulk: as if Tennyson would be less great or not great at all without most of his long poems; Browning too, and what about Gray? His themes are restricted: I started to make a list of them until it occurred to me that the same objection would exclude from the canon Milton, Herbert, Pope, Wordsworth, Keats . . . He turns his back on the modern world: next question. He made no technical innovations: get out of my sight. He archaises and neologises: so does Hopkins, so does Hardy, much more, and nobody turns a hair. He puts in classical stuff: yes, and gets it right, unlike at least two 'great' contemporaries of his.

Two objections to Housman that are more to the point, though they reflect no more credit on the objectors, are that he was not only a don but a hopelessly donnish don, easily seen as nothing more than the bitter, dried-up neurotic of Auden's travesty (effective poem as it may be), and that once the paper-thin shield over his homosexuality is penetrated, there is nothing in his verse to analyse or drag to light; one exception ('Hell Gate') is not enough. He cannot be made likable or interesting or even someone you feel you can understand or see all the way round. And, long before television, that sort of thing started to count for much more than what a man actually wrote.

91. 1887 (Housman). The year is that of Queen Victoria's Golden Jubilee.

themselves they could not save: an amazingly blasphemous reminiscence of Matthew 27.42: 'He [Jesus] saved others; himself he cannot save' (also Mark 15.31). It renders rather suspect the notions of God saving the Queen and of friends who shared the work with God. In fact it subverts the whole image of the poem as a straightforward hymn of thanksgiving. *the Fifty-Third*: the infantry regiments of the army bore only numbers until the year 1881, when they were given names corresponding to the parts of the kingdom in which they were recruited. So the 53rd Regiment of Foot became the 1st Battalion of the Shropshire Light Infantry (later King's SLI). So Housman's choice of number was not arbitrary.

92. Bredon (Housman). Pronounced Breedon, notes Housman.

93. Daffodil (Housman). What this achieves by saying nothing about its subject can be measured by a comparison with Robert Herrick's poem 'To Daffodils', which is very well in its way:

> Fair daffodils, we weep to see
> You haste away so soon:
> As yet the early-rising sun
> Has not attained his noon.
>   Stay, stay,
> Until the hasting day
>   Has run
> But to the evensong;
> And, having prayed together, we
> Will go with you along.
>
> We have short time to stay as you,
> We have as short a spring;
> As quick a growth to meet decay
> As you, or anything.
>   We die
> As your hours do, and dry
>   Away
> Like to the summer's rain,
> Or as the pearls of morning's dew,
> Ne'er to be found again.

94. Shire (Housman). *lady-smocks*: the lady-smock or lady's-smock is indeed in flower in May and is common in fields.

95. Be still (Housman). *quarry*: I can find no other meaning for this word than those in any dictionary, though clearly an image of the womb is intended here.

96. Terence (Housman). Here I think Housman wrote too much for once. He would have done better to stop after *In the dark and cloudy day*.

such tunes as killed the cow: to play or sing the tune the old cow died of is to offer advice instead of help or relief, from an old rhyme about a farmer who, when his cow had no fodder, sang her a song telling her to be reasonable.

97. Epigraph to *Last Poems* (Housman). Housman was fond of making his tune contradict his words but he never went further than here. The original, from Théodore de Banville, is glum all through. Actually.

99. Oracles (Housman). I suppose part of my immediate feeling of intimacy with this poem came from knowing about oracles and Mount Dodona and Delphi and the events alluded to in the last verse without having to have them explained to me. But I was not put off, attracted rather, by what were obscurities to me at first sight, not that even now they are all quite clear.

oakenshaws: Housman's own coinage, I think. One of the ways you got answers to your questions to the gods of Dodona was by interpreting the sounds made by the rustling of the wind through an old oak-tree. *cauldrons*: cooking-pots hung from the tree were also supposed to make interpretable noises with the wind in them. *the midland navel-stone*: the temple of Apollo at Delphi had a conical stone in it that was thought to mark the mid-point or navel of the earth, and presumably the wind made noises round that too. *The King*, etc.: the article on the battle of Thermopylae in any classical dictionary will illuminate the last verse for the ignorant. It might not say that, to a Greek, the King with initial capital but no other identification was always the king of Persia, prior knowledge of which I gloried in on my first reading of the poem. But any account of the resistance of 300 Spartans to some hundreds of thousands of attacking Persian troops will make it clear that the hair-combing habits of the former betokened no softness.

100. Enchantress (Housman). I named this as my favourite poem in an anthology of 1985 and would stick to that, though **89** may overtake it one day. Not that I am particularly keen on nature or often think of it.

traveller's joy: or old man's beard or wild clematis, noticeable for its seeds in autumn.

334

101. Knell (Housman). The last poem in *Last Poems*, the second and last volume of poems published in Housman's lifetime (when he still had fourteen years to live). After half a century of (intermittent) reflection I am still not sure what the title means.

I never thought that Housman had ever done anything like any of the things he describes in this poem, nor that he wished he had, nor that he should have done if he was going to write in such a strain.

upshot: an upshot is or was a final shot, so this must be the final beam.

102. Diffugere (Housman). The title is the first two words of the Latin poem and means 'the snows have dispersed' (*diffu-gio*, I flee in all directions). Housman's poem is not such a close translation as Cory's (**77**).

104. Thieves (Newbolt). The author is best known for patriotic poems like 'Drake's Drum' and 'Vitaï Lampada' ('Play up! play up! and play the game!') and when King George V broadcast to the nation, the first of our monarchs to do so, Newbolt wrote his script. This poem is among other things what might be expected of such a man, but the others I have reprinted are not.

105. Ireland (Newbolt). Reflects the fact that Newbolt was a Liberal in politics and a passionate believer in Home Rule for Ireland.

106. Viking (Newbolt). Anybody who thinks that writing about physical sex cannot be genuine or natural unless it is 'explicit' should consider this poem. The metaphor conveys much more – more tenderness and respect, for instance – than any imaginable direct statement could have done.

107. Nightjar (Newbolt). Written in his sixties, this shows Newbolt trying to develop a new, contemplative manner.

ſſ Kipling's confinement to the status of a minor poet is easier to account for than Housman's. The two oldest charges against Kipling still stand. First, he was inescapably the poet of Empire, and although the Empire, like the Third Reich, may have gone, no *Guardian* reader can ever quite forgive its most eloquent apologist. Nothing has happened to wipe out what was said of him in 1900, that 'for progressive thought there has been no such dangerous influence in England for many years'. And second, he was popular, and although that popularity no longer extends to the barely literate, it has gone on extending to the non-literary, and so much the worse for it. If this seems far-fetched, consider some of the reaction to the popularity of John Betjeman, the only subsequent English poet to have reached a comparably wide audience. Kipling's poetry needs to be read without preconceptions, and in bulk.

108. 1914 (Kipling). First published in *The Times* on 1 September 1914 and written in response to the events of the previous month on the Western Front.

the Hun: i.e. the barbarian coming from the east, the enemy of civilisation, not a racialist synonym for 'the German' or 'the Prussian'. *the gate*: that of civilisation certainly, but more immediately that of Paris. The German advance led the French government to quit the capital for Bordeaux on 2 September.

109. Deever (Kipling). *Files-on-Parade*: the imagined collective voice of the men of the regiment.

110. Tommy (Kipling). *makin' mock o' uniforms that guard you while you sleep*: George Orwell wrote that 'it would be difficult to hit off the one-eyed pacifism of the English in fewer words' than these.

the Widow's Uniform: the Widow of Windsor was Queen Victoria.

111. Mandalay (Kipling). *east of Suez*: one of the many phrases of Kipling's that have entered the language.

113. Children (Kipling). Kipling's only son John was killed in France at the age of eighteen. The father never referred publicly to this loss.

114. Copybook (Kipling). Copybook headings are conventional principles like caution and commonplace rules of thumb like 'stick to the devil you know', etc. For Kipling the values of the market-place are uplift, vision, pacifism and other progressive ideals. The market-place is usually understood as the place of trade, of commercial as opposed to ideological value, but Kipling must have had in mind the forum, in Ancient Rome originally the market-place, which in time became the scene of public debate, of political discussion. What he calls the market-place here we would now call the forum. 'The gods of the Fabian Society' is nearer what Kipling meant. It was careless of him to use the phrase he did use, and that and the title of the poem, also far from clear, may have combined to prevent this from becoming one of his best-known and most-quoted pieces. The year of publication is 1919.

115. Mary Moore (Yeats). Most of Yeats's poems, however appealing, are nonsense of one sort or another, some of it ('Easter 1916') vicious nonsense. But Kinsella makes sense in a petulant way and has a great gift of the gab, though his version of the priests' book shows up as rather precious compared with the one in **2**.

116. Cynara (Dowson). The title, from an ode of Horace, means 'I am not the man I was under good (good old, kind old) Cynara's regime' and incidentally establishes the pronunciation of the lady's name as *Sinn*ara. Dowson was the definitive Nineties poet, still incurring the disapproval of one's elders as late as the 1930s for 'dissipation' and 'excess' (whatever they exactly were), a frequenter of loose women (or so it was implied), dead at thirty-three and altogether irresistible to conventionally reared schoolboys of the era. This poem has enough energy and technical proficiency to remain attractive after the whore-worship convention has come to seem thin.

118. Ha'nacker (Belloc). *Ha'nacker*: a local pronunciation of Halnaker in Belloc's beloved Sussex.

119. Gipsy (Hodgson). This is one of several poems in this anthology that I try not to feel ashamed of liking. It is true that we tend to be most responsive to the poems we meet in adolescence, and in my case, given the natural time-lag, those belonging to the period 1900–1920 would be likely to be over-represented among them. Nor would the more innovative, forward-looking, etc., examples be prominent. But I am grateful for the other side of that, for the chance of appreciating some poems I might otherwise have undervalued or missed. And, to come off the defensive, I was lucky it was the period 1900–1920 and not 1930–1950, or 1950–1970.

∫∫ Our ultimate liking for poems that were early favourites

often comes after a long interval of indifference or hostility, and I suppose I have been further away from the work of Walter de la Mare (before turning back) than from anybody else's. From time to time, I now think, he got something exactly right, which must signify unless you think it was not worth getting right. And little more needs to be said.

120. Mad Prince (de la Mare). In reading lines 8 and 16 I have to be careful not to let into my head the voice of Fats Waller, whose works I was starting to come across in those same boyhood years.

127. Rolling road (Chesterton). *Kensal Green*: i.e. Kensal Green Cemetery in Harrow Road, West London. Opened in 1832, it shelters the remains of among others Thomas Hood and Leigh Hunt.

128. Lepanto (Chesterton). This poem will never be tolerated, let alone enjoyed, by a progressive intelligentsia to whom there can be no such thing as a just feat of arms. It may even irritate such people that Chesterton, though to them guilty of glorifying war, cannot also be plausibly accused of jingoism, since no English forces were present at the battle of Lepanto in 1571. Here in the Gulf of Corinth – the port of Lepanto is now known by its Greek name of Návpaktos – the naval forces of the Christian League, mainly Spanish and Venetian, under Don John of Austria routed a Turkish fleet under Ali Pasha. The consequences of the victory were the crushing of Moslem sea-power in the eastern Mediterranean and, more immediately, the liberation of some 15,000 Christian slaves who had rowed the Turkish galleys, as described towards the end of the poem. Chesterton had Roman Catholic inclinations and entered the Church in middle life, which makes a difference, and also no difference.

Anyone susceptible to poetry is likely to feel at some time for some time that 'Lepanto' is a very great poem, even if that time is likely to come early on and to last no longer than perhaps the rest of the day. I know I did, and for longer than that, and before I was quite clear what was afoot in the first two lines or could have told you anything about the Lion of the Sea or the Valois. Even now I should not much care to have to recite it in public.

his cruel ships whose name is mystery: i.e. the Turkish ships, those of the Soldan. *swat*: either these are the sort of slaves that work hard at their books, or Chesterton thought the word was a more dignified form of 'sweat', or it is a primeval misprint.

129. Elegy (Chesterton). Refers to 1914–1918.

ʃʃ Edward Thomas was a hack writer who turned to poetry at the age of thirty-five on the advice of one who had recently taken it up himself (Robert Frost from America), an admirably unsanctified and unpropitious way to the Muse's favour. He was even older – thirty-seven – when he enlisted in the army. His death in France in 1917 was as great a loss to English poetry as Wilfred Owen's in the following year. How a poet convinces you he will not tell you anything he does not think or feel, since you have only his word for it, is hard to discover, but Edward Thomas is one of those who do it.

132. Women he liked (E. Thomas). *cob*: here not a nut but a sturdy, short-legged riding-horse.

134. Adlestrop (E. Thomas). Adlestrop is between Stow-on-the-Wold and Chipping Norton in Gloucestershire. The station of that name, on the main Oxford–Worcester GWR line, was shut down in the 1960s, but there is a memorial to poet and poem in the village bus shelter.

140. Lights out (E. Thomas). To determine what kind of poet Thomas is, and is not, it may be helpful to recall what his daughter, Myfanwy Thomas, said about this poem in an interview:

> 'Lights Out' is one of the bugle-calls in the army and he's recalling it. It's about going to sleep but a lot of critics think he's talking about death. I am not old enough to have known him in an adult way, but my mother said that he would never write about death and call it 'sleep'. He never prevaricated in that way. He would never use a euphemism for death.

Mrs Thomas added:

> I remember my mother saying that to analyse a poem was like pulling a swallow's wings to pieces to see how it flies.

142. C.L.M. (Masefield). Clearly the initials refer to the poet's mother. She died when he was six years old and he was brought up by relatives.

144. Aspidistra (Monro). How this pot-plant, its name for some reason usually pronounced 'aspidestra', became 'often regarded as a symbol of dull middle-class respectability' (*OED*) is not known, but Monro's poem must have helped.

what-not: not a synonym for 'something or other' but quite precisely a (mostly nineteenth-century) stand with shelves for displaying ornaments, etc., and very much in the same department as an aspidistra. *étagère*: a variety of what-not.

145. Highwayman (Noyes). Another in the category described under **119**. Probably more difficult to do than it looks. I suppose some might wish it were impossible. They are not much to be envied. Noyes is described in *OCEL* as holding 'violently anti-Modernist views on [*sic*] literature'.

∫∫ Flecker spent some two years of his short life in the consular service in Turkey, where he extended his knowledge of Eastern culture. He died of consumption.

149. Samarkand (Flecker). *Samarkand*: historically, a royal city and centre of Moslem art from the tenth century, occupied by the Russians in 1868, but in Flecker's time still unwesternised. Now capital of the Uzbek SSR.

151. Nightfall (Squire). I used to think 'old Jack Squire' was nothing but the unfairly successful anthologist, parodist and literary journalist he seemed to be, only really keen on cricket and booze, until not many years ago I came across this poem.

country: district, not the whole kingdom.

∫∫ Even today some may need telling that Brooke was not a soldier, nor was he killed in the Great War. He was in the Royal Naval Division, died of dysentery and blood-poisoning on the way to the Dardanelles and is buried in the Greek island of Scyros, where there stands a repulsive memorial to him.

156. Soldier (Brooke). Even today sometimes thought of as glorifying war, though a glance will show that it is not about war at all. It is admittedly patriotic.

158. Breaking (Muir). Probably Muir's last poem; not written, then, in the immediate shadow or aftermath of 1914–1918 or 1939–1945.

160. Romance (Turner). *Chimborazo, Cotopaxi*: peaks of the Andes in Ecuador. *Popacatapetl*: a 'smoking mountain' or dormant volcano (5452 m.) outside Mexico City. From the poem's standpoint there is a case for the reader's continued ignorance of this fact and the preceding two.

161. Evening (Aldington). I knew this tiny poem for years without knowing who had written it. I like it for getting away from the solemnity that so often goes with Imagism.

162. Goods train (Ashley). All I can discover of Kenneth Ashley is that he published a collection, *Up Hill and Down Dale* (1924), in which this poem appears. There are very few free-verse poems that seem to me to make good use of their freedom, but this one does.

163. Realist (Hooley). I cannot discover anything about Teresa Hooley either. I came across her poem quoted, not admiringly, in Michael Roberts's *Critique of Poetry* (1934). Though nothing can ever be proved about a poem, and this one may conceivably be a conscious satire on female sensitivity, I take it as heartfelt and self-revelatory. In its unusual way it is a masterpiece. Some alternative titles have their merits, from 'The True Christian' to 'The Satyromaniac', but at the end of the day I think 'The Realist' fits it best after all. Well, the poor sod may even be married to her.

∫∫ Owen was not one whose poems they gave you at school in the 1930s, except perhaps for **165**, where the element of protest is small; it was Auden who passed him on to my generation. No poet has spoken against war, any war, as powerfully as he, and one is tempted to conclude that the war he fought and died in was what made him a great poet. Without it he could hardly have matured at such astonishing speed. Or so one says. He writes that his subject 'is War, and the pity of War', but that comes in his draft preface to a proposed book of war poems, and he had already had time to show, in **168**, **169** and elsewhere, that his imagination was looking further. As Philip Larkin put it, Owen was concerned with

> not particular suffering but all suffering; not particular waste but all waste. If his verse did not cease to be valid

in 1918, it is because these things continued, and the necessity for compassion with them.

Owen achieved an authority of statement and generalisation rare in English poetry. Surely, that of our own time would have been not only enriched by his presence but also improved by his example if he had survived into it and gone on writing until, say, 1963 and the age of seventy. But to be on the safe side I would have to stipulate *per contra* the early death of Hopkins, before at any rate he had had time to write 'The Wreck of the *Deutschland*'.

164. Insensibility (Owen). Owen introduced into English poetry the form of rhyme used in this poem and others, as killed/cold, feet/fought, known to critics variously as chime, half-rhyme, assonantal rhyme, pararhyme, alliterative assonance and no doubt other uncouth expressions.

165. Anthem (Owen). *Anthem*: not just a synonym for 'elegy' or 'hymn', but a piece sung by the choir alone as part of a church service, specifically the funeral service implied in the poem. *shires*: not just a synonym for 'counties' or 'neighbourhoods', but a reference to the shire regiments of the Midlands and North of England which suffered severely in 1917–1918. *a drawing-down of blinds*: until quite recently it was the custom to lower the blinds of a house on the day of a funeral.

166. Exposure (Owen). *grey*: also the colour of German uniforms. *since we believe*, etc.: Owen constantly showed how terrible the war was, but for him it still had to be fought and won. In his preface, he writes of his book that he will be satisfied 'if the spirit of it survives – survives Prussia . . .' The last two words have sometimes been glossed over.

168. Princes Street (Owen). *pale rain-flawed phantom of the place*: this is not very clear, but we must be meant to imagine a woman who has just read of the death in action of her husband, son, brother, sweetheart in the casualty list in the evening paper.

169. Roads (Owen). Never finally revised.

∫∫ Graves made a reputation as a poet of sexual love, the female or feminine principle in life and poetry, the Muse, the Moon Goddess, the White Goddess and such matters, but for me he seldom functions at his best with these themes and succeeds oftener with his less central interests. The poems of his that reflect the latter also offer less to write about and lecture on than the love-Goddess sort, and I think Graves's poetic standing may have suffered in consequence, not that that would ever have bothered such an independent spirit.

170. Cow (Graves). Reflects the poet's service on the Western Front in the Great War.

176. War (Graves). The war is again the Great War but the date of composition is twenty years later.

184. Experience (Blunden). *a green country*: Flanders, where Blunden experienced trench warfare.

185. Jig (Day Lewis). I bought the volume containing this and the next poem on Paddington Station in 1943, a most impressive tribute in the circumstances. One of my feelings about them was gratitude for a couple of poems by a licensed modern poet that I could take pleasure in.

188. Myfanwy (Betjeman). The poet has got me where he wants me all right with this poem and others in the same vein, but I have never been able to work out quite where that is. Nor has anybody else I know of.

190. Golf (Betjeman). For the record, I am bored by golf to the point of hatred. I never knew the poet to express any interest in the game. But there are plenty of other exceptions to Philip Larkin's rule that poetry is about yourself and only novels are about other people, enough to leave that rule looking fairly tattered.

195. Sunday (MacNeice). *Hindhead*: A handy first objective for a nice little drive towards the south coast from London, there and back in a couple of hours in the Thirties.

196. Wolves (MacNeice). Reflects rather early (1934) misgivings about what was happening in Europe.

197. Valediction (MacNeice). Powerful enough to appeal to those of us who have no connection with Ireland, North or South. Perhaps if I had some I could make a little more head or tail of the first few lines, but then perhaps as a Brit I am meant to be puzzled.

their verdure dare not show: a verse of 'The Wearing of the Green', the Irish national or nationalist folk-ballad, runs:

When law can stop the blades of grass from growing as
    they grow,
And when the leaves in summertime their verdure dare
    not show,
Then I will change the colour that I wear in my caubeen
    [cap],
But till that day, please God, I'll stick to wearing of the
    Green.

But then . . .

∬Having constructed a personal myth loosely based on
Scandinavian sagas, the poet used to boast Icelandic descent
and an Icelandic name. In fact 'Auden' is a form of a perfectly
ordinary English name, others being Alden, Olden and
Haldane, indicating at most a Scandinavian origin so ultimate
as to embrace half the present population.

Auden's poetry was for me an acquired taste: as a schoolboy I made nothing of it. Its obscurity put me off and still
does, though not enough since then to prevent me from
thinking his best poems as good as any in English in the last
hundred years. I now see that obscurity as intimately connected with his homosexuality. I do not mean merely that he
conceals what he (no doubt rightly) felt it prudent to conceal,
but that secretiveness spreads out in his work to become a
part of the style, an almost instinctive mystification, much as
in life some homosexuals are apt to be close about anything
and everything they may be up to, not just the special bits.
Further, secret societies develop codes, jargons, argots, with
the object not simply of maintaining security but, again, of
gleefully and for its own sake saying the unsayable under the
noses of the stupid police/British/white man/hetero/whoever.
All good innocent fun – and much nicer for the world in
general than calling a spade a spade; but to make public
poetry, to-be-published poetry out of a private language is to
work under a handicap only a great poet could have over-
come.*

*None of this, admittedly, seems to have affected Housman (though *More
Poems* XXIII and the famous *Additional Poems* XVIII, both published posthum-
ously, have some bearing). A difference of temperament, no doubt, or
something to do with the gap in birth-dates (1859, 1907).

A reader of the foregoing will at any rate see that I am apologising in advance for not being able to explain a number of references in the poems concerned.

Auden published many of his early poems without titles and I have followed his first thoughts here, rather than adopt the often silly and distracting titles he gave them in his *Collected Shorter Poems* in 1966. I have also followed his original texts.

199. Watershed (Auden). Worth saying that in 1927 it was not usual for a poem to mention tramlines, engines or flooded workings unless in a special 'realistic' tone of voice.

200. Taller (Auden). *Captain Ferguson*: who was he? Ah, wouldn't you like to know! An embarrassing frivolity in a deeply-felt poem.

202. Get there if you can (Auden). Dropped from the 1966 collection. The poem does say rather unobscurely what others of Auden's at the time were more reticent about. Not that that makes this one necessarily better.

Homer Lane: (1876–1925), American psychologist. Indirectly responsible for Auden's 'belief' that psychological states have physical manifestations (e.g. a habitual liar develops quinsy). I cannot discover in what dotty sense he was 'killed in action'.

204. Siren (Auden). It may be of interest, as an illustration of how wrong poets can go about their own work, to give here the awful verse that Auden must have thought was somehow better than his original last verse, since he substitutes it in the 1966 collection.

> Till our nerves are numb and their now is a time
> Too late for love or for lying either,
> > Grown used at last
> > To having lost,
> > Accepting dearth,
> > The shadow of death.

206. Johnny (Auden). This is one of 'four cabaret songs for Miss Hedli Anderson', otherwise Mrs Louis MacNeice. I have always thought it an inappropriately good poem to serve as words for anything like that.

207. As I walked out (Auden). This poem dates from late in 1937. In January 1939 Auden left England for America in order to continue the struggle against Fascism from there. War broke out in Europe in the September. He never after his departure wrote anything to touch his earlier work.

211. Crisis (Durrell). There is something not quite right about this poem, and the next one too, but the excitement with which I first read them still flickers.

212. Epidaurus (Durrell). This is the text as published in *Poetry London*, not the version in the author's collected poems.

213. Winter night (Fuller). The last line is as the poet first wrote it, not as he later revised it.

∫∫R. S. Thomas is or was a minister of the Church in Wales, but has retired from his position in it. He was born in South Wales and like the great majority of Welsh people he spoke English as his first language, though he later learnt Welsh and preached in a Welsh-speaking parish in North Wales. The poems of his I reprint are all in the early style he abandoned in the 1950s.

222. Hunchback (D. Thomas). Dylan Thomas knew no Welsh from first to last, though he is sometimes sloppily alleged to have 'thought' in that language. This poem shows him, for once in his life, writing about something outside himself.

224. Hero (Woddis) and Aengus (Yeats). There cannot be many completely serious parodies apart from this one, and I know of no other driven by indignation. It says more than any prose could.

∫∫ Asked in an interview of 1979 if he got much out of reading criticism of his work, Larkin said:

> Well, there isn't an awful lot of it. I may flatter myself, but I think in one sense I'm like Evelyn Waugh or John Betjeman, in that there's not much to *say* about my work. When you've read a poem, that's it, it's all quite clear what it means.

226. Climbing hill (Larkin). This was the only poem in Larkin's first volume, *The North Ship* (1945), that I really liked and felt I understood, and even so I greatly preferred the last six lines to the first eight.

229. Bleaney (Larkin). This was the name of the Junior Dean of St John's in 1942, and for Larkin and most others he was never anything else, though it was agreed that nobody who bore it could be interesting, literate, any good, etc.

234. Reference back (Larkin). *you*: the poet's mother.

235. Going (Larkin). Larkin writes that this was commissioned by the Department of the Environment, and that it was reprinted in his collection *High Windows* by permission of the Controller of Her Majesty's Stationery Office.

237. Cut grass (Larkin). *Queen Anne's lace*: better known as cow parsley.

238. Salamnbo (Bayley). *the amorous man*: Flaubert, knowledge of whose circumstances and of his novel *Salamnbo* will help understanding here, though I have always felt that the poem would still mean a lot to a responsive person who had never heard of Flaubert.

239. Time (Jennings). This poem first appeared in *Oxford Poetry 1949* (ed. K. Amis and James Michie).

ACKNOWLEDGMENTS

For permission to reprint copyright material the editor and publishers gratefully acknowledge the following:

Rosica Colin Limited for 'Evening' by Richard Aldington; Martin Secker & Warburg Limited for 'Lament for a Cricket Eleven' and 'Patch' by Kenneth Allott; The Bodley Head and the author for 'Goods Train at Night' from *Up Hill and Down Dale* by Kenneth Ashley; Faber & Faber Ltd for 'Who stands, the crux left of the watershed', 'Taller to-day', 'From scars where kestrels hover', 'Get there if you can', 'Who will endure', 'What siren zooming is sounding our coming', 'O who can ever gaze his fill', 'Johnny' and 'As I walked out one evening' from *The English Auden* by W. H. Auden; John Bayley for 'Salamnbo' by Oliver Bayley; Gerald Duckworth for 'Ha'nacker Mill' from *Collected Verse* by Hilaire Belloc; John Murray (Publishers) Ltd and the Trustees of Sir John Betjeman's Estate for 'Croydon', 'Myfanwy', 'Christmas', 'Seaside Golf', 'The Cottage Hospital', 'Remorse', 'A Lament for Moira McCavendish' and 'On Leaving Wantage 1972' from *Collected Poems* by John Betjeman; Mrs Nicolette Gray and The Society of Authors on behalf of the Laurence Binyon Estate for the extract from *The Burning of the Leaves* by Laurence Binyon; A. D. Peters & Co. Ltd for 'Thames Gulls' and 'Report on Experience' from *Poems of Many Years* by Edmund Blunden; the author for 'Watering Place' by Robert Conquest; Carcanet Press Ltd for 'The Garden Party' from *Selected Poems* by Donald Davie; The Executors of the Estate of C. Day Lewis, Jonathan Cape Ltd and the Hogarth Press for 'Jig' and 'Hornpipe' from *Collected Poems 1954* by C. Day Lewis; Faber & Faber Ltd for 'In a Time of Crisis' from *Collected Poems* by Lawrence Durrell and 'Epidaurus' by Lawrence Durrell; Martin Secker & Warburg Limited for 'Winter Night' from *New and Collected Poems* by Roy Fuller; A. P. Watt Ltd on behalf of the Executors of the Estate of Robert Graves for 'Dead Cow Farm', 'Love Without Hope', 'Love in Barrenness', 'The Presence', 'Callow Captain', 'On Rising Early', 'Recalling War', 'The Cuirassiers of the Frontier', 'Wigs and Beards', 'Cold

349

Lonely Farmer', 'Children's Song' and 'A Welshman to Any Tourist' by R. S. Thomas; Martin Secker & Warburg Ltd for 'At Birth' from *Poems 1953–1983* by Anthony Thwaite; the author's estate for 'Romance' by W. J. Turner; the author for 'The Hero' by Roger Woddis; A. P. Watt & Co. on behalf of Michael B. Yeats and Macmillan, London and Basingstoke for 'The Song of Wandering Aengus' from *The Collected Poems* of W. B. Yeats and 'John Kinsella's Lament for Mrs Mary Moore' by W. B. Yeats; Martin Secker & Warburg Limited for 'The Ruined Chapel', 'The Stockdoves' and 'The Shepherd's Hut' by Andrew Young.

INDEX

INDEX OF AUTHORS

Numbers refer to the numbers of the poems, not the pages

INDEX OF TITLES AND FIRST LINES

Numbers refer to the numbers of the poems, not the pages